**The Urbana Free Library**

To renew: call **217-367-4057**
or go to **urbanafreelibrary.org**
and select **My Account**

# MEXICO

ALSO BY JOSH BARKAN

Blind Speed
Before Hiroshima

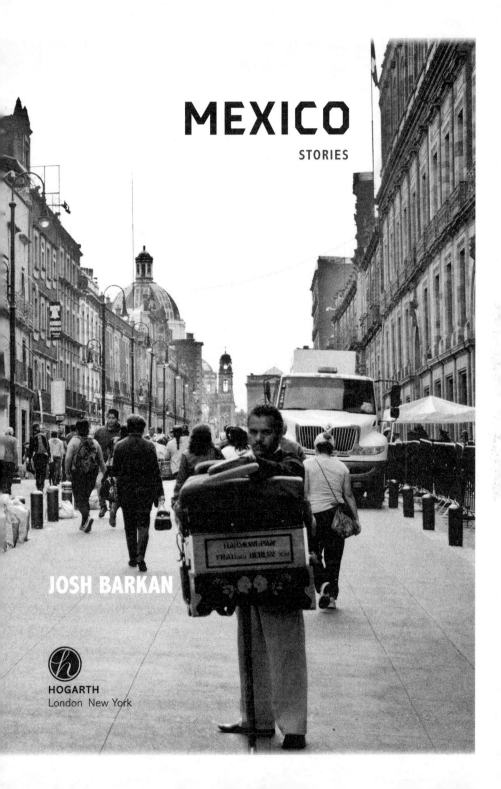

# MEXICO

## STORIES

**JOSH BARKAN**

HOGARTH
London New York

Published in the United States by Hogarth, an imprint of the Crown Publishing Group, a division of Penguin Random House LLC, New York.
crownpublishing.com

HOGARTH is a trademark of the Random House Group Limited, and the H colophon is a trademark of Penguin Random House LLC.

"The Kidnapping" was first published as the winner of the Lightship International Short Story Prize 2013, in *Lightship Anthology 3*, Alma Books, U.K., 2014.

Library of Congress Cataloging-in-Publication Data is available upon request.

ISBN 978-1-101-90629-3
eBook ISBN 978-1-101-90630-9

Printed in the United States of America

Book design by Elina D. Nudelman
Frontispiece photograph by Frederick Bertrand
Jacket design by Elena Giavaldi
Jacket illustration by Alexander Henry Fabrics

10 9 8 7 6 5 4 3 2 1
First Edition

FOR MARIANA

# CONTENTS

# MEXICO

# THE CHEF AND EL CHAPO

**H**ow the hell "El Chapo" Guzmán chose my restaurant to come into, I'll never know. It was just like the stunt he's done in a few other cities—Nuevo León and Culiacán. Guzmán—"Shorty"—it was him, with all his narco clothing. He had on a baseball cap with some of that digitalized camouflage the U.S. Army invented for Iraq, and a beige down parka. It was one of those cold days in June, after the rainy season has started, and the most badass narco in the country must have felt just a touch of a chill. Crazy! In my restaurant. With fifteen bodyguards swarming around him. The guards came in first. They all had AK-47s swinging in their arms. They came in fast and polite, rushing past the maître d'. The leader of the guards, a tall guy with a neatly trimmed thin mustache and a diamond earring, swooped into the center of the dining room and yelled out, "The Boss will be coming soon. Everyone give us your purses and cell phones and continue with your meal. Nobody leaves before The Boss is done. If you cooperate, everything will be fine. You'll get your purses and phones returned when The Boss is done. Leave your check. The Boss will pay for your meal."

I knew Shorty was short, of course, but when he came in, it was surprising to see just how small the biggest drug kingpin was. He walked in quickly, like he knew where he was going. He turned to the first table, to the left, and introduced himself. He removed his cap and said in polite Spanish, "Hello, my name is El Chapo Guzmán. Nice to meet you." He smiled and extended his hand to shake with one of the customers, an old man in a blue blazer who, fortunately, had the presence of mind to shake back. The customer looked like he'd just seen a ghost.

Guzmán went from table to table shaking hands like a politician asking for votes of approval. But the way he smiled, with a permanent grin and his eyes a little too focused on the clients, he seemed to be saying: You will like me! I'm not so fucking bad, right? After he reached the last table, he chuckled, cracking himself up. He was the most badass jokester in the world. He was the biggest gentleman, extending his hand of courtesy to every diner, after he'd killed hundreds.

Every day, I drive from the neighborhood of Santa Fe, in Mexico City, to the restaurant, and I pass guys selling tabloid newspapers in the morning. They run up and down the street, at the stoplights, trying to find clients, waving papers in the air, and the covers always have a narco like Guzmán with some gory detail like the bodies El Chapo dissolved in acid on a farm after he got pissed off at some other narcos, or like the photos of headless and handless bodies dumped in the middle of the streets of Veracruz. El Chapo killed the son of his brother-in-law. He's fifty-five and head of the Sinaloa Cartel, and he's one smart narco, because he not only escaped from prison—with the help of dozens of people he bought off, pushed out of a maximum-security prison in a laundry cart—he's managed to live to the age of fifty-five when most narcos never make it even close to being a grandpa.

Everyone in Mexico knows about him: how he married yet another young woman, some beauty queen, and how she had twins in a hospital in Los Angeles. How the guy controls all the cocaine, pot, and most of the meth and heroin that's going into the U.S. I've only been in Mexico two years, building the restaurant up, but anyone who's spent time down here knows the names of all these narcos like they're the heroes and devils of the soap operas that are on all day in every housewife's home and in every cantina.

So it didn't take a genius to know the guy who'd just walked into my restaurant was capable of killing me and every one of my clients, and I was the head chef.


EL CHAPO ASKED to be escorted to a private room, in back, where we sometimes have lunches for important business people. My restaurant is in the neighborhood of Polanco, on the border with the most expensive neighborhood of Las Lomas, where all the international banks are located. The food in my restaurant is a mix of French with new American cuisine—meaning anything is OK, fusion with Asian touches, wasabi with bourbon crab, pork with chanterelle mushrooms in a ginger cream sauce with Beluga caviar sprinkled on top, arugula salad with truffle shavings and Cointreau sauce.

I wake up early in the morning and go to the San Juan market, in the center of Mexico City, to buy the freshest produce I can find. The market looks typical, at first, in a wide concrete warehouse, but the stalls are full of the latest vegetables trucked in pickups from small farmers, and there are even a few Korean stands where you can find Asian vegetables that are less common in Mexico City. Fusion cooking has been the rage in the U.S. for thirty years, but in Mexico it's a new thing, so I've received more attention than a comparable chef would get in the U.S. That's one of the reasons I came to Mexico. A friend of mine, who was living in Mexico, came into a restaurant where I was the head chef in Pittsburgh, he tasted some cured duck breast I was preserving in the cellar of the restaurant, he slurped up the homemade vinegars we were using in the salad dressings and to pickle baby carrots and peas, and he told me I could be an instant hit in Mexico City.

My body is covered with tattoos, with bright oranges and blues swirling in sci-fi flames up my legs and arms, and the thought of going to somewhere new, out of the U.S., appealed to me. I had already done the "successful chef" thing in the U.S. I found myself staying after work with adoring clients who had watched too many episodes of *Iron Chef,* who thought I could throw knives in the air and prepare delicious meals in half an hour or less. The reality is, it takes time to make good food. Those shows are bunk. It takes hours of planning and experimenting. It was nice to ride the wave of the food obsession in the U.S., but I wanted to see if I could go somewhere out of my comfort zone, somewhere where food was not synonymous with pornography, where people still loved the food for how it tasted and not for what it said about them. So I jumped at the chance to open the new restaurant in Mexico City.

I needed clients with money to do the kind of food I wanted. But I was looking for clients who needed their palettes awakened, who hadn't already read about everything in some glossy magazine. I was looking for new markets in which to hunt down ingredients, for new adventures.

El Chapo was led into the back room, and he sent one of his guards to summon me. If it was adventure I'd been looking for, ironically I was going to get more of it than I'd bargained for.

There's a fine leather bench along the walls of the back room, and El Chapo was perched on the bench, leaning back, his legs so short I had the sense he was swinging his feet beneath the table when I came in to meet him. A guard blocked the door, to the left, to the main dining room. Another stood pointing an AK-47 my way. El Chapo sat, alone, waiting to speak to me.

"Sit down," he said. He spoke in Spanish.

I sat in front of him. He looked me over and then spat on the polished wood top of the table.

"What kind of chef's costume is that?" he said. "Don't you have any self-respect? I thought you were supposed to be the latest hot chef in this town. Fucking Mexico City. Everyone thinks they're so fucking important in this city. They don't know anything."

I never wear a white chef's hat. That seems ridiculously pretentious to me. I usually have on some T-shirt with a retro rock band that I like. I tend to wear bicycle riding pants and clogs in the kitchen, under my apron. I like to ride, whenever I get a little bit of time, and I tend to wear a bicycle cap or a baseball cap with some heavy metal logo. I had on a baseball cap, with the letters AC/DC on the black front. The truth is, El Chapo and I looked a little similar, each in our baseball cap.

"What kind of outfit do you want me to wear?" I asked, politely.

"Oh, have some self-respect, man. If this is the getup you have to make yourself feel important then don't try to change what you do for me. But you look like some kind of wannabe athlete, not a chef. Everyone wants to be something other than what they are. Politicians pretend to be saints. Crooks act like they love their wives. I would have thought a chef was something different . . . But I see you're a phony, just like all the rest."

"I'll try to do my best," I said.

This was going to be harder than I thought. I knew that if El Chapo Guzmán was coming into my restaurant, he was probably doing it for PR, to let everyone in the city know this was his territory, that he could come and go at will, that they could have a five-million-dollar bounty on his head and he could still make a mockery of every counter-narco cop in the country. If he could come into a fancy restaurant and pay for everyone in broad daylight, then it would be enough to strike terror into every last person in the city. I had heard this was the effect of his stunts like this in other cities. He seemed like a god who could come and go as he pleased, invulnerable to any human boundaries. But if he was coming into my restaurant, in particular, I guessed it wasn't just to make a statement. If he was coming into my specific joint, it was to see if the food was any good. My job then, like any great chef, was to be a magician.

A chef who's truly great sits a person down at a table, makes them wait longer than they want until they're beginning to salivate—to be a little cranky, to doubt the abilities of the kitchen—and then comes out with plate after plate of unexpected wonders, with flavor combinations that pop and surprise in perfect ecstasy, until the patron willingly pulls out their wallet, pays much more than they think they should, but without any regret, with a clamoring, in fact, for the next opportunity to eat more of the food. And all the while, the chef has to come up with just a few dishes on the menu that will please everyone. Each person eating thinks the magic has been made just for them, but it's been made for the eighty to a hundred clients of the day.

Reluctance, I was used to. Someone who was already saying I looked like a pansy was another thing. It was going to take more than the usual tricks to win El Chapo over. It didn't seem like he was the kind who would want to kill me if I failed to charm him, but it was always an option.

"Would you like something from the menu, today?" I asked El Chapo. I used reverse psychology. I knew if I asked him this way, he would say he wanted something made just for him.

"Do I look like the kind of guy who eats what all the other pigs out there are eating?" El Chapo said. He pointed to the door to the main dining room. Normally, there's a hum of patrons talking, eating, ordering fine wines, and privately licking their knives, even though that's gauche. You can tell how much your patrons like the food by how much sauce they leave on their plates. I always inspect the plates as they come into the kitchen. Where there are marks where people have been sopping up the sauce with bread, I take note and try to make those sauces more frequently, though you always have to try something new.

There was barely a sound from the other side of the door to the dining room.

"Something special, just for you, then?" I said.

"Do you know how I became the jefe?" El Chapo said. "It wasn't just killing people. Anyone can kill people. Anyone can be the baddest badass around. That will get you about twenty percent of what you need to be the capo." He leaned in closer to me, as if he were about to give me the secret key to the universe. "What made me the jefe was coming up with a better plan. What made me the jefe was someone else telling me what I had to do, and me coming back to them with something better than what they asked for. You want fifteen tons of the product in Chicago, by Monday? OK, I'll get it there. But I'm also going to build a tunnel under the border so we can ship over three hundred tons next week. And I'm going to ship two kinds of product on the same planes into LA. Those idiots. They were just shipping pot on the planes, when they could have been shipping coke." He looked under the table, as if he wanted to be sure there were no bugs in the restaurant recording what he was saying.

"It's making do with less to make more," he said. "So here's what I want you to do. I want you to give me something that tastes so good I almost cum in my pants, that makes me and my compadres slap you on the back and give you an extra million-dollar tip for cooking so well. And I want you to do that without salt, without pepper, and with no more than two ingredients. And if you can do that, then I'm serious. You're going to get some unexpected tip. And if you can't . . ." He gave his chuckle again, the same jokester laugh he'd given to the patrons, outside, when he'd introduced himself to them, the great El Chapo shaking their hands. "If you can't," he said as he put his right hand up to his head in the shape of a pistol, cocked his thumb, pointed into his ear, and released. "Pow!" he said, and he started laughing.


I CAME DOWN to Mexico City with my wife. We have a four-year-old son, and one of the pleasures of Mexico City has been seeing how kid-friendly, how kid-obsessed, the place is. Mexicans love their kids

more than just about any place I've ever been. There's a big park in
Polanco, not too far from my restaurant, called Chapultepec, and
on Sundays I walk with my wife and son, Jimmy, through the park. I
leave the cooking up to the sous chefs on Sunday. I close the restaurant on Monday. It was because of Jimmy that I opened a gourmet
hot dog restaurant in Pittsburgh, before moving down to Mexico
City. He loves hot dogs. He takes a dog in both fists and shoves it
in. There's something primal about the way kids eat food, shoving
the good things into their mouths, tossing what they don't like onto
the floor. Behind the hidden-flavor sophistication in a fine restaurant I want the patrons to feel that primal energy, to feel like they're
pushing food in and tossing it out on the floor, all as they constrain
themselves to holding a fork delicately in front of their mouth and
then popping it in.

I like to watch the patrons eat like animals. I like to see them roll
their eyes upward in delight, just as Jimmy does when he eats a hot
dog with mustard and all the fixings.

A couple days before El Chapo came into the restaurant, Jimmy
was in Chapultepec Park, next to one of the big artificial lakes where
the fountains spout water into the air, and he dashed away from my
wife and clambered over the lip of the stone border around the water
before I could grab him. He went straight into the water. I thought
he could drown, even though the water is no more than a couple
feet deep. I had my riding pants on, since I'd gone into the restaurant
earlier in the day to check up on how everything was going. (Sundays are a day off, but sometimes I pop in, unexpectedly, to make
sure everything is keeping up to standards.) With all my clothes on
and shoes, I jumped straight over the lip of the lake into the water
and grabbed Jimmy, and threw him up into the air, out of the water.
"Never do that again, Jimmy," I said. He'd scared the living daylights
out of me and my wife. Jimmy thought the whole thing was hilarious. He laughed and spit water out of his mouth, into my eyes. He
had no sense of the danger he was in.

So this wasn't about me anymore, I realized, as I went back into the kitchen to cook for El Chapo. This was about me and my wife and Jimmy and all the patrons out in the restaurant. Going to a restaurant is putting trust in the chef. A chef is meant to do more than delight. He's meant to block out the pressures of the world, for a few minutes. For a couple hours, the patron sits at the table, with a nice white tablecloth, and they're allowed to forget about the outside world, to forget about their business deal going sour or their dying grandmother, or the problem they're having with their spouse. Food, at its best, can be like an amulet, something that wards off evil like a magic shaman. I could feel the weight of the magic that I needed to perform as I went into the kitchen.

It may sound crazy, but people like to eat what they are. If they have voracious habits they can't change, they like sweet foods. If they are tight with their money, they prefer to eat bread and mashed potatoes. If they are flamboyant they like elaborately thin vegetables, fried and piled up high like a fancy hat. We are all cannibals, eating ourselves, eating the secrets we have within. There's a reason the pedophile has poor dental work, teeth that have eaten too many sweets.

I went to the main meat fridge in the kitchen, and I started to pull out things that I thought El Chapo might like. El Chapo was a short bull. He was an animal. He was dark and earthy. He snorted when he spoke. Beef, alone, wouldn't be enough to get his attention. I needed something darker. I thought of some wild boar I had in the fridge, some elk or venison. The boar meat might be close, but the elk and venison were too delicate. If I could have found a slab of water buffalo, that would have been about right. I ate a piece of cured water buffalo meat once, in a restaurant in Sri Lanka, and it tasted as black as the thick skin on the animal.

And then I realized, only one thing would make El Chapo absolutely happy. Human flesh. I knew human flesh would do it. But I couldn't give him what he wanted unless I could cut that flesh off of

myself, to save the life of me and the other patrons outside, waiting
to see if they would make it to another day.

I found a block of Wagyu beef and took it out of the fridge. I
sliced it in thin delicate shavings and then piled the shavings up on
six different plates, for El Chapo and some of his henchmen. The first
ingredient would be the beef. The second would be human blood.
I took one of the sharp knives off the wall of cutting utensils and
cut my thumb. I squeezed drops of blood onto the beef, letting the
crimson color sink into its thin wafers. The plates looked colorful
and there were only two ingredients. I made the plate for El Chapo
bigger than the rest, to fit his big ego. I was about to tell the waiters
to bring the dishes out, but then I stopped, for a second, and tasted
the meat. The ingredients were wrong. The dish was close but not
quite right. There was a bitterness, a tough saltiness to my blood that
wasn't quite perfect, as if the totality of my experiences in life came
out in the flavor of the blood, and I realized normal blood wouldn't
be enough.

El Chapo had eaten everything. He had eaten, I guessed, in the
finest restaurants of Vegas and in London, Tokyo, and Paris. His
empire was global. I knew he was a billionaire. This dish had to be
unlike anything he had ever eaten in any of those fine restaurants.
But normal blood wouldn't do. I thought of the baby piglets, lambs,
and veal that were the staples of every great restaurant in Europe.
It was precisely the tenderness and innocence of those animals, the
very thing that made vegetarians cringe at such dishes, which made
meat-eaters relish such food. Like old people rubbing on creams to
remove their wrinkles, the restaurant patron craves baby carrots,
the youngest peas, and other new-grown shoots and lettuces to pass
across their tongue before they are chewed and ingested. The desire
of someone like El Chapo—who had devoured young women like
his wife, and who dressed like a teenage hip-hop star—to avoid his
true age, was strong. He needed to dominate all the people around

him, like a dirty old man who preys on young girls. So I knew, suddenly, that I needed the blood of a kid.

I went out the door and into the main dining room. There were a dozen of El Chapo's guards there, watching the patrons eat. Most of the diners' plates were empty, and they were waiting for El Chapo to finish his meal so they could go. When I came into the dining room, I heard a few gasps from some of the clients and saw an older woman start to cry. I had no idea how bloody my apron looked. I saw a young girl with two long pigtails running down the back of her hand-knit blue sweater. Her mother was holding her tight by her side, telling her, gently, not to be worried. I came up to the mother, well done up with makeup, who looked like she went to the spa once a week. I had to convince her to give up her daughter.

"My son's name is Jimmy," I said. "He looks about the age of your daughter. Please trust me if I tell you I need your daughter to come into the kitchen for a second."

"Why?" the mother asked. She looked tortured, like she was in the middle of a bank robbery and I'd just become one of the bank robbers.

"There will be time to explain later," I said, in as calm a voice as I could manage. I tried to be commanding. A command would be the only way to get the mother to relinquish her daughter. I said in a soft, but firm and commanding, voice, "I need your daughter to come back to the kitchen with me."

"Only if I come, too," the mother said.

So I told her all right, she could come, too. The guards of El Chapo told me to hurry up. "What are you doing wasting time?" the head guard, with the diamond in his ear, said. "Get in the kitchen and give The Boss his meal. He's hungry. He's been waiting for you."

I went back into the kitchen with the daughter and her mother. I stood in front of the plates of Wagyu beef growing moister and plumper as it absorbed the blood.

I put my thumb up to the face of the mother, where I had the slice from the knife I had made before. The wound was pink and the blood was sticky. "You see this?" I said to the mother. "I need to do the same to your daughter."

She looked at me like I was a crazy terrorist. She tried to pull the knife out of my hand. I had a choice: Give in, let the girl go, admit that I might be crazy, a Dr. Frankenstein in the kitchen, admit that the whole thing was an overreaction on my part. But I have learned, in life, that you have to go with your gut. I didn't think, I just took action. I put my hand up against the mother's mouth and made her stay quiet. I grabbed one of the dish towels and stuck it into her mouth. Her eyes pleaded with me not to do anything to her daughter. I picked up the knife again, I pulled up the hand of the child and cut her thumb, deeper than I would have liked in the heat of the moment, and blood came pulsing out. I lifted her high into the air, with her pigtails flailing behind as she cried out for her mother, who was trying to yell, and I squeezed the blood of her hand onto El Chapo's plate.

The waiters looked at me like I was insane, but the rule in a fine restaurant is to never question what the head chef demands. They brought the food out to El Chapo, and I made sure they brought the plate with the young girl's blood specifically to him.

I followed out a few minutes later, and I could see El Chapo licking his thumb, picking up the plate to get more of the sauce on his lips and into his mouth.

"There are only two ingredients in the dish," I told El Chapo.

"What is it? It's fucking good. It's fucking delicious," he told me. "The others agree. I've eaten all over the world, and I've never eaten anything this tasty."

"It's Wagyu beef with human blood," I told him. "The blood is mine." I held up my thumb to prove I wasn't lying. There was the cut, irritated and sticky with drying blood. I didn't mention the girl. If El

Chapo knew, he might develop a fetish for young blood. He might look for her in the main dining room and take her away. He might rape her. There was no telling what kind of habits he could develop. I've read, from survivors of airplane crashes, that once the taste of human flesh is tried, once the taboo is broken, it's hard to go back.

"Son of a bitch," El Chapo said. "You think I'm an animal. Some kind of cannibal." He spat on the table with venom, like a rattlesnake. I couldn't tell if he was going to pull out a gun and shoot me, or not.

"I don't think anything," I said submissively.

"You people in the 'normal world,' you know nothing about who I really am," El Chapo said. "A cannibal! Nothing could be more ridiculous." He picked up his plate and held it in front of his face, looking into a mirror. He threw the plate against the wall and the white china, with blood, broke into pieces.

"But I never lie," he said. "Even if someone attempts to trick me. I'm the most honest person you'll find in all of Mexico. Come here!" I approached, as commanded. He took my thumb and squeezed my wound until I cried out, hoping my finger wouldn't burst. New blood came forth from the thumb. "You should be happy just to keep your life," El Chapo said, looking me straight in the eyes, letting me know he could kill me every bit as easily as he'd tossed the plate. "But I challenged you, and you gave me something with two ingredients, and it's the best thing I have ever tasted."

He ordered one of his guards to bring me my tip. He pulled out a couple thick piles of hundred-dollar bills from a brown briefcase, and left the money on the table. He put my thumb on the money, until some of the blood seeped into the face of Ben Franklin on the bills. "Now you are guilty of entering the world of blood, too," he said.

He stood up quickly and walked into the main dining room. The girl was back with her mother, sitting at their table, the mother still in tears. I prayed El Chapo wouldn't discover she'd been involved with the meal. I hoped he wouldn't see the girl's thumb was just like mine.

El Chapo looked around the room and saw the girl, next to her crying mother. He stood in the middle of the patrons. "What's wrong, little girl?" he said to all the customers. He walked up to the girl. "Didn't you like your meal? Please finish eating, everyone. I hope you've seen the great El Chapo isn't such a bastard after all. Please enjoy your meal. It's compliments of me and my associates." He waved his hands wide in appreciation to his guards and bowed to them.

The mother held her daughter, hiding the girl's face from the "great" El Chapo, and he left with his hands raised in the air like a boxer accepting applause after winning another fight, though the room was silent. The guards returned everyone's purses and cell phones, and then disappeared.


TWO MONTHS AFTER El Chapo came into my restaurant, I went with Jimmy to the Museum of Anthropology in Polanco, not far from where I work. The museum is enormous, with a courtyard where Jimmy can run around, so I like to take him there when I can. At the far end of the museum, like a magnet drawing all the visitors forward, are the rooms with the remains of the Aztec empire— high stone temples covered in alabaster, which had reached up to the broad sky at the center of the ancient city of Tenochtitlan in the middle of what is today Mexico City. The halls with Aztec art are filled with clay statues, and one is of a god that looks like a robot, square with big round eyes. This is Tlaloc, the god of rain and thunder. He controlled the water, necessary for the corn to grow. The Aztecs prayed to dozens of gods, and at the top of their pyramids they sacrificed thousands of people to keep the gods satisfied.

Jimmy ran ahead of me in the Aztec galleries, past stone knives with small eyes made of turquoise that the Aztecs used to cut out the hearts of the sacrificed people. Young victims were always considered the most worthwhile for placating the gods. They had more potential energy for the rest of their lives stored within, so they were believed to be the most valuable offerings.

For two weeks, I hadn't been sleeping well. I didn't know what to do with the money El Chapo had left me as my tip. I kept thinking about what he'd said to me, that now I was guilty, too. My wife had told me I should be practical and use the money to keep building up the restaurant, or to put it into the college fund for Jimmy. She told me I would be turning bad money into good, taking it from the drug dealers and making it into something positive. She told me I should be proud I'd saved everyone in the restaurant that day. But whenever I looked at the money, and thought about the possessed way I'd lifted the girl to put her blood on the beef to give to El Chapo, I wasn't so sure I was a hero. It wasn't just that I'd tortured her mother and cut the girl's finger; I was playing with black chef magic, thinking I could outsmart El Chapo. What if he'd reacted differently to my dish? What if he'd reacted in anger and killed me, or more people? I was just as guilty of giving in to my ego, of thinking I could control him, as El Chapo thought he could control the world.

"Come over here," I told Jimmy. He was lost, wandering among the Aztec gods, and I had to call him a couple more times before he complied. I'd told his mother I wanted to go with Jimmy alone to the museum. Jimmy and I came to a stone pyramid altar, twenty feet high, which used to sit on top of one of the pyramids of Tenochtitlan. From my backpack, filled with snacks and a juice bottle for Jimmy, I pulled out a big envelope with the twenty thousand dollars El Chapo had given me. The envelope was new, but you could still see, faintly, the blood on some of the bills within. "Take this envelope up to the top of the pyramid," I told Jimmy. "Put it on the round stone." I told him to go to the place where the Aztecs used to leave the sacrificed hearts. I looked around to make sure there were no guards coming.

"Keep going! Put it up there," I said to Jimmy. He placed the envelope just where I told him, on the stone altar. He made a face at me. He told me he didn't want to come down. "It's fun up here," he said. I could hear the guard coming. I told Jimmy to hurry. I told him we had to go home.

# THE GOD OF COMMON NAMES

This is a Romeo and Juliet story. But it's set in Mexico, where I live and work as a teacher.

One day, about a month ago, this black SUV pulls up in front of the private New Hampshire School where I teach in San Jerónimo. The New Hampshire School is one of those precious schools where rich Mexicans send their kids to give them an exclusively foreign-feeling education. English is spoken in half of the classes. The students take ski trips to Vail, in Colorado, over Christmas break with the other students. They dream of getting into places like Harvard and Yale, but most end up at places like Bucknell University or, if they're less brilliant, the University of Miami, Florida.

Three blocks up the street from the school, there's a fantastic bakery where you can get croissants stuffed with walnut paste and a dog-grooming store where they import weight-loss dog food for breeds like yellow Labs. There's a wine store with two-hundred-dollar bottles of imported French wine and an electrolysis beauty salon that keeps humming with one laser plucking after another. I'm told permanent Brazilian waxes there are the thing.

Black SUVs aren't all that uncommon at our school. The kids come with their drivers and bodyguards, who bring them in the morning. But what made this SUV unusual is that it showed up in the middle of the day, when the kids had already eaten lunch and were all in their classes. The other thing that made the SUV unusual was that no kid came out of it. I could see the Cadillac come into the parking lot. I was teaching my usual tenth-grade class in American History and Culture. We had just done a unit on American outlaws like Jesse James and the Chicago gangsters of the '20s, and the kids were into that.

Two of my students, who almost never pay attention, had perked up during the unit. One was José Cachez Jiménez and the other was Sandra Fernández de Guanajuato. I make up a seating chart at the beginning of each semester, where I place the students randomly in new desks. I do this to avoid having cliques form, and I do it because one of the big social differences between American students and Mexican students is how everything in Mexico revolves around the group. American students, of course, like to hang out together, but they tend to break off in groups of two or three after school. But in Mexico it's all about big groups of eight or so buddies or female pals. They do everything together. They play soccer together, go to the movies together, have parties together, and then work together or swap business deals together as they get older.

In any case, Sandra and José ended up randomly in my class sitting next to one another, in the back. There's some strange law about teaching that even when you seat students randomly, the ones in the back tend not to pay too much attention. I would hear them tittering, a few weeks into the class, when my back was turned to the students, while I was writing on the board. I'd see Sandra and José casting glances back and forth, even while taking exams.

Sandra's face is long and thin; she wears her hair with a lot of wavy curls that she's spent hours combing so they cascade one below the other in bountiful thick semicircles, frozen perfectly with lots of hairspray. If Frank Gehry were a hairstylist instead of an architect, this would be his kind of head of hair. She wears red lipstick that she regularly freshens. Excessive makeup is illegal in the school, but the definition of what's excessive is different in Mexico. Unless you have false eyelashes, you're OK in the New Hampshire School. Outside of school, I saw Sandra in an upscale mall, once, with tight jeans with sequins stitched on the back pockets, in the shape of crosses—but coquettish, round crosses that let you know she's religious and she believes in God but if some boy wants to come along and find his way into her pants, that would be OK.

In class, the students all have to wear uniforms with green and blue plaid skirts for the girls and blue blazers with the New Hampshire crest for the boys.

José is the kind of guy who likes to have his blazer always unbuttoned. He sneaks in a soccer shirt when he can, under the blazer, of the national soccer team or of one of his favorite teams in Italy.

I never turn the kids in for clothing violations, because I figure the whole pretension that the kids are future Ivy Leaguers is ridiculous. And besides, they're kids. All I'm interested in is that they learn to read a bit better, that they start to understand just a little of the wide history out there that most of them are oblivious to, and that they consider the possibility there's more than only one right answer. If they can get away from the idea that history is a right or wrong answer, with only dates to memorize, then I feel I've done my part.

The man who came out of the SUV was wearing a white cowboy hat. He was tan in a way upper-class Mexicans around Mexico City don't like to get, meaning his skin was rough and leathery. He had on a crisp, Western-style shirt with fake cowboy stitching on the pockets, and he was wearing a pair of mirrored aviator glasses. Needless to say, this isn't the typical kind of parent that comes to pick up their kids at the New Hampshire School. Two men in black suits, with white shirts and pink ties, who looked like private security guards, trailed behind the man with the cowboy hat as he came into the school.

For another couple minutes, I forgot about the man I'd just seen in the parking lot. I continued with the latest course section about American Prohibition and the women's suffragist movement, how women finally fought to get their full right to vote.

Then a knock came at the door to the classroom. I turned away from the blackboard, where I was writing, and went to the door. There was the guy with the white cowboy hat. I looked through the glass window of the door, and for a second I had the certain feeling I should leave the man outside and call security. But I also had the feeling I was going to be in deep trouble if I didn't open the door. So I did. Or, more like, after we made eye contact the man with the hat let himself in.

He turned to the class as a whole, and there was suddenly complete silence. He walked toward the back slowly, letting the sound of his white crocodile-skin boots click precisely until he got behind José and stood next to Sandra. "Your romance," he said in Spanish, "is over. You hear me?" He turned to everyone in the class and said, "It's over."

He took his son José by the collar of his green Mexican national soccer team jersey, holding the shirt beneath José's blazer. The boy stood up obediently and bent over, like a little child hoping not to be caned by his father, even though he was about five feet ten. The father pulled José up through the middle of all of the desks until he got to me. I watched the whole rebuke in silence, holding my textbook, trying to think how best to respond to let the father know I was the boss in this room. But get real. He was the boss. So I just stood there silently, obediently, with his two guards at the doorway. "And you," the father said when he got up to me. He spoke in English to let me know he could tell me what to do in English, too. He had a thick Mexican accent to his English. It made "you" sound more like Jew. "Jew," he said. "I am going to hold Jew personally responsible for these two. If they ever—ever—do anything together again, I'm going to come kill you. Is that clear?" He paused for a second, as if he realized the way he had just spoken to me in public was too much, a bit outrageous for a school, and then he added, "Look, these two people, they're from different families. That's all you need to know. I'm asking you to keep them apart."

He took José away, and Sandra sat in the back of the room crying.


APART FROM THE tremendous fear I felt from the man threatening me, it was funny that he called me a Jew. Not funny in the way of *ha ha,* but funny that he made that mistake of pronunciation, because I am a Jew. I'm a secular Jew, maybe even an atheist Jew, meaning that I grew up as a Jew in Chicago, and my parents sent me to temple, but I don't believe in God. But I do feel an extreme sense of ease in a temple, so it was with great surprise, when I came down to Mexico eight years ago, that I discovered there was a large group of Jews living in Mexico City. The thought that there could be Jews in Mexico had simply never occurred to me. Mexico was a place of tamales and tacos, mariachi bands and guacamole. What would a bunch of Jews be doing in a place like that?

When I first arrived in Mexico City, with a backpack, with no real plan other than to find some eventual work, a friend of mine who worked for the U.S. embassy let me stay in her apartment in the neighborhood of Polanco. The first day I arrived in the city, I walked outside to get some groceries. I wandered around the upscale neighborhood. It was a Friday, and around evening I saw all these men walking with black fedora hats and long black jackets toward who knows where. At first I just saw one or two, who stood out oddly against the other people walking to a nearby mall, where there are stores like El Palacio de Hierro, which is like Saks Fifth Avenue. The men looked like they'd been Photoshopped into the scene from Brooklyn or Jerusalem. The few Orthodox men I saw grew into somewhat larger groups as they walked into the distance, to the end of the sidewalk.

When I got home to the apartment I was staying in, I asked my friend what these Jews were doing in the neighborhood. "Oh, there are lots of Jews here," she said. "Maybe forty thousand of them." My friend was from El Paso, Texas, and she'd definitely been raised Catholic: hence she used the "them," which is the way even I thought of the Jews, as "them." We were a "them." Always had been, since the days when the Jews first went to Egypt. Even as a nonreligious Jew, it was part of my identity that I was a "them."

The next week, when Friday came around, I followed the men to temple. I was clearly not dressed appropriately to enter. I stood at the door, watching the men go in, feeling like I should stay outside. But curiosity got the better of me, and I asked one of the men, in broken Spanish, if he had a yarmulke I could borrow. He looked at me suspiciously, at first. He eyed my corduroy pants and white button-down shirt. It wasn't a suit, but it was the best I had in my backpack, and I'd ironed my clothes neatly, and he must have seen the good intentions in the crisp creases because he nodded slightly toward the door and let me in. He gave me a tallit, he found me a yarmulke, and he took me inside the main temple, and in the center of the room I saw the scrolls of the Torah eventually revealed, with handles gleaming so brightly that even in the dim light of the temple they shined like silvery moons.

I returned to the temple the next week, and while the women were separated from the men, and while I still didn't believe in God, and while I fumbled through some Hebrew as the other men recited together in unison, I was dragged to a Shabbat dinner afterward, in the basement of the temple, where candles were lit, and where I first set my eyes on Sara.

She had soft freckles and her cheeks were a bit pink and upwardly round, her eyes were a turquoise that pulled me into her gaze. She wore a long black skirt and plain black shoes with stockings, as was required for an Orthodox woman to be considered modest.

What can I tell you about the walks we took throughout the city the next six weeks? They were the kind of ambles where the sun feels warm and perfect on the skin and on the brow. They were the kind of walks where birds seem to constantly sing. We wandered through the Parque Lincoln, where all the trendy restaurants are located. We saw the people eating their meals happily, laughing, raising glasses of wine and seeing people like us as passersby. We watched the dogs play in the park, leaping for balls thrown by their masters. We walked by the beautiful fountains in the Bosque de Chapultepec. We walked to the ice cream store called La Michoacana, where they served us mango and guava sorbets.

But after six weeks, one afternoon after I'd taken Sara home, as I stood outside of her apartment under her second-story balcony—not going upstairs because I knew her father was very strictly Orthodox and didn't approve of me—she stood on the balcony waving at me below, and then the screen door opened and her father came out and he stood tall with his black pants and black jacket and white shirt, and with the fringes of his tallit just poking from under his shirt, and he looked down at me with the beard on his face looking heavy, with the weight of gray crowding out the rest of his once-brown beard, and he raised his hand like a hammer, banging it in the air, and he said in Spanish, "You. You sir. You! Go away. You are not good for my daughter. You are not a real Jew. You! That's enough. I don't want to see you around here anymore."

AFTER SCHOOL, I coach one of the girls' basketball teams at the New Hampshire School. It's part of my contract. I have to coach a sport. It's part of the motto of the New Hampshire School that students will excel not only in the mind and in the heart but also on the field. Growing up, I used to love to watch the Chicago Bulls play basketball. I marveled at Michael Jordan flying through the air and reverse-dunking the ball. It was like he had escaped the bounds of this earth and the bounds of his background in the 'hood.

I was never a natural-born basketball player, myself. I'm too short, only five feet eight. But I'm pretty quick with my hands, so I could always play as a guard.

I remember on one of those early dates with Sara, as we walked through the Parque Lincoln, I saw some kids shooting hoops in a made-up basketball court. A ball came rolling over to me, and I picked it up and dribbled for a few seconds. I thought of throwing the ball from the distance to show Sara I could make a long shot, but then I thought that would look like showing off, so I decided to throw the ball to her, instead, and when the ball came into her chest, where I expected her to grab it, she didn't know how to fully raise her hands properly, to spread them wide to catch the ball, so it went straight into her chest, hitting against her plain white shirt, smashing her breasts.

She gave me this look of betrayal, like I had just intentionally hurt her. I went running up to her as she sucked in air, looking at the smudge of dirt on her shirt. "Why did you do that?" she said.

"I'm so sorry," I said. But I was more than sorry. I was afraid we wouldn't be able to go out anymore. I was afraid the distance between us might be too great. While I'd been growing up watching TV, and Jordan hit the hoops, she'd been wearing long, modest clothes, and occasionally playing jump rope. Attraction is one thing: turquoise eyes, a beautiful smile. But maybe there was too much to overcome.

I thought about that moment with Sara—it was years ago, before we'd gotten married—as I watched Sandra come out to play on the basketball team. She wasn't very good as a student in class, and she may have spent hours combing her hair in perfect curls, but on the court she was an aggressive tiger, wearing her hair back in a long ponytail.

You might think that after the incident with José's father, earlier in the day, Sandra would have gone straight home, but I think, like me, she must have been terrified of deviating in any way from the normal routine.

So, there she was in her basketball shorts and white court shoes trying to go through the motions of shooting hoops from the three-point range. Usually, she was a good shooter. Usually, the ball went in with a nice swish, her hands following through in a delicate downward dip after the shot. But she was missing them all, today, and I saw her shoot even an outright air ball.

I called Sandra over while the other girls continued throwing hoops.

"Are you OK?" I asked.

"You have no idea what it feels like to have him take José away like that. It's none of his business," she said.

"Excuse me," I said, trying to be genuinely polite, "I know it's not my place to ask. But what did you and José do together that got him so mad?"

"We've just been hanging out," she said. She looked at her shoes. She chewed her gum a little, dejectedly. She knew gum was forbidden during practice.

"Just hanging out?"

"His father and my father— They don't get along. They're from the same business. They compete against each other, and whenever one gets the upper hand they get furious at each other."

"And what business is that?" I asked. But I already had more than an inkling of the answer. I'd heard the same rumors all the kids in the school had heard. The rumor was the fathers were both in drug cartels, high up.

"Just a business," she said. "A very lucrative business. So sometimes they get pissed off at each other."

She looked at me stone-faced, as if wanting to let me know she didn't appreciate me asking that kind of question. "So if José comes back to class," she said, "what are you going to do? Are you going to make him sit apart from me? Are you going to tell the principal and make us stay apart?"

"I don't know what I'm going to do," I said, and I meant it. I didn't have a clue what to do. There was the very real possibility I could get involved in something violent if I didn't do what José's father said. There was the very real possibility that José and Sandra had been making love in some motel, somewhere in the city, and that I shouldn't be encouraging their sex at that young an age. There was the very real possibility I should just shut up and go about my business teaching and pretend this day had never happened. But beneath all those clear, rational ideas was the vision of Sara's dad yelling down at me from the balcony telling me I wasn't a real Jew, that I had no right to be with Sara, even though we knew we wanted to be together.

**LATER THAT NIGHT,** I asked Sara if she remembered our wedding day.

"Of course I do," she said. "Why must you bring up something so bitter?"

"Well, do you think your father was right?" I said. I genuinely wanted to know. I truly needed to know.

Her father had refused to attend the wedding until the end of the ceremony, and just after I broke the glass beneath my foot, indicating that I hoped for a life of happiness together with Sara even as we remembered that joy must always be tempered, her father came into the temple and yelled it was an abomination that we had just married. He stood like a prophet foretelling doom, shaking his hands in the air, yelling against us with so much force that drops of his spit seemed to fly out like bullets, caught in the shaft of light coming down from the highest window of the temple. He was a well-respected man in the Orthodox community, so no one tried to shut him up, but there were a couple of men who walked up to him, put their arms around his shoulders, and tried to give him comfort. The question I wanted to know was whether Sara felt I had been an impostor that day, dressing up for a Jewish wedding when she knew I did not believe in God? And I wanted to know if she thought her father had been right, that the divide between us was too big to overcome? Sara had certainly paid the price in marrying me. We had married in a temple different from the one where she grew up. We had married in a Conservative, but not an Orthodox, temple. There is no such thing as Reformed Judaism down in Mexico City. You are either a Jew or not a Jew. The shades of gray, as found in the U.S., don't exist.

Her father had never spoken to Sara again, after our wedding. In the end, during the last words he said to her, he stood frozen like a statue as he yelled in the temple, shouting out to his daughter, "Sara, how could you do this to me? You, who were always my favorite daughter."

There was probably nothing crueler I could have asked Sara after she'd made such a sacrifice of her father in order to marry me. But I felt, following the events of the day with Sandra and José, I wanted to know after eight years whether she was happy with her decision, or with *our* decision.

We had just eaten some tacos from around the corner—I had ordered some pork tinga tacos and she had her usual beef. She rarely went to temple now, and we didn't keep kosher at home, but she still never ate pork.

"I will always feel, in some ways, that a piece of me was cut out that day," Sara said, looking at me with the same intensity she'd looked at me the day the basketball flew into her chest. "I will always feel sad that my father couldn't understand that a good man is a good man whether he is Muslim, Asian, or whatever. You're a good man. That's why I married you. But if I could have married you and kept him happy at the same time, I would have done that. My father used to tell me to never burn any bridges. He used to tell me you never know when you will have to walk back over a bridge you have left behind. I miss the community sometimes. Of course I do. But I don't miss the irrational exclusivity that keeps people in and out. It felt like a prison. That's why I left. And you already know all this, so why are you bringing the subject up?"

I felt, after dragging her into the muck of our marriage, that I owed her an explanation for what had brought the thoughts of our marriage day back to me. The night before our wedding day, her father had come to me where I lived in the south of the city, far away from his neighborhood of Polanco. I was living alone then. Sara stayed residing with her family until our wedding day.

Her father came to my apartment building. Like Sara, I lived on the second floor, and like Sara, I had a balcony, though not nearly as nice, or as big, of one as the apartment where she lived. Her father had come all the way to the south of the city, but he didn't want to get too close to me, so he didn't knock on the door—at least that's why I think he didn't knock. Maybe he thought somehow I could infect him if we came too close—me an atheistic, secular Jew, him a pure man who studied the Torah into the wee hours of the night. So instead I heard a small rock tap against the window of my balcony door. I went out onto the balcony, and I looked around. I couldn't see anyone, at first. I only heard the sound of a forlorn whistle, the haunting wail like a steam train of a *camote* wagon, which roasts bananas and sweet potatoes. I thought maybe I had heard a tap that wasn't really a tap, from the stone. But just as I was about to go back in, the form of a black fedora hat and a black jacket, and the silent, bluish-white glow of his shirt became clearer, below me.

"I have tried with warnings," Sara's father said. "I have tried with reason. Reason is what the Torah teaches us. Two things that are different should not be joined together. But if you will not listen to reason, then I will ask you as a humble man who loves his daughter. Please. Please! I'm begging you. Don't do this to an old man. Don't make me die before my time. Let my Sara marry someone worthy of her. Don't let me lose her."

He was not such an old man. He was no older than sixty-five. His pleading was haunting, touching, and certainly I felt for him. I asked him if he wanted to come upstairs to talk to me. I asked him, couldn't he come upstairs so I could convince him I was worthy of his daughter? But he just shook his head in the moonlight, bending down on one knee, praying as if he could no longer hear me. I went downstairs and opened the door and walked up to speak to him, and when he saw me coming he told me the only way I could redeem myself was to not show up at the wedding tomorrow. "Better not to come. Better to break her heart than to ruin her life," he said.

"Me, ruin her life?" I said. "Haven't you already ruined it? Look at you. Just look at your pale, wrinkled face. You quiver and worry, wringing your hands like some kind of medieval caricature of a Jew in the shtetl. You claim you're the only person who knows right, that there is only one way to live, and that I'm not a real Jew, that I'm a dirty atheist. You negate life itself, wrapping yourself in a small bubble of virtue, blind to everything outside your community, fearful of it, cursing it, and demanding your daughter do the same."

I could no longer hold my tongue. I no longer felt the impulse to try to placate him. Who was he to tell me I shouldn't show up at my wedding tomorrow? It was Sara's and my decision to make alone. I told him so. He put his hands up, against his ears, to block the sound of my voice, and then he ran off.

He disappeared within the shadows of the curvy streets of the night like a chimney sweep, darker than coal. "It's not my fault, it's yours," I whispered after him, as he ran away.

But now, years later, I wondered if I had done wrong to separate his daughter from him forever.

"There are these two kids in my tenth-grade class," I told Sara, "and today the father of one of them came to school and said they should break up, they shouldn't be together." I told her the rest of what had happened that day.

"How can you equate the kids of two rival narcos to us?" she said, at the end of what I told her.

"I'm not," I said. "I know it's different. But is there any real reason why the two of them should be kept apart, if they love each other, other than that their fathers hate each other?"

"You complicate your life," Sara said. "Stay out of it. Let the fathers take care of it. Or, if you really feel like doing something— before you meddle with the two kids in your class, go visit my father and make things right."

"Make things right? You know the fault was never mine. It was him."

"It takes two to build a wall," she said.

IT WAS A windy, sunny day three weeks after José's father had come into the classroom. The days were getting longer. Spring was in the air, even though the seasons don't change all that much in Mexico City. But it felt like a spring day, with a gentle breeze and the sky bluer than usual, without the frequent pollution of Mexico City, and I stood in front of one of the small motels that litter the city, made for romantic affairs, usually between bosses and their secretaries, or between married men and their lovers. This motel was called Amor del Paraíso and was located near the Central de Abasto, a market where every kind of food is sold, and where all the restaurants of Mexico City come to buy their fish in the football field's length of stalls.

I had parked my car a block away, after following Sandra and José riding in a small, black BMW that belonged to José. As they drove through town, I saw them lean into each other at the traffic stoplights, José kissing Sandra as she turned into him, and I could see him twist his head back, occasionally, to see if any of the security guards of his father were following, or the guards of Sandra's family. He must have sensed someone was on his tail, but the mind sees what it is inclined to see, so he couldn't imagine his teacher was following him.

I had listened to Sara, and also to José's father when he'd spoken to the students in class. I separated José from Sandra, as far away as possible, placing him in the front right corner of the classroom, near the door where his father had peered through the window before telling me what to do with my class. It was embarrassing to move José. It meant admitting to everyone in the class that I wasn't their leader: that I was a coward, that I would teach them the rights and wrongs of history and about great leaders like FDR but that in this class I wouldn't practice what I would preach. It's hard to talk about the women's suffragist movement when you won't even let a tenth-grade boy and girl, who love each other, sit next to one another.

Beyond separating them, I went and told the principal what had happened in the classroom. This was the ultimate cover-your-ass move. I hated reporting on Sandra and José. I hated reporting on José's father, too. It went against every fiber in my body. But Sara had asked me to do this, and she was right that it was common sense. What if José's father came back with guns? What if he became more violent? The administration had to know what was happening inside the classroom and to decide what to do next. The principal shook her head as I told her of the incident. She wiped her palms on her tight wool skirt and said she agreed José and Sandra should be separated in the classroom. We discussed the possibility of expelling both of them, because of the threat of violence in school, but we laughed at the very moment we said this. That may have been the right punishment, but you don't play God with the cartels, you accommodate yourselves to them. For the same reason, no extra security was placed around the school. Everything was left as before, to imply nothing had happened, except the separation of José and Sandra in the classroom to comply with the father's will.

That was the official response. The unofficial response was that I wanted to see what José and Sandra were up to. You could certainly call this voyeurism. It's what it was. But I liked to think of it as chaperoning the two of them. I know it might sound insane—me, a defenseless teacher without any weapons, and the people who wanted to hurt Sandra and José, narcos with guns. Certainly, in class, I hadn't found the strength to stand up and protect them. But it was precisely because I hadn't been able to stand up to José's father, so far, and because I felt such cowardice was wrong, that I fought to find the strength to try to take care of Sandra and José in private. Any teacher worth their salt feels the students in their class are there more than to learn; they're there to grow safely into adulthood. A teacher is as much psychologist, protector, and nurturer as the teacher of a subject. This is why they have parent-teacher conferences. This is why they take care of the students at prom, to make sure they get home safe. This is why they spend their short lunch break trying to help the poor student who doesn't have anyone else to speak to in class. In whatever limited way I could, I wanted to try to protect Sandra and José. If I could find a way to keep them safe from their parents, I became determined to do that. So, every day for three weeks, I followed them.

This was the fourth time in three weeks Sandra and José had come to this motel. The first time they'd come, I'd stood far in the distance, not approaching closer, waiting a couple of hours until I saw them exit the hidden curve of the motel's in-and-out entrance. They were safe, still together, still unharmed, still undiscovered by their fathers, and I breathed a sigh of relief as they came out, José looking carefully left and right to make sure none of his father's security guards were watching.

The second time, the man working at the check-in desk asked me if I needed anything, and I said I just wanted to know the rates of the place for future use. I was too scared to go any closer, and I left early, back to my home and to Sara.

The third time, I grew so bold as to walk into the area of parked cars until I found José's car in front of one of the doors. I put my ear against the door, and I could hear them laughing with two friends, the four of them smoking pot. I heard the high laughs and rambunctious jumping on a bed of four teenagers goofing around. That was enough for me. I didn't need to know more. But I kept following them, feeling like I was their guardian angel. If I had to castigate them, or separate them in public, at least I could protect them in private. I looked for ways they might be able to escape from the motel. I checked out where there were exits and what roads anyone who wanted to harm them would come from. If I knew the exits, maybe I could lead them to safety when the time came, alert them to get the hell out of the place before it was too late.

This fourth time, as I stood across the street waiting for José and Sandra to come out, I saw two black Cadillac SUVs approach from the right, down a one-way street that led to an on-ramp of the highway that passed in front of the innocuous motel. I couldn't tell who the bodyguards inside the SUVs belonged to—Sandra's or José's family—but I knew they must have something to do with them. By now, I'd discovered there was a small rear entrance to the motel. It was made for the cleaning crews, so they could take laundry in and out. I'd had far too much time to explore the place—the bland beige paint that covered everywhere except the blue palm trees stenciled on the interior courtyard, where the cars were parked, and a red heart painted on the door to the check-in desk.

When I saw the SUVs approach, I ran across the street behind them as they pulled in front of the motel, and I hurried along the dying cacti and volcanic rocks littered with juice boxes, condoms, and other trash thrown along the side of the motel. A furniture construction warehouse, small and old, with sawdust flying to the ground toward the motel, ran along the path to the back, and I squeezed between the two buildings hearing the sound of a whirring table saw. It was the sound of wood being ripped in two for cheap pine furniture in poor homes. I reached the back door. It was jammed for a second. I picked up a rock and smashed at the lock. The door wasn't closed with a key, it was just stuck from loose hinges, causing it to lean sideways. When I came into the inner courtyard, I looked fast to see if José and Sandra were in their usual room, parked on the left, and they were. Across the thirty-yard courtyard, I could see the two black SUVs. The men had gotten out from the SUVs, and they were entering the check-in area to ask, no doubt, for the check-in book. I'd looked before, the second time I'd visited the place, to see if José was smart enough to use a fake name, and he was. At least he had no illusions that no one would come for them. It might take a couple minutes for the men to pry out of the man at the front desk where the two of them were staying. But it wouldn't take longer, so I knew I had no time to waste.

For a moment, as I stood in front of their door—the cheap wood dry with the dust of the city, the unmistakable sounds of the two of them making love—I thought about turning and fleeing. What the hell was I doing here? What if I was wrong about the guys in the SUVs? What if the men dressed in black that came out of the SUVs wanted nothing to do with them? What if they were looking for someone else? There's an edge, at the point of a knife, when you can fall to the side that gets cut or to the side left safely behind. But I didn't waste time knocking when I found the door unlocked. I opened the door and saw José on top of Sandra.

Her hair was sweaty, spread to all sides. José looked at me and said, "Son of a bitch! What are you doing here? I'll kill you." He reached for a gun, beneath the bed. He was ready for what he knew was coming. I put my hands in the air and held them there. José stood up, his chest hairless, thighs firm from playing soccer, hair still held back from gel and from Sandra's fingers combing through his hair. He was a naked man with a gun. Sandra tried to cover herself quickly with the blanket, but one of her legs strayed out from beneath the covers, and she could barely hide her breasts.

"What the fuck?" José said. "Mr. Jacobs. What the fuck? What are you doing here?" He was still holding the gun pointed at me, but he lowered the 9mm a little.

"You have no more than two minutes to get out of here," I said. "There are security guards. Coming. Fast. At the check-in desk. You have two minutes to get out of here, at best, or they're going to find you."

"How do you know this?" Sandra said. "What are you talking about?"

"Get out the window, quick," I said, pointing at the window that led to the pathway between the motel and the building where furniture was made. "Open it and get out now. Or come with me to the back entrance."

"You're crazy," Sandra said. "If they've come this far they're going to cover every way out. They're not going to let us escape."

José put his pistol down, threw on his jeans, and grabbed his pistol again. He ran barefoot, without a shirt, to the window and tried it, but it was locked. I told them we had to go. I told them we should run out the way I'd come. I waved at them to follow me, but José and Sandra wouldn't listen. I ran back into the motel parking lot and hoped that if I led by example, they'd follow. I'd done as much as I could. I'd stuck my neck out way too far to stay around to see what would happen next. I ran to the back of the motel, farthest from the check-in desk, heading to the door I'd come in before. When I got to the back, I turned around and saw the men opening the glass door at the check-in desk, and I knew I didn't have time to fully escape, so I hid behind a Coke vending machine.

I can only tell you what I heard next: the sound of men running with polished black shoes over the pavement. The sound of the men running up to the room where Sandra and José had been mating. The sound of glass breaking. Perhaps from a chair? José told Sandra he'd broken the window. He told her to go out before him. He must have had his arms behind Sandra, trying to push her out the window.

The sound of a small gun firing, which must have been José shooting at the men running after them. The sound of the guards letting out round after round of their large pistols. The guards weren't from José's father. They were from Sandra's. They shot José. "Come with us, you slut," they yelled at Sandra. But she told them she'd rather die than leave José. "If you come any closer I'm going to kill myself," she said, and she must have found a pistol, because there was one more gunshot and then she didn't make any more noises.

A WEEK AFTER the death of Sandra and José, I was in Polanco, in the evening. It was Friday night and I saw the Jewish men dressed in their black fedora hats, heading to temple. I had walked in the Parque Lincoln earlier in the evening, with Sara, after school. I felt I needed to be back in the park where we used to stroll. I needed the calm order of the tall palm trees that spread over the park, protecting the walkers below like umbrellas. After the shooting of Sandra and José, I had told Sara immediately what had happened and where I was at the time of the shooting. I had even confessed to her I had been following Sandra and José for three weeks.

"You crazy, irrational man," she said, but then she held me tight, stroked my head, and let me know she loved me as much as ever. By her fingertips, I could tell it was precisely the fact I cared so much about Sandra and José that had moved her to give me comfort, and to marry me in the first place.

As we walked in the Parque Lincoln, and I saw some of the Jewish men gathering to go to the synagogue, I said to Sara, "Why don't we go to temple? Why don't we find your father and tell him we're sorry he's so far apart from us?"

Sara looked at me sternly. She gave me a look that said it was better not to stir up old wounds. What she actually said was, "But you don't believe in God."

"Well, I don't," I said. "If ever I needed proof of the absence of God, look at what happened to Sandra and José."

"That's not proof of anything," Sara said. "That's proof bad things can happen to good people, or to people who don't deserve what they get. But that's proof of nothing. Besides, you can't prove whether God exists or not. That's why they call it faith."

"Why should your father care whether I believe in God or not?" I said. "Isn't it enough I'm proud to be Jewish? Isn't it enough I try to live my life in a good way?"

"For me, it doesn't matter," Sara said. "For me, I can see your intentions are good, and that's close enough to God for me. But for him, God is God and you've betrayed his faith."

"I'd like to go to temple and find him," I said. "I don't want us to live the rest of our lives feeling he has disowned you because of me. I'm not comfortable with that burden." Following Sandra and José's death, I felt a need to go to the temple to find him.

Sara relented, after we had a few more rounds discussing the futility of seeking her father out. I saw a man with a black fedora, black pants, and shiny shoes, walking down the Calle Goldsmith toward Avenida Horacio, and I decided to follow him. Sara followed with me, though I could feel her lagging half a step behind, the weight of her resistance wanting to pull me back to the park. There was no need to follow the man; we knew, of course, exactly where we were going. There was no doubt where the temple was where Sara's father would be walking to this very moment, and who knew if this other gentleman was going to the same temple or to another? We walked together in silence for ten minutes, and then came to the imposing door of the temple with Hebrew letters written above the door.

"I'll wait outside," Sara said. "I'm not dressed properly to go in."

"Please," I begged her. "Do this for me. For us. With a gesture we can repair things. You were the one who told me a wall is built by two people, not by one."

"You go in first," she said.

I paused in front of the long handle, feeling the weight of the door, the weight of the thousands of years of tradition the temple represented. But I am a man of faith, too, I thought, even if I don't believe in God. I am a man of faith in the brotherhood of all men, and I belong to my tradition as much as Sara's father, I thought.

When I came into the temple the men were already grouped below on the bottom floor, davening, listening to the rabbi lead the prayers and reciting to him their responses to his calls. The women were upstairs in the temple. I saw Sara walk behind me, and then upstairs to the section for women, as I went inside the main temple area, below, to find her father.

There he was on the right-hand side, in back, as I remembered his place had been eight years before. It was as if he had stood in the exact same spot, praying, the whole time. His beard was now fully gray and his yarmulke sat sternly on his head like an anvil. I didn't want to surprise him too much, by coming up from behind, so I chose to enter his bench row from the center left, where he could see me for a while as I came closer to him. The wood of the long bench, as I moved sideways toward him, was worn smooth from gen-erations of congregants coming every day to pray, especially every Sabbath. When I came close to him, I could see his eyes wander left and he seemed to see me. But he showed no immediate expression. He continued praying, looking at the book with Hebrew lettering in his hand, and calling out in response to the rabbi. It was as if I weren't there, as if an iceberg had come close to his ship, the *Titanic*, and he refused to acknowledge any ice. His ship was impenetrable, a fortress, impregnable. I came closer and closer, and was close enough that I could easily reach out to his hand to touch it. But still he made no motion to acknowledge me. It was now or never. I could leave this second with things as they were. I could leave with the same wall of silence between him and me and his daughter that had lasted eight years. For a moment, I considered moving back to the left, sidling

into the center of the temple, and leaving. But the thought of Sandra and José came to me, the sound of Sandra shooting herself, and
I whispered into the old man's ears, "Your daughter loves you and
would like to talk to you. And I love you, too."

At the mention of the word "daughter" his eyes widened for a
second, then they resumed their half-open shape of deep meditative
prayer. If this plea wouldn't work, then I thought I would try one
more. I turned to him and whispered, "I'll do anything. I will do
anything to make you happy."

He turned up to the balcony to see if Sara was there. He must
have found she was. He turned back down, not acknowledging my
presence. Then he turned to me directly and said, "Will you accept
there is only one God, that he is the God of Abraham and Isaac, and
that he is your God? Will you denounce that you don't believe in
God?"

What he wanted me to do was to denounce who I was. What
he wanted me to do was to be only who he wanted me to be. What
he wanted me to do was to believe in rote faith for no more reason than that I had been born into a faith. And even if I did that, I
knew he would find other problems with me: that I wasn't Orthodox enough, that I didn't keep kosher, that I didn't follow my daily
life as he wanted me to. He wanted to find divisions; and wanting
to find divisions, he would always find them. Who was he to try to
tell me what to do, when I had done nothing but try to treat him
with respect, and to give love to his daughter? Sara wasn't asking me
to make this choice. She had asked me, in fact, not to come see her
father. She had had that wisdom.

And yet, looking up at the front of the temple at the scrolls of
the Torah, it came to me that what the man was asking me to do
was to give a name to a feeling that was mutual. We both believed
there were mysteries to the universe. We both believed the ways and
reasons why men acted were often unknowable, and that they were
often worthy of punishment. We both believed a life should be lived

as morally as possible. He wanted faith, and faith I couldn't give him. But there is wisdom in seeking common ground, in breaking down walls that don't need to exist. If his faith meant I would honor him and his daughter and that I would seek to live a moral and just life, then I would say what he wanted me to hear. In naming, each hears the name they want to hear, and if it's the same name it will be heard as the same, even if it is different. "Yes, I have come to tell you I believe in God," I said. "I will no longer call myself an atheist."

He turned to me and hugged me, coldly, but with a pat on the head that let me know he was giving me forgiveness. He looked up at Sara and nodded for her to come down so he could talk to her. He went out behind the main room of the temple to the entryway to speak to her. And as he went up to Sara and hugged her, and whispered something into her ear, speaking to her for the first time in eight years, I thought to myself, I believe in the God of family. That will be my God, however we have to name it. It was not that I would believe in his God. I couldn't. But I would believe in the God of common names.

# I WANT TO LIVE

I was waiting in the waiting room of the Spanish Hospital in Mexico City. I'm a nurse. Or at least I used to be, until I retired down to Mexico. I came down, in part, because the cost of living had become more than I expected in the U.S. and mainly because, at a relatively young age, I decided I wanted to live my life to the fullest. I didn't want to die with the regret I never did all the things I would like to do. So, at the age of fifty, after working as a nurse for twenty-five years in Cleveland, I came down to Mexico City. For five years I integrated myself into the city and the culture. I learned Spanish, taking intense language classes and generally speaking to everyone I could.

Things were going swimmingly until three weeks ago, when I came in to get a checkup at the hospital for the first time. I hadn't exactly come in with no idea of what they would tell me. My mother died of breast cancer and my aunt died of breast cancer and my grandmother died of breast cancer. It runs extra-prevalently in certain families. The same way some families have heart disease or mental health diseases, others have a risk for breast cancer. I usually avoid sharing such information with doctors, precisely because I am afraid of what they will tell me. My whole adult life I was a nurse giving out logical, rational information to patients, but the minute the tables were turned on me and I was a patient, it felt the other way. As a new patient at the Spanish Hospital, three weeks ago, they gave me a sheet with a checklist of all the health problems that might be troubling me. I could honestly check *no* for almost everything on the list. When it came to a history of breast cancer in the family, I checked *no,* at first. Then I scratched out my check mark. Then I left the yes box blank. And then, after tapping the pen they had given me on the clipboard, I finally checked *yes.*

After a brief talk with Dr. Rodriguez, the general practitioner who examined me, they brought in another doctor, Jiménez, a specialist in breast cancer. "I see you have mentioned there is a history of breast cancer in your family," Dr. Jiménez said. I explained to him who had died in my family. He insisted we do a standard genetic test to see if I had inherited the gene for having a high probability of breast cancer. The test was arranged that very day; they took a sample. And a week later, two weeks ago, they told me I had the gene BRCA1, which gave me an 87-percent chance I would develop breast cancer, unless I had a double mastectomy.

It was under these circumstances that I was waiting in the waiting room when I saw a woman across from me waiting, too. She was quite young, no more than thirty. She had long, brown, perfectly combed hair and a stunningly beautiful face. Her eyes were wide and round in a way that reminded me of Japanese anime dolls. Her cheeks were fleshy and healthy. Her ears were petite, and she wore a couple of big fake diamonds that seemed an effort to show off her whole face. It was hot in the waiting room. We were in the waiting room for reconstructive surgery. I was very torn by the idea of having my breasts removed. I wasn't sure, at all, that this was something I was willing to let happen. At the same time, I was deeply worried about the consequences—a near certainty of getting breast cancer, sometime in the next five years—if I didn't.

Looking across at the other woman, I couldn't help but say,

aloud, without thinking, "It must be nice to still be so pretty and perfect."

The woman stared at me, then turned sharply away. I saw her fold one hand under the other in her lap. The suddenness with which she moved her hands struck me as odd. She played at the hemline of her skirt. The skirt was long and floral and accentuated the fact that she had a surprisingly fit body. She was in all ways, it seemed, a near perfect specimen of beauty, and it certainly didn't escape my notice that *her* breasts were perfectly intact. She had on a red silk chemise that attracted attention to her breast area, and when she bent forward and down to fix the hemline of her skirt, smoothing it, I couldn't help but see her young, well-formed breasts. Her body was evenly tan and her breasts curved firmly upward, so that even with her bending forward, the firmness of the curve, and the health of her breasts, was more than evident.

"It's so unfair," I found myself saying, involuntarily aloud. "Look at you. Just look at you." There were only the two of us in the waiting room, so there was no way for her to avoid me or to misconstrue what I was saying. She looked simply gorgeous in the most stereotypical of ways. She looked like she could be on the red carpet of an Oscars awards ceremony, with cameras taking photos of her. "You could be a movie star," I said. "And me, now they want to take away my breasts. Option A, they say, is to do a double mastectomy. Option B is to die. I used to tell patients about these kinds of crazy dilemmas and I would tell them all rationally, just like they have told me, but it's different when you're suddenly on the side of being a patient . . . But you, the gods seem to have made you perfect."

In the quickness with which the woman in front of me kept moving her hands, I could only notice her perfection, even her perfume smelled sweet. The woman tried not to listen to me; she looked away and laughed, a kind of shocked laugh when I continued insisting on her beauty, but when I declared the gods had made her perfect she shot up her right hand, holding the palm in my direction, and on her palm I saw, carved in a pink hideous X, a large scar that took up the whole of her hand. She raised her other hand, and the palm had the same hideous scar. She was marked with two Xs, puffy and thick, fleshy and with a rawness that indicated they would most likely never disappear, even with the best of reconstructive surgery.

She turned away from me and lifted her perfectly combed hair, held with hairspray that kept it perfectly in place, light brown with streaks of blonde, thick and rich. She bent to show me her neck even more clearly. It was a thin, pale brown, delicate long neck made for caressing; only, in the center of the back of her neck there was another X, marked as crudely as the first two.

"I'm so sorry," I said. "How did it happen?"

"Some things are not meant to be shared," she said. She spoke in Spanish. "You're asking something too private."

"Yes," I said. "I'm listening." Over the years, as a nurse, I have learned that what everyone really wants to do, what they really need to do, is to tell their story, locked inside. If they can just get the story out, it can do more good than even the surgery they are facing. I have learned that—more than running around changing IVs and helping doctors prepare for surgery and changing bedsheets for patients— the biggest role a nurse plays is psychologist. "Yes, tell me. Tell me," I said. "Tell me and maybe your story will help me feel better, too."

"You want me to tell you such a personal story, but you want me to tell it for you rather than for me," the woman said. "Do you think you can stomach such a story?" She held her palms in the air for me to clearly see the two Xs. It wasn't like me to blurt things out the way I'd done. I must have looked tense, an animal lost at sea. I had no family in Mexico. I was, completely, all alone. She was right, I wanted the story for me and not for her.

"Yes, I'm sure I want to hear about the scars," I said. "I'm all alone, here in Mexico. I'm waiting to see if they're going to remove my breasts. I never had kids, and the man I was once married to left me. I'm divorced. I could use hearing your story. I'm in deep trouble. I don't know *what* I will do if they get rid of my breasts. I think I'll feel like I'm just going to die, like they're getting rid of my body and soul."

She sucked in deeply and examined me. I must have looked well on my way to becoming a grandmother. She must have felt pity for a woman my age having to confront breast cancer alone.

"Forgive me," she said, "but I can see you are a foreigner. Only a foreigner would insist so much I tell a personal story for them. Yet, since you insist, I'll tell you, because it seems it might help you—on the condition you don't judge me before I finish telling you the entire story."

"Oh, I won't judge. I can see someone did something wrong to you." Since she spoke to me in Spanish, I did the same.

She leaned back and closed her eyes, as if retreating to a time far away. She kept her eyes closed as she began to speak, opening them only as she got into her story, so rapt in her tale she barely saw me as she talked.

"I have been a very foolish person. I have used beauty like a drug. But I became the person who did so much wrong, I think, or who participated in so much wrong because I grew up with nothing, first. When I was a kid, I was completely an orphan. I grew up in Sinaloa, and I grew up in an orphanage. My father ran off, away from my mother before I was even born. I have no idea where he went. He was a man who just wanted to plant his seed in every woman he could find. I hear he was from Brazil, but I really don't know. He came and went, arriving on a boat in a storm and leaving only a few weeks later, after he had wooed my mother. My mother was very beautiful, they tell me, and she died when I was two. She had been raised as an orphan also, so when you say the gods have made me perfect and that everything has been given to me, I laugh, because the only thing I know is that life is like a wheel that circles and circles. What happened to my mother was passed on to me. She chose a bad man to live with and to have a baby with, and I guess I did the same.

"But I loved my bad man. That's the thing—I suppose I loved my bad man just like my mother loved hers. Bad men are like addictions. They lure you in with sex and fulfilling whatever dream you have, and they make your heart rush with their masculinity, and that's what Enrique did to me.

"But every addiction starts somewhere, and my addiction to my beauty began when I lived in that orphanage. I didn't know that I was beautiful, and what the power of being beautiful is, until I was six years old. Yes, of course, I knew that people always looked at me longer than they looked at other kids. When you are beautiful people envy you, they look at you and they want to get close to you. But they also want to punish you and harm you because you are everything they want to have and what they are jealous of.

"When I was six, a wealthy woman came to the orphanage where I was growing up. The orphanage was run by nuns. There were children crying all over the place. Each group of children had to look after the others. One room had the kids who were infants, on up to three-year-olds. Another had the kids who were from three to eight, which is where I lived. And then there were the oldest kids, who were, by then, considered untouchables who would never be adopted by anyone, destined for failure. The three- to eight-year-olds were expected to change the diapers of the babies. I was changing the diapers of one of the infants when the wealthy woman, La Señora Elvira de Castilla, came into the orphanage. She had a long face, full of wrinkles that had been stretched tight with plastic surgery. Her gray hair was as brittle and dry as dusty straw. She walked with her body rigid, like she was afraid of bending over because it might hurt her bony figure. She was someone, I would discover, who always looked in mirrors. The mother superior took La Señora around the orphanage, bringing her into each room, and when La Señora saw me she said, 'Stop. Stop. That one is beautiful. She is exactly what I am looking for.' She grinned at me like a cat looking at its prey. She came up to me and stared deep into my eyes, seeming to see a reflection of beauty too alluring and powerful for her, which reminded her of whom she had once been, or wanted to be. She pinched my cheek until it left a sting I could still feel the next day, when I was delivered by a nun to her dark, front house door.

"La Señora didn't treat me like an adopted daughter. She treated me more like her servant. She made me sleep in the servants' quarters with the other old muchacha she had. She made me wash the floors and clean food in the kitchen and dust the banisters of her house, where she lived, otherwise, alone. She made me wind up the grandfather clock in the old study where her husband had once worked, before he'd died. She made me stand behind her as she sat at the boudoir for hours putting on makeup, having me comb her hair, one long brushstroke after another, the gray, long hair, like pieces from a skeleton, coming off in my brush.

"She would barely let me go out, since she barely went out. She had caged birds in her house, in large cages I had to regularly clean. The birds stank, even though they were beautiful, exotic tropical birds from South America, and I would watch them gnawing at the bars of the equally exotic birdcages.

"So it shouldn't be surprising that, like those birds, I searched for any way I could get out of the house. I looked for excuses to go to the market to buy fruit and vegetables. I never had any money of my own to go shopping. La Señora would give me exactly the small amount she wanted me to spend on the food. She never gave quite enough, so she knew I would have nothing to spend on myself. It was always embarrassing to come to the end of the shopping and to find, with one of the last vendors, that I would have to tell them to take some of the food back because I didn't have enough money to pay for everything. I would walk home eating a mango or plum, and when I got home La Señora would tell me she knew I was eating some of the food and that I shouldn't be such a little thief.

"At the age of sixteen, then, it shouldn't come as any surprise I ran away, one day. I left without any extra clothes. I was afraid if I left with anything that seemed unusual, La Señora would notice and slam the door before I could leave, or she would immediately call the police and have them search for me. So I ran away with only the black dress I had on, with a white lace top like a maid's bib attached to the dress. For six days, I wandered the streets. I slept in alleyways so no one would find me, in the corners of stairwells, and once even behind a garbage dump, because I had looked in the garbage for food and then had fallen asleep, so tired. It was the day after that that I found Enrique, or, I should say, he found me.

"I am not going to lie and say he did not look like a drug dealer, or a pimp. He looked like a criminal, straight-up. He had on a white suit with a red handkerchief. He had on a pair of shiny, gray alligator-skin boots that were so polished they looked like leather mirrors. His black hair was gelled back with tons of oil, and his eyes were hidden by dark sunglasses. His smile was almost nonexistent. If he smiled, it was despite himself. But when he took off his dark glasses his eyes looked through me, and through everyone he saw. His eyes came to black points that shined like glass, which seemed to calculate and take everything in all at once, figuring out the value of anything before him, what kind of gold he could turn something into that looked to others like nothing. He had the eyes of someone who won at cards, who could sit down at a table, assess the situation, and walk away with all the money on the table.

"He took one look at me and said, 'Allow me, please, to take you out to breakfast.' He spoke to me like a gentleman, even though, by that time, my clothes were covered with dirt, and the lace bib attached to the dress was gray with filth.

"He took me to one of the fanciest places for breakfast, on the main plaza of the city. When he walked into the restaurant, the waiters all stood at attention. The headwaiter came up to him and said, 'Señor Enriquez, your usual seat?' and they took him to a table that looked directly out onto the plaza. He ordered me a large breakfast of huevos divorciados, a plate of fruit, coffee with fresh cream, sweet rolls, and an extra plate of strawberries. La Señora Elvira had never allowed me to eat with her, only to serve her. I truly didn't know how to eat in the company of a man who was well-dressed and who wanted me to sit at his side. I ate, sometimes, with my fingers, because I didn't know any better. I picked up some of the pieces of strawberry with my hands, without thinking, though I tried to eat with a fork and knife because I knew that was what a lady was supposed to do.

"Enrique watched me eat like a wolf, and at one point he began to laugh, after I told him a little about working for La Señora, and as he watched me eat the fruit with my fingers. 'She tormented you,' he said. 'She turned you into an animal. That's what I like, a beautiful animal. The regular women out there, they are either too soft or—if they are tough—they have no physical beauty. But you have both, because of the way you were raised.' He told me he was going to buy me all the clothes I wanted. He told me he was going to let me see just how beautiful I was. He told me I was the most beautiful young woman he had ever seen. He was no older than twenty-nine, but I liked that he didn't look like a boy. I wasn't looking for a teenager then, like the boys I had sometimes stared at with longing in the marketplace. I wanted someone who could keep me safe, and he had everything I needed then."

She stopped, suddenly, and came out of her dream for a second. She looked over at the secretary in the waiting room, but it was clear there was no movement forward from the doctor to speak to either of us. We were two patients who were going to have to wait to see the doctor. It was a Tuesday around lunchtime, and who knew if the doctor was even with a patient, or if it was just going to be one of those waits, in Mexico, that can take forever?

"And the scars?" I said. "What happened with the scars?" The lady's story was engaging, but I had to admit I was getting impatient to hear about the scars. I was still trying to figure out what any of this had to do with my potential double mastectomy. The lady had suggested there was some connection. I was glad she was getting her story out, and I wanted to hear more, but I was feeling anxious about what the doctor would tell me, and this story wasn't necessarily comforting me.

"The scars are always there. Even before they give them to you. But I told you, you will have to let me finish the story. You want everything to be revealed quickly, you want this story to be immediately about you. Just listen. This story is not instantly about you. It's about me. And you will have to not judge me."

"I promise," I said. "I guess I promise." I was beginning to lose my patience, a bit.

"Do you want to hear, or not? Just listen to what someone else has to say." I heard her say the word "selfish" under her breath. She shook her head and pressed her hands, anxiously, one against the other. She looked at the palms of her hands, where the scars were. She looked at them, seemingly in disbelief, and continued.

"Over the next two years, once Enrique picked me up off the streets, I began to shop and to buy clothes, voraciously. I bought long, bright gowns, purple and gold, with sequins sewn all around the necks of the dresses. I was only sixteen when I met Enrique, and I had never had a quinceañera party, so Enrique gave me a sort of party like that, even if it was a year too late. He invited the various other small-time leaders of the drug cartel he was in. It was a way of trying to move up the ranks. At the same time as he was selling more drugs and killing more people and proving he could be tough enough to become one of the bigger leaders of the cartel, he wanted to show me off as his girlfriend and as the woman he intended to make his bride. A couple hundred people were going to come to the party, and he wanted me not only to look good but to be able to perform something for the guests. 'I think you could be a good entertainer,' he told me. 'Most of those singers who get all the attention on TV, they start out like us—people who the rich try to keep down—but then they show their pure soul and their talent and they prove the rest wrong. I don't see any reason why you couldn't be a famous actress or an entertainer. Just look at you. You're more beautiful than Ninel'—a popular singer, at the time. 'We're going to turn you into something, too. You and I, we're going to rise, together.'

" 'Really?' I said. 'You really think I can be something? You really think I could be someone people would admire, with talent?' When I said 'talent,' I was thinking of the soap opera stars. It never occurred to me to think of a serious stage actress or a serious opera singer, or a simple singer in a church choir. I wanted to be like the pop stars and the soap opera stars and the stars of the movies in the theaters, which La Señora Elvira had never let me go to, and that I went to with Enrique religiously.

" 'With your beauty, anything is possible,' Enrique said. 'Life is for the taking. You have to take what you want. The people who want to stop you from becoming what we want to become are everywhere. But I'll be your prince. I'll make you into what you want.'

"So I started to take dancing and singing lessons. I started to pose in front of the mirror as I sang, and to practice my moves. I learned to sway dramatically in those most sentimental of moments, when you want to hold the audience enraptured with your song. I started out learning traditional songs, because tapping into the traditional songs was all I knew, at first, and they were easier to learn in voice lessons. I put on more and more jewels. Fake ones, at first, much bigger than these fake diamonds you see me wearing now. I covered myself in big hoop earrings and rubies. I watched videos of the pop stars, and I did the same moves with them on TV, walking back and forth on my imaginary stage. Jumping and shaking and twirling. Enrique told me I had always had the talent within me to be a star, it's just that others were preventing me from being what I could be.

"You see, we were in this together. The idea was we were going to both rise up until people could admire us the way Enrique said we should be admired. That's why Enrique wanted me to compete to be a beauty queen, and that's why he was strategizing and working so hard to move up the ranks of his cartel. And I want to tell you, I could see how much we needed each other. At the party for me that he threw with his couple hundred guests, he would pull my hand, bringing me forward from one group of invited men to another, showing me off, telling everyone I was his novia—his girlfriend. He told me to wear a bright red dress, because he knew no other woman would have the guts to be dressed so brightly, so young, and at a party where I was meeting all these men for the first time. As each of the men would come up to me and Enrique, to shake his hand and to show their loyalty to him, or for him to show his loyalty to them, the men would whistle under their breath, as if to say, 'Oh my god, how did you get such a beauty?' They gave Enrique the look that said, 'I wish I could be in bed with her. Caray!' They shook their hands rapidly in front of their faces up and down when speaking to the others, just next to us, after they had met me with Enrique. It was the waving of hands that said: 'She's too hot! Fuck, man. That Enrique is one lucky cabrón.'

"You might think a young woman would feel like a cow on display, like a sex object these crude men wanted to rape, if they could. And you might not be far off, if you did think that. But that's not how I felt, at the time, at all. What I felt was that I was radiating. What I felt was that, for the first time in my life, I was the object of attention, not because I was the servant being called to attention by La Señora Elvira but because I was envied and admired.

"When I sang at that first party, up on stage with a group of sixteen mariachi players Enrique had brought in just to make me look good, I sang so-so. I looked beautiful on stage, but my voice wasn't as good as how I looked. Enrique was furious with me, afterward, that my voice wasn't good enough. 'You are going to have to do better,' he would tell me. 'You are simply going to have to do better. I am not going to let you embarrass me in front of the people who I invite to my parties.' And then he hit me. It was the first of many times he would hit me on the cheek. But out in public, after I had sung that first time, he came up confidently on stage, holding the microphone so close it gave a reverberation feedback, a wince-inducing high-pitched echo as everyone watched Enrique on stage, and he said, 'Wasn't that just beautiful? Please, everyone, give a round of applause for Esmeralda Sanchez. She is going to be the next movie star and pop star of Mexico.'

"People clapped politely, but without much enthusiasm. Enrique went backstage to tell me to do better, and he hit me. I felt the pain so sharply, after having tried my best, after feeling I was finally beginning to be someone more than what La Señora Elvira had told me I was, after having been presented to all the other men at the party. But I didn't take this as a sign Enrique was at heart what he, of course, was—a violent man. I took it as a sign I had failed and that I needed not to fail the next time. I would need to work harder.

"And so, I did work harder, one dancing and singing class after another. Pushing myself harder and harder. Singing with records and tapes in the dance studio Enrique constructed for me. The dance studio began to feel like one of those birdcages La Señora Elvira had in her house. At times, I felt I wanted to stop practicing, but Enrique would come and check in on me. He would even lock me in there, occasionally, if I told him I was tired of practicing so much.

" 'I need a break,' I told him, once.

" 'You can take breaks another day,' he told me. 'Everyone out there in this city, they think the only way to make it in this world is to be born with connections, to be born rich. But you and I know otherwise. When you have nothing, you have to make it yourself. I'll be your connection for you, but you have to have the talent, too.'

" 'And how do you show *your* talent?' I asked him.

" 'Excuse me?' he said, with indignation. 'Are you saying it

doesn't take talent to lead my business? To make my business decisions every day?' He was building up his section of the cartel, more
and more. He was rising, quickly, in the cartel. This is what he told
me regularly, and it was something I could see, as well. The men
around him were becoming more solicitous. They started to walk
with him, his old friends, less as equals and more as men showing
respect to their leader.

"A year later, I finally fulfilled Enrique's dreams. Not his final
dreams for me at all, to become a big star, but his dreams for me in
Sinaloa, as a first step to the big time. I competed to be Miss Sinaloa.
My makeup was caked-on thick, and I had extensions on my lashes.
I posed in evening gowns and in a green bikini with bows. I crossed
one leg alluringly in front of the other. The men whooped, in the
audience. They hooted and hollered with lust. The announcer had
to tell them to keep their shouts down and to show some respect. I
felt the heat of the lights and the sweat on my forehead, and I worried the heat might somehow ruin my makeup, that something out
of my control might cause me to be just a little off and to lose the
contest, which would cause Enrique to lose faith in me and to hit
me, as he had done, by now, a number of times. I began to associate
my beauty with the pleasure of Enrique's adoration, but also with
the pain when I disappointed him.

"But on this day, when I completed my dance and singing routine, I was relieved to see I had not failed Enrique. The announcer on
stage, dressed in a tuxedo with big white ruffles, placed the crown on
my head, and I felt like a true princess wearing that tiara. I felt the
love and adoration and appreciation of the crowd. I began to cry on
stage, as all beauty queens cry, but I was crying not only because all
of my hard work had paid off, and not only because I knew Enrique
would be proud of me and would love me more, and because he was
right, he had pushed me hard and proven to me that with hard work
I could be something more than I thought; I was crying because I
felt for the first time I had escaped the clutches of La Señora Elvira

and the clutches of the orphaned life, the wheel of life that had first made my mother an orphan and then me. I was escaping from that past. The wheel of life could no longer control me. And so, I cried on that stage, letting my mascara run a bit beneath my eyes, a mark of imperfection that was perfectly meant for the moment.

"Enrique didn't wait to meet me after the contest, behind stage. He ran up the side of the stage and took the microphone from the announcer, who looked at him as if this was a bit odd, but by then everyone knew who Enrique was and that they shouldn't disappoint him, or their personal safety might be on the line. Enrique lifted my hand in the air, as if I was the champion boxer of the country, as if I was not the beauty queen of Sinaloa but the real queen of the city and nation. 'Ladies and gentlemen, this is my queen,' he said. 'And I wish to announce we are going to get married.' I was as surprised as everyone in the audience. Enrique hadn't said anything definitive about marriage, up to this point. He had kept me close, as if I was the only one who mattered to him, but I knew well that a man like Enrique could lose interest and suddenly want to be with another woman. He was tough and full of intensity, full of whatever he needed at any moment. Announcing the marriage, on stage, I was both filled with elation and relief, a sense that now he would be mine and I would be his, that we would truly fulfill, together, our dreams and his dreams. As I said, I felt he knew more than me at that point. But I also wondered why he hadn't asked me, in private, as he should have. The side of me that had been caged for so long could not help but ask him, behind stage, why he had made the announcement before asking me what my intentions were.

" 'Are you disobeying me, mi amor?' he said. 'Do you think I don't have good reason to tell everyone out there?' I could see the well of anger within him bubbling to the surface at the idea I had challenged him, for a second. And then he switched moods, entirely, pretending I had said nothing and that he had said nothing that was acrimonious. He swept me off my feet, with my tiara on my head, and told me he loved me and adored me and that he wanted to make me the happiest wife I could ever be. He pulled out a big diamond ring, which was a real diamond, not like the other fake costume jewelry I so often wore. He slipped the ring on my finger and pulled me out to the car, a long, white limousine he had rented just for the occasion. There was a sunroof. We drove around in the limousine, with a jeep of his cartel compadres carrying weapons in front, and a black SUV with support in back. The three vehicles drove around the city, honking, letting everyone know I had just won the Miss Sinaloa contest and that we were going to get married. Once in a while, Enrique would tell me I should stand in the back of the limousine and peek out the rooftop and wave at my public. 'Go ahead, wave! Wave to them. They are all your people, now. They all adore you.' I did as he commanded. I was with my prince, the man I was going to marry. I stood with my head through the roof, waving, with a crowd in the central plaza waving back at me, and Enrique standing next to me. He held my hand, fingering the diamond he had placed on my ring finger. He gave me a big kiss on the lips, in public, in the central plaza. Shouts, egging him on to be manly, made him kiss me again. I wrapped my arms around him, and for a fleeting second, despite the fact I knew I was more and more his possession, despite the fact I knew he was the leader of a cartel that others feared, despite the fact I knew his cartel must be killing hundreds of people, despite all those things I grabbed him closer to me and I felt, 'This is my man.' "

Listening to the woman, who I now knew was Esmeralda Sanchez, who I thought for a second I had seen on TV, once, in a cantina—now that she'd mentioned she'd been elevated to Miss Sinaloa—I could see she was reliving each experience as she told it to me. She sat in the waiting room waving her arm as she'd once waved at the public. Only now her hand had a scar on it.

"And the scar?" I said. "The scars . . ." I tried to remind her she was supposed to be telling me about her scars.

"The story of the scars will come soon enough. But I cannot just tell you the story about them right away, or you won't understand, and you won't understand why this story is important to you and why I'm telling it to you." She stood and straightened her long flower skirt and walked to the far end of the waiting room and filled a cup of water from a watercooler. She went to the bathroom to freshen up, it seemed. I asked the secretary if the doctor was back yet, and she said he was still busy with another patient, or maybe out to lunch. I'd wanted the doctor to come quickly, before, so I could talk with him about whether I should have the mastectomy or not, and to have the certainty of a decision made crystal clear. But now, before I met the doctor, I felt I needed to hear the rest of the beauty queen Esmeralda Sanchez's story. I hoped the doctor wouldn't come before she could tell me what I needed to hear. It seemed to me all of a sudden that she must have the answers, like a fortuneteller, as to what I should do, she was telling her story so passionately.

She came back from the restroom, sat down, and began to tell her story, again.

"Three years went by, with Enrique's business in the cartel growing and growing, with other narcos feeling more and more threatened by him as he took over more of their territory in the drug business, when one night, on June second, a date I will never forget, a group of men broke into the house where we were living, who worked for another cartel. By this time, we lived in a house on the beach that looked out over the water, with high ceilings, crammed full of the art and objects that Enrique felt proved he had made it in his cartel work. He had been collecting large jade and malachite Buddhas and scenes of ancient fantasy landscapes, in the clouds, from China. He bought them not only in Mexico, from dealers who brought to him the art they thought he would like, but also from places like Hong Kong, where he occasionally went for his work. He had a collection of French crystal statues of sports cars, over fifty objects in a case at the base of the stairs leading up to our bedroom. The objects were truly rare, and at his command a number of lights lit the sports cars when he showed off his crystal to guests. At the front door, when visitors came in, there were porcelain cheetahs; and, in an effort to please him, I'd selected red fur coats and suede leather couches of purples and aquamarines, which made the whole place feel like a very upscale home, with rococo designer furniture. A Porsche 911 and two Porsche SUVs sat in the garage. He'd attained more and more of what he wanted, but more was never enough.

"I saw him less and less because of his work, and because I tried to appear in movies and TV shows, just as he desired. I had a bit of success but not nearly as much as his. I had the looks but not, necessarily, the full talent. And soon, I had even less of the looks. Much less.

"The night when they came and hurt me so badly, a group of three men, the rival narcos, came into the bedroom. Two held me down on the sprawling, custom-made bed. They did not rape me. I will never understand why, though I think they understood it would torment Enrique more if he could never know, for certain, whether they had raped me. Instead, they carved one of the Xs on one of the palms and the scar on the back of my neck, and an extra scar which I haven't shown you, an X that is the same as the others, on my stomach, just over my belly button. It is important to know they did not make the scar on my other hand. That would come by me, later.

"I could go into gory details of how they carved the scars into my body, but why turn this into a horror movie? The facts are bad enough, aren't they? The fact they took their time as they cut me. The fact they knew what they were going to do, before they came. It wasn't a crime of animalism, in the heat of the moment as they fought with my husband—who, in fact, was not there. It was a crime of meditation, a well-thought-out act to send my husband a message that his most precious object, the one he had shown off for years as the beauty queen of Sinaloa, was not untouchable, was scarred and belonged to them, and was deflowered.

"Only, my husband had already, even before the incident, begun to care less and less about me. He was already beginning to lose interest in me. He was already beginning to look at other women, and I suspect to sleep with them, and once I was scarred by these men—in the middle of the night, with blood soaking into the sheets, and especially with the mark over my womb, which had failed to produce a child for us—he lost all interest, completely. He simply almost never came home.

"The absence of his attention, even though he had hit me over the years, even though he had always treated me more as his possession than a mutual love built by the two of us, made me feel more and more insecure, more and more desperate to win his attention back. I bought brighter and richer clothes, if that was possible. I went shopping for Louis Vuitton and Prada handbags, dresses from Versace, not the most expensive haute couture dresses because those were out of Enrique's league, but I bought whatever he could afford and whatever he would allow me to afford. I bought gold and platinum baubles and sat in front of the mirror and combed and recombed my hair, feeling the brush scrape against my neck, sitting in front of the boudoir off the room where they had scarred me, combing my hair just as La Señora Elvira once had me comb her hair for hours. Once free of her, I was now acting as if she still possessed me, as I tried to repossess Enrique.

"But Enrique was with other women now, barely hiding them anymore. Once, when I confronted him about an especially young woman, who looked as young as I'd been when Enrique had first found me on the street, but whom, looking at her at a party, I felt had none of the charm I had originally had, none of my toughness, I wondered what he saw in the woman he was nudging up to so closely at the large party, a party now with five hundred. I had sung at the party, and people had politely clapped. I sang better than that first party Enrique had me sing at. I had the moves down now, after years in the profession. But I was still the mediocre performer I had started out as, a beauty queen who was no longer all that beautiful, with the scars on my hand and neck and on my womb, which I now hid. 'What is it about her that makes her so perfect for you?' I asked him at the party. If it seems strange I asked him then and there, directly to his face, it was no stranger than when you, earlier, asked me why the gods had made me so perfect. What I am saying is, the question was involuntary, a question I should not have asked, unless I wanted to be nearly destroyed.

" 'What makes her so perfect,' Enrique said, 'is that she is what you once were but no longer are. She has potential, and what kind of potential do you have now, with the scars they did to you? But I want you to know I am not rejecting you because of your scars alone, though they are hideous. I am rejecting you because you have lost your edge, your talent, your drive, your animalism. Look at you now, so soft and draped in all of these clothes. I can barely see the puma inside of you that I once wanted. You have failed to give me a child. You have failed in the most basic task of a real beauty queen. Infertility is hardly becoming. Every king needs his heir. Every king must have his concubines. And I have to say, when I look at the scars on your body, I can't help but wonder if they raped you, too, but you just won't admit it.'

"They were words, in short, of pure bile. Pure hate. They were words to hurt me like a boy who holds a magnifying glass in front of an ant, keeping the focus of light that is too hot on the ant until it burns and dies. And here is the part where you will surely want to, and have to, judge me. Because after that evening, when he said those things to me and touched his new, young female thing, I went up, into the room in the house where we lived, and I took a sharp knife from the kitchen, a small one usually reserved for paring apples and potatoes, and by my own will and with my own self-loathing and with loathing and anger for Enrique, I took my left hand out, a hand that had never been scarred by the three men who had tied me down, and I carved slowly and methodically, and then faster and deeper, with punctures of pain, with pain more that I had let myself become Enrique's thing and his object, and then that I could no longer be that object of desire for him. I wanted him to know I was in torment. I wanted him to wake up from his smug certainty that he knew everything and controlled everything. I wanted him to feel for a second, when he would hear about this carving of my flesh, and when he would be forced to see it, that I loathed him now and myself now so much that I had had the strength, the animalistic strength, to do this self-mutilation.

"After sleeping, most likely, with the other young woman at the party, he came in the door at four a.m., smelling of sex, with the smell of his cologne mixing with the perfume of another. He came up to his bedroom. By then, we didn't sleep in the same room. Like a phantom, I walked into his bedroom, once he was undressed and getting into his bed. I held my palm up in the air, with blood dripping on the carpet, on a tiger skin rug he had brought from Hong Kong, which stood at the base of his bed. I held the palm up in the air until he could tell something was wrong, something was desperately wrong.

" 'I did this,' I said. 'I did this because of you!'

"He rushed up to me and looked at the hand, and the wound was so fresh even he could not deny what he had done. 'Oh, Esmeralda, Esmeralda, what have you done? What have you done? You should never have done that. Never.' He looked at me with a look of pity, and yes, some concern, and maybe even, oddly, a bit of pride that I could be, momentarily, an animal. But I was no longer the queen he wanted. There was a new queen. She would be his new pretty face. The concubine, in those old Chinese tales I would read later, replaces the queen, and even my most desperate cry out could not win him back.

"The rest of the details of my story are hardly worth noting, how the police and military finally set up an operation to take him out. Usually they took their cut and left Enrique alone, but one day they came in force to kill Enrique, and he got word of their plan first. He

met them in a full gun battle in the center of town. The one surprise
for this story, perhaps, is that I fought beside him. I, too, carried an
AK-47 and fired in the direction of the police who were firing at my
husband. We hadn't had sex for a year, when he was shot and killed.
The bullets, they truly riddled his body and he fell in the street. He
had taken me with him to flee to the next compound. He had re-
jected me in almost all ways, but he still seemed to want to keep
me in the cage of his house, and he still insisted I continue to try to
make it in the music business, though my recordings were fewer and
fewer. But when the cops came, I was standing next to him, a loyal
follower to the end, admiring his drive and talent, loathing my own
body, wanting to do what I could to please him. He was my man, and
I foolishly still loved him.

"But it was not then that I learned what I needed to from the
experience. It was two years later, long after all the furs and clothes
and houses and boats had been confiscated by the government, and
I was living in a very small house that I could barely afford, renting
only a room in the top floor which had an attic that was too hot. The
police had determined I was not a real narco, just the wife of a criminal, and they had let me free. I was already twenty-six. I was walking
through the town, one day, and I saw a young girl, and I could see
she was an orphan from the same orphanage where I had grown up.
I followed her, as if involuntarily, back to the orphanage. There, despite all the changes to my body, was the structure of the orphanage,
almost identical to when I had left. Time had flown by, my body was
now permanently marked, and I had attempted to run away from
this orphanage for so long, and from the orphanage somewhere else,
unknown, where my mother had grown up. And standing in front
of that door I realized I had spent my whole life running away from
that door and that building instead of running to something. I had
been running with the subconscious fear that if I did not become a
beauty queen, if I did not please Enrique, if I did not do what everyone else wanted from me, I would end up in the orphanage forever,

not just the orphanage in front of me but the orphanage of a trapped spirit, a trapped soul. And in my fear I had ended up scarring my body more than anyone else could have ever scarred me, trying to live for others, instead of ever truly living for me, or ever even truly living. 'I want to live,' I told myself. 'I want to live for me and for me alone and not for anyone else and not out of any more fear.' I opened the gate of the orphanage. I walked into that door, the porthole that had marked the gatekeeper of my greatest fear, and I walked inside. I looked around the rooms of the orphanage—first in the room for the babies, where I had once changed the diapers of the smallest infants, and then in the room where La Señora Elvira had come and snatched me away, when for a fleeting moment I had felt some hope, until the once beautiful witch had dashed my hopes. 'I have paid for my beauty,' I told myself. 'I have paid more than enough.' I walked up to the head nun. I raised my palm to her. 'Mother Superior, I have sinned against myself for not loving myself.' I walked around the old orphanage, looking into the corners of the place that had once been my deepest fear. I was not going to let the place dominate me anymore, if I could. I was no longer going to run away from myself, couching my fears in my body. I was going to find some other orphanage to work in, a place where I could help some new young girls."

She stopped her story abruptly, opened her eyes, and looked straight at me and told me she had gone to work in an orphanage. She had completed her promise to herself. She was exhausted from telling her story, and she quickly walked to a sink in the corner of the room to wash away tears that had come to her.

While she was at the sink, I thought about her story. It seemed foolish to try to reduce what she had said to one idea or two. Was she saying beauty is only skin-deep and that I should worry less about any scars to my body, because she had suffered much worse? Was it that I should worry less about my fears, and that I should confront them head-on? Was it that I should escape the cycles of life that she had been caught up in, just as my own family had cycles and cycles of breast cancer? Or was it what I think she was really getting at—that to give means more than to take? It was all of these things, perhaps, but when I walked into the doctor's office, when he finally came, after I'd thanked the woman for telling her story to me, a telling that I believe and hope was of some cathartic use for her, as it was for me, I walked into the doctor's office and I told him I needed a double mastectomy; I told him I had made up my mind firmly and said to him, "You see, doctor, even with all the pain and cruelty and torture out there in the world, I want to live." There was nothing more magnificent, more surprising, more awe-inspiring, more mystical than being alive in the world. I thought of the woman with the scars on her body, who had told me the story. I thought of her in her new orphanage; and even with her scars, because of all of her suffering, because of her honesty and her fortitude, her spirit unbowed by the pain, and because she had been there for me when I needed someone to comfort me when I was alone, she was the most beautiful woman I had ever met. She had given me something when I was feeling wholly selfish and afraid. She was much more than her mother could have ever known.

# ACAPULCO

At 3:42 a.m., according to the police report, we left the nightclub. But don't take the reports too seriously down here in Mexico. They're a joke. That time seems about right to me, though. I have a watch, an expensive Piaget my father once gave me, and after the whole shooting was through, I heard the faint Swiss, precise ticking and the time said 3:50.

I ended up in the nightclub because the client wanted to show me a good time. Never mind that I have a girlfriend/partner who I've been living with for two years. She and I are going to get married in a few months. But the way business gets done in Mexico, the older men—say about fifty-five—they don't care about being faithful to their wives. They have "lovers" on the side. They go to motels on the edge of town to have sex with their secretaries or with their hidden "gem." Me, I'm not into that kind of tradition. It smacks of a macho culture that I left behind when my parents sent me to study architecture at Harvard School of Design. I grew up in Mexico City. My whole family is from Mexico. But I'm halfway in, halfway out. I consider myself proudly from Mexico, but I'm a citizen of the world. I'm as happy eating sushi in Tokyo as having a quesadilla on the streets of Mexico City.

We went to the nightclub to close the deal. Gonzalo was the client. Sixty years old. The usual paunch that most older, rich Mexican men have. It's the paunch of the *felicidad*—the happiness. Gonzalo wears a gold Rolex. It's the kind of flashy watch I would never wear because I come from old money, and his money is new. Who knows from where? There are some questions it's best not to ask, with all the cash floating around Mexico these days. If you're an architect, as I am, you don't ask where the dough is coming from, you just ask, "What kind of pool do you want?" You give them an option—large or extra-large. I've designed pools that extend off the house and into the ocean, with a long jetty that slices into the Pacific. To me, it's never made sense why a client needs a pool right next to the warm water of the ocean, but for the clients the pool is where the action is at, the trophy, like the trophy bride, that is always immaculately clean, radiating turquoise up to the sky, the center of their personal temple. And believe me, for the clients, their house is their personal temple.

My own taste is toward the modern. I'm a good architect but not a great architect. I can do nice, sweeping open-floor plans. I can get you that view you want that makes you feel like your house is worth a few million. I do my best. I struggle to get the details. I love the clean, white look of *pilotis* from an architect like Le Corbusier. But no one is ever going to remember me. Fortunately, you don't have to be amazing to make a living down in Mexico. You just need to be willing to give the client what they ask for. There is a long tradition of great architects in Mexico, like Luis Barragán, and, as is usually the case, most people don't buy their homes or know about them. Bad taste reigns supreme, everywhere. I try to find the clients who have less bad taste so they don't give me too many problems. I build them what they want, and then, in a few smaller places, I try to design what I really care about. It's the life of an architect. So it goes. And it goes easier, since my father is a fairly well-known architect in Mexico.

WHEN WE CAME into the nightclub, the first thing I noticed was the pole dancing. This club was on the edge of Acapulco, out of town about fifteen minutes, up on one of the side hills and at a sharp pullover. The club stands alone, with no other stores nearby, and it has a sign with two cartoon-cutout women dancing with martini drinks in their hands, all lit up with fifty flashing incandescent bulbs. Some of the lightbulbs are gone, so the sign looks like some teeth are missing.

Gonzalo's driver parked his Mercedes-Benz. Gonzalo got out and I followed him in. It was the third club we'd been to this evening. In Mexico, everything's about excess. If you have a party, the music volume has to be at eleven. If you invite one of your cousins over for lunch, you have to invite their parents and their sisters and brothers. It's the same in business. There's no such thing as going to one club to close the deal.

When we came into the club, the driver waited by the door, acting as a security guard. Most of the drivers do that for someone like Gonzalo. He was traveling light this evening. He only had his one driver for security. Often, a guy like him drives with two extra cars around as his security detail—one in front, one in back, hugging close to him through traffic with a couple bodyguards in each car to make sure no one kidnaps him. This isn't just for nefarious people. This is for anyone with money. They never know when some group of professional kidnappers or hit men will try to get them. The guards look like Secret Service details. They dress in dark suits and have earpieces to communicate with each other. The main difference is they don't have to hide their weapons as much in Mexico. They let people know they're nearby. They try to be a presence, without bothering anyone at the party or at the business meetings.

I think Gonzalo was traveling with only his driver as his guard because he wanted to be able to take me to some of the smaller, seedier bars, and with four guards it would have been too intrusive. He told me at the beginning of the night he wanted to take me to some of the traditional nightclubs because the women were better there—not so jaded, he said, not so phony. "I like them with fat butts, you know what I mean?" he said. He put his hands up in the air and squeezed, as if he were squeezing a big, round ass. "For me, if they don't have a pretty face, it's a plus. It means they like what they're doing. It means they probably have a sweet boy back home that they take care of. They're mothers. I like the mothers . . ."

That chain of logic made absolutely no sense to me. If they're mothers they were working in the clubs because they had to, not because they wanted to. But I think it's fair to say Gonzalo had a Mommy complex. He needed some kind of mother he maybe never got as a child, and he wanted me to share his fetish. Me, I wasn't interested, but the guy wanted me to design a four-million-dollar home off one of the nearby golf courses, so I was willing to go along for the ride.

It was just like what you might expect for a cheapo porno bar. Up on stage, to the left as you came in, the lighting was red and dark, a single white spotlight on the woman at the pole. If she was a mother, she was a young mother, no older than twenty-five. Her nipples were big and brown, so she probably was a mother, and her ass was wide, just like Gonzalo wanted, but otherwise she was slim. She shimmied around the pole. She wore a pair of black-velvet high heels. She had on a red G-string. Otherwise, she was naked, cinnamon brown. Gonzalo walked straight over to her. He pulled out a five-hundred-peso note. The lady turned, with her ass in front of his face. She jiggled it up and down, back and forth, like she was playing the bongo drums, or like some Disney porno film version with her ass as some bongo drums. The standard rule with the pole dancers—as I'd learned earlier that evening, and with other clients closing deals—is that you don't touch the dancer. You can push money in her G-string, but you don't touch the merchandise. For that there are lap dances, and there are always plenty of women circling around the nightclubs to offer lap dances and to fill your drink.

Gonzalo came about as close as you can to violating the rule. He put his hands up behind the dancer's butt, he came within a millimeter of touching her, putting his hands around each cheek and pretending to squeeze in the air. This was the third time of the evening he'd done this, as if he thought it was hilarious each time. One of the advantages, from his point of view, seemed to be that for a moment his face and hands were caught in the spotlight, so everyone could see he was the big man, the guy putting in the five hundred pesos. After he stuck the money into the strap, he turned around to me and gave me this look like, Not bad, eh?

I gave him the look of approval he wanted.

To the right of the door, as you came in, there was a long bar-table with a view of the stage to the left. I took a seat at one of the stools and Gonzalo wended his way back to me. He chuckled as he sat down. His hair was combed straight back like some kind of Latin American dictator from the '80s. He had on a pink button-down shirt, the collar wide open showing some black hairs mixed with gray. He had a number of gold teeth fillings that were more noticeable whenever he put his hand with his Rolex up by his mouth, while laughing. There was an old scar over his left eye. His face was smooth from eating a lot, full of fleshiness, and he had a constant slight sweat from eating and drinking. He seemed to feel a bit hot and sweaty wherever he was.

The whole evening he'd said normal things to me, talking about girls, asking me about my girlfriend, asking me about my father. There wasn't much to say, he kept the conversation light, but now he leaned in close to me and put his heavy arm around my shoulder and whispered in my ear, "You're a pussy, but even though you're a cunt they say you're a good architect. I want a palace. You give me a palace and I'll be happy and you'll make some good money. You fuck up, you give me a house that other people don't like, and I'll make your life miserable."

There was no mistaking his words. It was some kind of strange

threat, from out of nowhere. How did I get this client? My brother
Rodrigo had a friend who played golf in Acapulco. That friend had
said he knew Gonzalo on the golf course. Three degrees of separation. In Mexico there's usually a personal link, or nothing happens.
Rodrigo's friend was the link. I was going to kill him.

**THE WHOLE TIME** we were in the club it was pretty empty, other than
the women working there, the bartender, and Gonzalo's guard, but
there were a few bunches of clients randomly scattered at the tables,
some in pairs, chattering, some alone staring in wonderment or, like
depressed junkies, up at the pole dancer. There were just enough that
I didn't notice two guys who slipped in after we had been in the club
for an hour. When they came in, I didn't know they were the reason,
but Gonzalo excused himself and said he had to go to the bathroom.
That left me alone for a while, sitting in the club without having to
pretend to be interested in Gonzalo's conversation. I had a chance
to take in the soft Latin beat of the music. There were a few trumpets. It was supposed to be happy music, but in the sad red light falling on the pole dancer on stage the trumpets sounded forlorn, and
I wondered what I was doing in this club, so far from my girlfriend,
Julieta, in Mexico City. She was under the covers now, sleeping like
a babe, with our dog, no doubt, on the floor by her side. We live in a
loft I designed in the center of the city, with modern lines that were
clean enough to get *Wallpaper** magazine interested. They did a photo
shoot of the loft—a mix of the modern within a traditional Colonial
building, downtown. The truth is, I ripped off the style of another
architect whom I admire who isn't that well known. The loft looks
beautiful, but it never would have gotten into *Wallpaper** without the
connections of a friend of my father. My father is one of those great
architects of Mexico, who people in the outside world know. I got to
thinking about my father, and I asked myself why I was in this dump

with Gonzalo, trying to get him as a client, and I realized the only reason I was sucking up to Gonzalo, or tolerating him, was because I wanted to prove to my father I could make it without him, that I could get my own big clients by myself.

My father's clients are serious. They're famous writers, like Carlos Fuentes, or big industrialists who own steel and tuna factories, or telephone and TV companies. You know where their money comes from. They're old, established families that have owned Mexico from the time of the haciendas or who came over from Spain to make their fortunes. I'm not saying they're all nice, or all have good taste, but in as many deals as my father has told me about, I've never heard him say he went to three crappy strip joints, on the edge of town, to keep the customer satisfied.

While I was having these thoughts, Gonzalo's driver came up to me and asked me to please follow him to a back room where Gonzalo had gone, earlier, following the two men. The back room had floor-to-ceiling mirrors on the walls, and a mirror on the ceiling. There were cheap chandeliers, barely casting an orange tiger glow that perfectly imitated the clothing of the three women who were on the gold vinyl couches next to Gonzalo and by the two men who had come in. The women wore leopard-skin bodysuits. They had long nails and they put their arms around the three men. One stuck her hand on Gonzalo's hairy chest and stroked him. There was a low coffee table in front of them—a rectangular cube made of mirrors—and on top of it the two other men had made a bunch of lines of white powder cocaine. A lady in a leopard suit grabbed my arm and made me sit in front of the cocaine. One of the two men slapped me on the back and said, "Take some. It's good. It's good quality." I told him, politely, thanks but no thanks. That's one rule I had for myself. No coke. Ever. I didn't do that, and I didn't need Gonzalo so badly that I was going to get trashed that way. It was one thing to drink shots of booze and to go from cheap club to club to get my 10 percent of a four-million-dollar home that many future clients would walk around along the beach of Acapulco. It was another to be told, like a dog, that I should snort coke with a fat client like Gonzalo.

"Hey boss," one of the two guys said. His face was thick and his ears were missing some of their flesh, like a wrestler who's had them pulled at too many times. "This guy—what's his name?—he says he's not interested." He pointed at the coke. "What kind of faggot is he? Where did you find this guy?"

I couldn't tell if Gonzalo had snorted some of the coke, or not. He seemed way too subdued to have taken any. He seemed the opposite, not up but down. He had his head leaning back on the couch, and his eyes half shut, and he was taking in the rubbing of the woman in the leopard suit assigned to him. He was staring up at the mirror on the ceiling.

"I don't really like him, either," Gonzalo said in a fairly muted voice, like he was underwater. "He's been a party pooper all night. He does look like a faggot. But he's not. His girlfriend lives with him at Corregidora 38, in the Center. They have a dog and they live together in a loft. He's an architect who's going to design my next house for me. And if he screws up, if he makes any mistake on the house, his girlfriend is going to be in trouble."

I had never given him my home address. I had never told him I had a dog. I had never told him I lived with my girlfriend.

"Hey faggot," Gonzalo said. "You've been avoiding the lap dances all night. I've offered you women in each of the clubs and in each place you look at your Piaget watch like you have better things to do and like you don't like my Rolex. I don't care if you think I'm a cheap, fat guy with nouveau riche money. Every penny I have, I made it myself. I started my business myself. I don't sell drugs. I didn't make money the cheap, fast way. These guys are not drug dealers. They're just snorting a little coke. Big deal. Every penny I made, I earned it myself. I didn't come from some family where my father was sending me off to Harvard to go to architecture school. I would have liked that. Anyone would have liked that. But that's not the way it was for me. So, here's what you're going to do. You're going to take off your pants right here, right now, in front of all of us, and then you're going to get a lap dance from one of these women."

I was more and more convinced he didn't earn his money, pulling himself up by his bootstraps. If he'd made his money the honest way, people would have told me where his money had come from— but before we got together, no one knew. They said he just had it. I was more convinced than ever he was a small-time drug dealer, one of those mini-jefes down the totem pole who thinks he's a big shot. This kind of scum was getting bigger and bigger in Acapulco. It was infecting the whole country like a cancer.

In Mexico, earthquakes are common. Every architect has to learn how to build around them. You put big buildings on springs that can move with the earth when it ruptures. You reinforce the beams with thick steel rods. You put on extra concrete so the elevated freeways don't fall. If you do it right, the structure survives with only minor cracks.

The smart thing to do would be to listen to Gonzalo and just do what he said, to go with the flow, to bend. Who cares if it was humiliating? I could take off my pants. I could take off my underwear. I could let the women rub me until I got hard, with the other men watching like animals. I could be the circus animal and design his house, and take the money that I knew was from illegal sources, and get the house printed up in one of the big Mexican architecture magazines that would lead to other clients. It would be a small price of humiliation to keep climbing up the ladder. My father would see me doing better. He would have to admit I could make it on my own. I stood up with one hand on my belt, trying to decide what to do. Should I open my belt or not? If I opened my belt it would be capitulation.

I opened my belt, and I justified it to myself that it was better to live than to be a dead example of someone who had stood up for his principles against these thugs.

"That's it," Gonzalo said. "That's it. Now dance, dance with one of these lovely ladies." One of the older women with long, red nails opened my pants. I stood in front of the other men, and she felt me up while the men laughed at me like I was a circus monkey.

SOMETIMES, I THINK about my watch. There are a million things happening around the world at any second. There are an infinite number of split seconds in a minute. If Zeno's paradox is right—that between any two points there are an infinite number of halfway points, so we should never be able to get anywhere—then the same must be true about choices in life. What if I hadn't opened my belt? What if I hadn't let myself stay in that room for a stupid lap dance that I feigned interest in? I didn't care about the woman who was, supposedly, turning me on, and I cared even less about her twenty minutes later when Gonzalo finally came out of his stupor enough to say he wanted to leave. The two goons who'd been cutting up the coke on the mirror asked Gonzalo, suddenly, when they were going to get paid for some work they had done and for the delivery of a load. I couldn't hear well, since by now I was standing fairly cold while the woman assigned to me gyrated around my body.

"Just shut up," Gonzalo said. "You'll get paid when I tell you."

The goon with the ears partially missing said, "Nothing is free, jefe. You pay up soon or things could get nasty."

Gonzalo's driver came in, and he wasn't having any of this discussion. He told the two goons to calm down. He was sober. He told Gonzalo he had to go to the car now, that it wasn't safe to stay anymore. He said he would deliver me back to my hotel.

"We're not going to his hotel, yet," Gonzalo said. "He's coming with me and these two women." He grabbed ahold of the woman

who had been dancing around me, who'd tried to give me a blowjob in front of the other men—she wasn't fully successful because I
willed myself not to get it up for her.

It seemed like the evening was falling apart, completely. Whether
I would get the contract to build the house or not, suddenly seemed
up in the air. In the morning, when everyone is recovering from
their fiesta, there are times when people pretend whatever happened
the night before never happened. And that could mean I would have
a contract for the house or not, the next day. Oddly enough, though,
and one of the reasons I had opened my pants—other than wanting to live—is that I knew these jefes lived according to their own,
perverted code. If they said they wanted me to build the house, and
even more so if they threatened me, it meant they had fixated on me
for some reason, and they wanted it bad. And once they wanted it
bad, they wouldn't let go.

Gonzalo's driver hurried me into the back of the Mercedes-Benz
with the two women—one for Gonzalo and one, supposedly, for
me. I had hopes the driver was just humoring his boss, that Gonzalo
would finally calm down and let me end the "fun" of the evening
and go home to my hotel.

"You'll get your money next Monday," Gonzalo said to the two
goons, and this calmed them as we got into the car.

For a moment, sitting in the back of the car, I thought there
would be a happy ending. I was sandwiched between the two women.
Gonzalo was in front, telling his driver to go faster. The engine of
the Mercedes accelerated hard and we swooped around a curve at
what must have been ninety miles an hour. On the straightaways
the driver was going a hundred. The precision of the machine, the
precision of European engineering, was comforting, and I leaned
back into the plush leather thinking this was it, a minor moment
of humiliation survived, a day I could live with. My head was foggy
from the late night, and the bad perfume of the women next to
me pressed into my nose, but I began to think of the house I would

design for Gonzalo on the beach. I would build it four stories high, one more than usual to give it the prominence he wanted. There would be circles and triangles throughout, primary shapes, just as Louis I. Kahn did in his Center for British Art at Yale, but I would come up with my own style for this house. I vowed I would never let myself rip off the work of any other architect again. This house would be a turning point in my work, a moment of maturation where I would go from cribbing others. And I would do it precisely because Gonzalo had humiliated me. I would give him a house that was better than he deserved, because it would be for me and not for him, and I would use his filthy money to do it.

The car slid sideways as the driver slammed on the brakes when the headlights pointed out a tree across the road. From a hundred to zero in six seconds. The women next to me came out of their soft leaning-in, tired from their work, ready for sleep, and screamed. I angled forward once the car came to a stop, with the bright lights against the green branches of the tree in front of us. It was a large tree, masking what was beyond. Gonzalo yelled at the driver, "Get back. Turn this around. It's a trap."

The driver punched the car in reverse, and I was thrown forward and then back hard into the leather seat. Bullets came from the right as the wheels whirled against the pavement. *TaTat! TaTat! Tattat-tattattat.* When the projectiles hit the front, they didn't break the glass. There must have been bulletproofing. But the bullets kept coming, the glass bending and molding inward, until there was no more resistance, Gonzalo yelling at his driver to go faster, the front window pocked with flying metal, the women grabbing at me and trying to get down, Gonzalo's head flying back and then his body slumping forward, the driver's foot coming off the accelerator as he slumped, too. I hid beneath the bodies of the women on the floor of the backseat. I couldn't see anything, but I heard some men running up to the car and then away from it.

"They're dead," I heard one shout. "Come on, let's go, they're all finished. We got them."

Then another opened up his machine gun against the side door, in the back. He unleashed a wave of bullets. They hit more and more into the door, just behind me. I felt a sting and a piece of metal go into my body somewhere. I heard someone open the door and look in.

"Yes, they're all dead," he said, and he left the door open and ran away.

How I'd become twisted, with my back against the floor, I'll never know. My hand was splayed above me and I heard a faint *tick, tick, tick,* with the precision of a Swiss watch, and saw the time: 3:50. One second earlier, and I might have had a different outcome—I might never have been in that car.

A COUPLE DAYS ago, I went to a funeral. It was of the woman who gave me the lap dance. Before the funeral, my girlfriend asked why I had to go. I'd told her everything that had happened that night. I didn't want any secrets between us before we got married. She came and saw me in the hospital, from Mexico City to Acapulco, and while it wasn't clear, at first, whether I would live, I told her, through the breathing mask stuck to my face, what had happened. I didn't want to leave any detail out, so I told her about the strange way I'd ended up in the back room with the mirrors and how Gonzalo had insisted I have a lap dance. I told her about the house I wanted to design for him.

"Why would you want to design a nice house for him?" she said.

"Because I wanted to prove him wrong."

"But you don't have to prove anything to anyone," she said. "Not even to your father."

That's why I like Julieta. She tells me what I want to hear. She didn't understand why I'd want to go to the funeral of the women who worked in the club, but she didn't try to stop me.

The funeral was in a small church in a small town outside Acapulco. The priest started his sermon as a hundred people listened, crammed into the pews. In the front of the church I could see the two children of Gloria, the woman who'd danced for me. I knew her name, now. The children were ages three and five. Two boys. There was no father present. They stood with their grandmother.

The priest told everyone gathered that as hard as it was to accept, there was always a reason for everything that happened. Everything was God's will. The ways of the Lord were unknowable and mysterious.

I could think of no reason, whatsoever, for Gloria's death. So a man like Gonzalo could get his sexual kicks? So a man like Gonzalo could make enough money to build a four-million-dollar home? I was just as complicit as her, just the same, trying to make a buck off a guy like him. I had let my ambition get the better of me. I was revolted that I'd let myself stay that night in the room with the mirrors, and that I'd let myself "dance" with Gloria—not because there's any shame to sex, but because I had no interest in that sex and because Gonzalo had made me do it.

I walked into the parking lot, where there was dirt around the old cars. I picked up a stick. And in the dirt I wrote, "For the memory of Gloria, who deserved none of what happened." I held on to the stick. I drew circles and squares. I was going to make a memorial to her, in a small place by the beach. I wouldn't make the memorial too big. It wasn't for me, wasn't for me to try to get some recognition in the magazines, it was for her. I drew a tower into the air, which represented me and my hopes. I was going to do better. I was going to try to make something of myself while I still had life.

# THE KIDNAPPING

Ten seconds before they kidnapped me, son of a bitch, I was walking my dog, Azteca. There are little stalls all over my neighborhood in downtown Mexico City. They sell everything—paper, plastic beach balls, bolts of cloth, straw hats, tight jeans with sequins, bright plastic Tupperware, blow-up superheroes, chilies, tacos, fried pig skin, speakers for local bands, tools, and wedding cakes. You name it, it's being sold down here in the center of town. I like to watch the hot women walking around my neighborhood. I like to even check out the tranny prostitutes—not that I'd ever want to sleep with one of them, but man, they do it up all the way, you know what I mean? They go whole hog.

So I was walking my dog late at night. Another dog was barking ferociously from a rooftop. I don't usually go the way I was walking after 10 p.m., 'cause walking down that way gets a little hairy. During the day, it's fine. But at night, you gotta be careful. Normally, no one messes with me 'cause of the dog. I have a Xoloitzcuintle, which is some kind of pure-race dog from the time of the Aztecs. It's one of only three kinds of 100-percent pure, authentic, Mexican dogs. People come up to me all the time to try to get close to the dog.

They're a little afraid, but they're curious, and they're especially curious 'cause I'm an American, and they know something ain't right with a white-looking guy, a güero, with one of these pure Mexican dogs. So it gets their head spinning and they come up and ask me what my dog's name is, and I say Azteca, and that gets them laughing, 'cause it's almost like calling your dog George Washington, or something unduly serious and patriotic like that, and since my dog's big, they keep their distance, and they like that my dog is big.

But man, those motherfuckers, when I was walking late at night at 11 p.m., trying just to get to my studio where I do some of my bigger paintings, or more conceptual type of work that takes up some larger space—those dudes just came up to my dog and shot him, point-blank, one shot right through the rib cage, and Azteca twisted his ears first toward them, even before they got the shot off, but he didn't have a chance. It was cruel to do that shot. Azteca got blown down. He cried while his rib cage was jerked around. And then my dog, which had always guarded me so well, was kaput.

I was standing on one of those empty streets downtown, in the center of the old Colonial city, where there's always garbage littered around in the middle of the night after all the people coming and going have bought and sold whatever they're going to take home for the day from the stalls. So I was standing naked in that street, other than my dog, the harsh mercury of some streetlights in the distance the only thing making the street safe. Usually, there's at least someone on the street watching, hanging out, talking with their buddies, but these dudes who did the kidnapping, they knew what they were doing. They must have been watching for just the right moment. There was no one, and I mean no one on the street when I finally saw them coming and when they shot my dog.

One shot. I looked up the alleyway. A car comes screeching up from the shadows. These two dudes, who smell like a combination of too much piss, alcohol, and bad perfume, push me into the car. One of them puts a gun to my head. He tells me to shut up, in really

fast, crude Spanish. He tells me to bend over. They put a blindfold
on me. They tie my hands behind my back with the leash from Azteca. Azteca was gone, of course. They left him back on the street,
stone-cold dead. I tried to tell myself to stay calm. I told myself just
to do whatever they wanted me to, 'cause I usually have this attitude
that if you stay calm everything will work out. But it wasn't doing
me any good. This one jerk, and I mean that with the greatest of all
understatements, he spit in my hair, he told me I was a filthy pig and
that my mother would never see me again unless I begged for mercy.
Beg, he said. Beg, now. Beg for your life. So man, I begged. Oh yeah,
I begged. I tried to do it calmly. I tried to do it with all the sincerity I
could muster. I'm gonna beg until they get whatever they feel comfortable with, I thought. One of them hit me on the back of the head,
and when I came to I had a large welt on my scalp.


I'LL TELL YOU what's terrifying. It's not being alone in the place where
they take you after they kidnap you. It's the fact that you're *not*
alone, that there are other people with you who you know are going
through the same hell they're putting you through.

Here's what they did every day for five straight days. They woke
me up in the middle of the night, they slapped me on the side of the
head, they did all this after I listened to them cut the finger off some
young woman in the other room, and then they took me in the back
of the car to an ATM, where they forced me to take out all the money
I could, the daily limit, before they slapped me on the head again,
beat me in the chest, and stuffed me back in the car. You're like a
gerbil on a spinning wheel, while they do this. You're in the ninth
ring of hell. I mean, you don't know what day it is—whether it's the
same day as the day before. Whether they're just gonna fuckin' waste
you right there. Whether they've already found a way to get in touch
with your family, and whether your family is gonna pay. It's just one
big, black hole of no information. Maybe you'll live, maybe you'll

die, and that finger they cut off the woman in the next room—that's real. That's her begging for them not to do it. That's them coming in, in a posse of three, and you hear them scuffling with her, and you hear them shouting at her in Spanish, "They aren't paying, señorita. They aren't holding up their end of the bargain. So they're gonna have to be convinced."

The cry from that woman, there was no faking there. They take a pair of kitchen shears. They run it up along the skin. They scrape your knuckles with the edge of the blade of the scissors, until they bleed. I know how they do it, 'cause later they took one of my fingers off and sent it to my family. This is what they do. They tease you. They make you shit your pants. They have you saying, Please no, please don't do it. Please. No. For Christ's sake, I'm a painter. I'll do anything. I'll get you more money. I'll get you any money you want.

There were two guys when they did it to me. One was the man I saw shoot Azteca. He had a couple Fu Manchu hairs growing out of his jaw, his face was trapezoidal, his eyes sunk in, his skin leathery like a burnt turtle. He had all the look of a Neanderthal you could imagine. He had a tattoo on his right upper bicep that said MAMÁ, with a heart below, and a dagger through the heart. The other guy was skinny, like he was addicted to heroin. He never said anything. He would just hold my arm down against the wood table. He was a lot stronger than you'd expect for a junkie. It was like all his junkie-ness, all his neediness, came out in his grip. He'd hold my bicep, while the Neanderthal threatened to cut off my finger, and then one day the Neanderthal did it. Blood was gushing all over the fucking place. They cut my pinkie. They said they were gonna start with the small fingers first and then go up the scale, with each request to my family that didn't come through for money. One thing about Mexico, it's impossible to send any mail. You can't get any letter anywhere in less than a week. It takes a full eight days just to get a letter sent from one side of Mexico City to the other. So these guys aren't dumb. They use

FedEx. They work for the cartels. They aren't some loners. They're pros. They FedEx'd my finger to my family in Pittsburgh.


MY FATHER, HE'S as straitlaced as they come, as straight a shooter as possible. He never lies. Or, if he does, he does it for a good reason, to help someone. He was the football coach at Pitt for twenty-five years before he retired. I'm forty-four. He's seventy-eight. I'm one of seven kids. I used to joke my parents had kids until they realized the Pope wasn't watching anymore.

My father, his idea of cruelty was making his players run fifteen miles. He'd have them woken up by his assistant at 5 a.m. on a Sunday, and make them run to our house out of town and press the doorbell. Then he'd have them run back into town before breakfast. If he was torturing someone, it was for their own good. He'd tutor his students personally. When the army called him up, he went. There was no question in his mind ever, what you did; you did the "right thing." The guy has a heart of gold, but he has this sense of duty that sometimes blocks out everything else. So if the FBI told him he shouldn't cave in to any extortion, that it was just going to make things worse, that giving in to kidnappers usually results in having someone killed, that he should just listen to the cops and be firm and not negotiate, but only say a deal could be cut—if they gave me back, no charges would be pressed—then that's what he did. It pained him. This kind of decision pained him. It's not the kind of decision he'd like to make for himself, but the FBI had more experience in these matters, and if that's what they told him then that's what he should do.

My dad coached a lot of winning teams. He's probably the smart one in the family, but if it hadn't been for my mother, I'd probably be dead now. She sent the first amount of ransom. She sent ten thousand dollars behind my dad's back. She sent the money, so they stopped cutting off my fingers for a while. But it was never clear if they were stopping the finger-cutting exercises because they were just gonna kill me.


**I'M NOT SURE** what the purpose of life is, but I can tell you this, every person has a reason to be on earth, and that reason isn't to be kidnapped, isn't to die in some war, isn't to end up some puffy body left in a trench or to be the residue of some crazy drug war, like what they've got down in Mexico now. I kind of think the purpose of life is to sing. I don't mean, literally, always to sing, but to sing metaphorically, to sing in some way of beauty, to raise the spirits of our voices in hope.

So here's something I did one day, while they had me kidnapped, sitting on the floor with my hands tied behind my back, my head leaning against a hard concrete wall. I started to sing "Mary Had a Little Lamb." I've got a bit of a gravelly voice. I like to smoke my share of stub cigars. I like to drink mezcal, if it's offered to me. Or, more like, I like to give it to friends if they come around. I like to have spontaneous parties. I like to get a bunch of people together and buy too much food. There's a tranny who works in a restaurant below me, and she makes the best plantain empanadas this side of the world, and just looking at the pride on her face when she brings up the food for a party, that's what I like. I want people to be happy, you know what I mean? So I started singing "Mary Had a Little Lamb." Amazingly, they let me sing, at first. I started singing louder and louder. I wanted the woman in the next room to hear. She'd been going downhill. She'd lost two fingers already, and I thought, if I can sing this song loud enough she'll come back to life. So I just started singing. I don't know why in the hell I chose that song. It's just the one that came to me. It's easy, you know. And after I'd been singing for a bit, I swear I heard that other woman singing, too. She wasn't singing the same song. She started singing some Mexican song. But there it was, some other nice song in Spanish that some-how fit together, perfectly, with "Mary Had a Little Lamb," and even though her voice was weak, she was singing with some kind of inner strength, in perfect harmony with the melody of my own song, and the two of us sang to the concrete ceiling, feeling like we'd stolen a moment, going round and round, repeating the songs a few times, like some kind of chorus of monks but with more joy. They shut us up, of course. They came in and hit me on the mouth. But it didn't matter. It's those moments of joy that make life worth living. It's that harmony, when all around you there's dead silence.

HERE'S WHAT I was deadly afraid of when I was kidnapped in that room. It wasn't that I was going to die. After a while, you get exhausted, you start to lose your energy, but what you're really afraid of isn't that you're going to leave this world, it's all the things you never did outside that room.

I mean here's the thing that was getting to me. I'd never had a relationship for more than two years with any single woman. Like I said, I'm a free spirit. I like to drink, I like to have sex, I like to roll around the world like a nomad. I've been to Cuba six times, and when I'm there I'm happy to find some women, to have a good time, to do whatever comes to me in the moment. But while I was kidnapped, I got to thinking about this one moment with my last girlfriend in Mexico, who I went out with for two years. I'd been shuttling back and forth from New York City to Mexico City for thirteen years, mainly living in Mexico. The rawness of the place intrigues me. It's cheap, and I was able to get started as a painter late in life, at thirty-three, after studying to be an architect.

I wanted to live life large. I didn't want to be stuck just in NYC, like all the other wannabe artists. I wanted to paint with all my heart and soul, with everything I've got, and Mexico was a raw place where I could work, a place that inspired me with the Wild West spirit.

My girlfriend, she'd been in a band. She was the lead singer, but she was really a good girl at heart, from a pretty wealthy family. She said to me, "Jakob, you can go around the world wherever you want, you can paint the best painting in the world, but until you find that stone within that makes you distrust everything, that makes you fail to put down roots, that makes you think everything is just of this moment and never of another, just a bang, you're never going to be happy." She told me this when I said I wanted to break up with her. I wasn't 100-percent certain why I wanted to break up, but like I say, I'm a nomad, I need change, and at some point, anything—even something good—gets too familiar to me, and I cut things off.

So I'd sit there in all the dead time during my kidnapping and think about that. Being kidnapped isn't like in the movies. Most of the time, they're not beating you up. Most of the time, they're not torturing you. Most of the time, you're just sitting slumped on the floor, with complete dead time on your hands, with time to think over who you are and what you want and why normal life is so hard.

Like a rolling stone. That's what she meant. I'd been a rolling stone, chasing after the bottom of the hill. Maybe I needed to take the time to grow some moss. I sat on the hard concrete floor and cried.

The reason I was crying was because I'd been an SOB cheating on her just before we broke up. I mean, sure, things had already fallen apart between us. She was using coke. She was taking too much of the stuff, and I'm just not into that. That shit will mess you up. I stay pretty clean with just mezcal and tequila, beers and some occasional ecstasy or something like that. But coke, that'll mess you up. And she was hiding her use of all that from me. She was pretending she wasn't using that shit, and that's not OK with me. I like to be up front, you know what I mean? If there's a problem, I like to be up front about it.

So I was in Cuba taking photographs for some new art project.

I'm mainly a painter, but I like to go wherever my interests lie, and the changes and things happening in Cuba were just totally interesting to me. Fidel was sick and it seemed like the place was already changing a bit, even though his brother Raúl still had the reins. I went over to take pictures of the things happening. We went into every nook and cranny of Havana. We got great shots of people living in their poor homes, of people waiting in lines, of guys wearing Nike sneakers—when Nikes had been forbidden, forever. One day, we started taking photos of these two young girls, they must have been seventeen. They thought it was just amazing, us taking photos. I went with this photographer partner of mine. And the two of us, we started charming the girls. We went out to a nice bar with them. We took photos that made them feel like they were superstars that were going to be on the cover of *Vogue*. We never promised them anything. We never said we were shooting for any magazine like that, but you know the hopes of young girls. They saw these white dudes with expensive cameras, and they got excited.

I like to wear a straw trilby hat and a Hawaiian floral shirt, with a good pair of jeans. I've usually got some gray stubble on my face, and these girls, looking at the photos you can see how wide-open their eyes are. We each had our own room, and I took one of those girls for a romp, while my partner did the same with the shorter, brown-haired girl. And, oh my god—the one who I had in my room. She was so frickin' hot. She did all the moves on top of me. She took it all off, I didn't have to even do much of anything. And that's just the way it is, you know, for me. I've got to be in the moment. I've got to be taking it all in—everything, from the blade of grass to that mural of Che Guevara. I want it all.

While I was on the floor with my hands tied behind my back, I got to thinking what a dick I'd been. How it didn't matter how hot those girls were. There was nothing exploitative about it. They wanted it just as bad as we did. But what kind of power relationship is that? I mean, doing it with some seventeen-year-old girl while my girlfriend was back in Mexico with a drug problem. That just wasn't cool. That was pathetic. So I cried.

After I cried, I got to thinking that a person can justify anything. If I could justify sleeping with that girl in Havana, then why would one of those kidnappers feel anything bad about cutting off one of my fingers? They looked like assholes. They looked like trapezoidal thugs, but each one of them had a family—some mom and sister somewhere who they were probably sending money to. Don't make the mistake of thinking that a kidnapper working for a cartel is some kind of heartless, psychotic goon. They may not have gotten enough love from their mom when they were young, but in their mind they're doing the right thing. Christ, Idi Amin thought he was doing the right thing!

**I'M OF TWO** minds as to whether there's a heaven. My logical mind says no way. I like the art in churches. I love the old wood cherubs painted with such bright cheeks in all the beautiful churches of Mexico. Those statues are incredible. But it's some kind of make-believe Disneyland that's just fun to look at. Whether there's a plan for anything, I doubt it.

But something let me stay alive. And I don't just mean the ransom money my mom sent, which, obviously, was essential. There are stories all the time, down here, of people who pay everything the kidnappers want, who follow every last instruction, and in the end they kill the person they kidnap anyway.

So the question is, what makes one live and another die? It could just be the luck of the draw, it could just be the way the dice tumble and fall. But I don't quite see it that way. Or I see it that way, and a little more.

I think I have more to do. I think each person is like a plant—

they have a length of time they're supposed to live, like a tomato until it gets ripe. And my ripeness just hadn't happened yet.

Those son of a bitches. They kicked the shit out of me. They came at 2 a.m. It was the same guys who'd cut off my finger, and two more guys. Not that they really needed four to kick the crap out of someone already sitting on the floor, tied up. But they came and took turns kicking me. I was half dazed when they did it, at first. They turned on the one bare bulb that lit up my room. There was gray peeling paint on the wall. The bulb shocked me, so suddenly bright, and I looked up at it and a boot came smack into my face. I swiveled my legs around trying to get one of them to fall, but he jumped out of the way. When you try to fight back with your hands tied behind your back, you mainly pull at yourself, tying yourself into knots. I tried in any case, and I was thrown on the floor by the force of the kicks. Some blood bubbled up from my lip and they carried me out, still trying to struggle with almost no force left. I think I got a good jab with one of my legs at one of them, though. Then it was pretty dark, my head blindfolded, but a little light seeped through as lights from the streets penetrated the cloth. You notice the smells at a time like that. The smell of old vinyl in an old car. The smell of upholstery in what's probably a stolen car.

They dumped me in the middle of a street, Donceles, in the center of town, with my hands tied behind my back, my legs tied up with Azteca's leash. It was like they wanted to remind me they'd killed my dog. They left the blindfold sack over my head. When they threw me out of the car, one of them said, "Hijo de puta—chinga tu madre!"

After fifteen minutes, I heard a street dog come up to me. There was a whole pack of them. They do that, sometimes, the homeless dogs of Mexico City running around at night. They come in all stripes, almost all mutts, but every once in a while a purebred gets stuck amongst the others, lost from its fancy neighborhood. I felt the dogs sniff at me. They put their noses up close against my crotch. They sniffed my shoes. They pulled a bit at my pockets. One of the bigger dogs tugged at the sack over my head and then I could see up, the face of a black and brown tiger-striped dog holding the bag in its mouth, the burning lights of a mercury street lamp shining like in a concentration camp, a small star in the sky in the infinite beauty and depth of the universe almost hidden behind.

**THE PARTY WAS** over. Everyone was gone. It was a month after the kidnapping, and I'd had all my friends over to celebrate the fact I was still alive.

There was the residue of the party all over the place, glasses and bottles. I've fixed up an apartment in the center of Mexico City. I bought it cheap, for thirty thousand dollars—in an old building from the seventeenth century—and even though the building, as a whole, looks like a dump, I've done a ton of work to fix up my apartment. I have high ceilings. You can see the old beams from the time when the Dominican monks and the Inquisition ruled the day.

The tranny brought up all the food, earlier. As always, I'd ordered too much. That tranny has been through everything. She's been through kicks and shouts. Mexico's a macho country, and it's not easy being a transvestite. They cackle at you as you walk down the street. But I've never seen a trace of anger on her face. She's got the height and slim hips of a man, but she plays up her freckles.

I ate one of the plantain empanadas that was left. The leftover tostadas looked like a mess, with the lettuce wilted and the tomatoes looking like they had sweated and over-ripened into the sauce. But the plantain was still just right, the filling inside good. The air smelled of smoke. There was still the smell of cigars, and we'd smoked more than a few short Cohibas I'd brought back from Cuba. I caught sight of my pinkie as I took a bite out of the empanada, or of where my finger should have been, where the stub ended with a raw skin wound.

I could view it as a wound or as a badge of promise. I could be tough like the trannies I admired. There was a lot more for me to paint. I went into my studio. I have two studios, one the one I was trying to walk to the night they kidnapped me, the other just off the space I've renovated in my old building. I pulled out a canvas. I put it up on the wall. I took out some spray-paint cans, which I sometimes use for background, and I put on yellows and bright greens. I shook those cans as hard as I could. I sprayed on thick the happiest colors I could think of. I wasn't going anywhere. I was going to stay right here and plant roots. I spray-painted an abstract form of a tree with roots. I added a stone in the middle that wasn't rolling anymore. I might call my ex-girlfriend in the morning. I had no intention of getting back together. We were through, but I wanted to call to check up on how she was doing, to make sure she was hanging in there, to be certain she was more or less OK.

# THE PLASTIC SURGEON

I am a plastic surgeon, and down here in Mexico it helps that I'm tall and blond. I'm six feet two, I like to play basketball, and during the summer when I take a vacation up in Seattle, where I have a house and come from, I like to row on the rough waters of the ocean. I don't spend that much time looking in the mirror. I spend more time looking at my hands, my tools, to make sure they're smooth and in working order. But I care about my body. I like to feel sculpted. Like most of my clients, I think it's important how we look. I'd rather my body look good via hard work. My nose is a bit long, and according to most standards of beauty it's not beautiful, but that doesn't bother me because I think people looking at my body can tell I work out, can tell I do the hard work necessary to make myself look good and healthy. Others don't have that kind of discipline. They might want an easy way to look fit, and while that's not my way, I'm more than happy to do the work for them in surgery, to suck out those extra pounds of fat with liposuction, around the hips and abdomen, or to design what they think is a more perfect face. It makes them happy, which is reward enough for me, and every patient is a challenge, a raw tableau to shape, a goal to work at hard, like paddling from one end of a large bay to the other along the most efficient route possible.

Some patients are more challenging than others, however. Not everything always goes smoothly. Sometimes the best calculations go awry, and that's what's been preoccupying me lately. I had a patient die a week ago. I've been trying to calculate why and how he died, and whether his death is going to mean I have less time left to live.

The patient was Paco. That's a made-up name, because I'm used to keeping the privacy of patients, and he has a long drug-cartel name in Spanish that means Lord of the Heavens. They called him this, in the Juárez Cartel where he came from, because he hired a fleet of Boeing 737 jets to transport cocaine from Colombia up to Mexico, flying in to municipal airstrips around the country, before sending the coke on to the U.S. through an extensive network he'd built up. Paco was one of the most wanted narcos in the country. It's always hard to tell if the Mexican government really wants to catch its fugitives or not. After all, how else do you land your own 737s around the country, with drugs hidden in the payload, day after day, year after year? After Paco died, I heard estimates he'd acquired a fortune of twenty-five billion dollars. That's a lot of smackers. But I can tell you, for sure, after the DEA came to visit my clinic, the U.S. authorities had been hell-bent on capturing him.

I'M NOT SURE how Paco found my clinic. My office is one of the smaller ones in Mexico City, in the neighborhood of Polanco. It's on a side street with shady trees, and the usual mix of private homes and guards and upscale apartments you might find on any street in Polanco. The U.S. embassy owns apartments at the end of the street, and there's an OfficeMax supply store around the corner and a Carl's Jr. hamburger place. I'm not one of the top plastic surgeons in the country, and as you can tell by my description, while the neighborhood is nice, and close to clients who can pay, the area is less chic than Las Lomas, where many high-end plastic surgeons have their offices.

Paco, I'm told by the DEA, had been running from the law a couple years by the time he came into my clinic. I don't mean that's when he began his life of crime. From what I understand, he was born into a cartel family in Sinaloa. Sinaloa is the Sicily of Mexico for drug mafias. It's a bit in the middle of nowhere, on the Pacific coast two-thirds of the way up the map of Mexico toward the U.S. If you're like me, these are just names—places of intrigue where Mexican narcos come from. But something changes, crystallizes, when one of the names that flits across the pages of the newspapers comes into your clinic and you're expected to operate on him.

Paco didn't announce who he was when he came, but he didn't seem like a usual patient. My clinic is called Verde, or Green, and it's meant to give off a clean, fresh spa feeling. Most of my patients come for routine Botox and collagen treatments, to add firmness to their lips and cheeks. I can do it all, however: blepharoplasty surgery for women who feel their eyelids are too dominant; rhinoplasty, reducing the thickness of a nose, adding an angular point, or reducing overprominence of the nose in profile; breasts can be augmented and shaped with silicone and saline implants or by reshaping the areola. Many women need breast reduction to reduce the pain and heaviness of large breasts and to create a firmer, more youthful look. Depending on the surgery, my two assistants can do most of the preparatory work; or, if the case is more traumatic, as with a burn victim, I take over from the beginning. Burn victims are complicated. The more surface area, the greater the risk without a full surgical hospital on hand, and unless the skin area is small enough, I send that kind of patient to the big hospitals, where they can get proper treatment.

Paco's hair was long and uncombed when he came into the clinic. He had a six-inch beard and a thin face, and he looked like he had a brown lion's mane around a face that was too skinny for all that hair. He had a long-sleeve, thick cotton shirt, his sleeves were rolled up, his hands dirty, and his jeans dirty, too, which made him look like a car mechanic or one of the homeless guys that sometimes live in the park along Avenida Horacio, nearby. I thought he might be lost and asking for directions, or wanting some change, when he walked into the clinic. He gave a fake name to the secretary and told her he wanted to speak to Dr. John Franklin.

"Right here," I said to him in Spanish.

"We need to go into your office," he said. He didn't ask if I wanted to do this, he told me what was going to happen. He looked alone, when he first came in, but two others with mirrored sunglasses, dressed in plain clothes with similar jeans and shirts like him, holding AK-47s, came in. They told the secretary to clear out any waiting patients. Veronica, my secretary, is probably smarter than me. She has a way of sizing up every patient as they come in. She often guesses what a client is looking for, before they fill out the forms or have their consultation with me. She wasted no time telling two women, waiting in another room, that she was very sorry but could they come back tomorrow?

Fortunately, we'd only been open half an hour. It was 10:30 a.m., so no one was in the surgery room.

Paco refused to speak in the reception area. His guards surveyed the front door while he took me into my office. I have a photo of my girlfriend there—things haven't been going well with her. I have a photo of my girlfriend's golden retriever. I've been in limbo, never quite rooted anywhere enough to feel I can have my own pet. I take off, suddenly, to go sea-kayaking on the coast of the Yucatán. So I've never made the commitment to having an animal.

"I want a full makeover," Paco said, when we were sitting in my office.

"I'll be happy to do whatever I can," I said. "But what, exactly, do you mean by a 'full makeover'? That can mean a lot of different things to different people." Some men ask for a tummy tuck or complete removal of the wrinkles around their eyes. Others want things plastic surgeons have nothing to do with—penis enlargement or cures for erectile dysfunction. Ninety percent of my patients are women, but I have an increasing number of men who want to enhance their body.

"What do you think a 'full makeover' means?" Paco said, sarcastically. "I want to change how I look so completely, even a master of disguises won't know who I am. I want this beard gone. I want my nose changed. I want my face altered. My teeth. My stomach. I want to walk out of here a ghost no one can recognize."

"That kind of surgery can take weeks of planning," I said, "to do safely, to assemble the right team, to make sure you approve of the plan."

"Do I look like I have fucking weeks or even days?" he said. "I've come to you because I heard you're good—good enough, but not famous. They're unlikely to look for me here. You're a somebody but a nobody, and I'm telling you you'll give me a complete makeover—today—or I'm going to kill you."

By the look of the guards, I knew he wasn't bluffing. If it hadn't been for them, I might have thought he was a schizophrenic with fantasies. In Mexico, the surreal can suddenly become real. One minute you're in your practice with Botox patients, the next a narco is threatening to kill you.


IN THE POPULAR imagination, a plastic surgeon is a greedy guy who makes millions, who cares only about sucking money out of the vanities of his patients. The patients drive BMWs, they can't accept they're getting older, and they ask the plastic surgeon to give them a "boob job" so they can keep their rich husband, or the male clients want to get rid of the wrinkles so they can keep their CEO job and their sporty looks. I'm not going to say there's no truth to this. But in my experience, there are far more women who scrape together all the money they have to make one significant change to their body.

They're women working as teachers, secretaries, police officers, and in bakeries. They're not hoping to look like the centerfold in *Playboy*, and they aren't ditzy women or rich bitches, they're women with souls, and hopes, and dreams, just like anyone, and often they had the misfortune to be born with something less than what society says is attractive. They didn't create the norms of beauty. Society did, and judges them. And often they had fathers who told them, when they were growing up, that they weren't beautiful, or, even worse, mothers who belittled them. That's one of the reasons I choose to have my clinic in Polanco. It's a place where I don't have to cater only to the super-rich. It's a place that feels more accessible to the full variety of patients. I charge different rates for different kinds of patients. I don't tell them this, so they don't feel like charity cases. I ask Veronica to use her judgment, as she watches the patients come in, as to what they can afford.

For me, plastic surgery is like any other medicine. It's a form of healing. And often I'm healing psychological wounds as I reshape the body. I consider it vital to adhere to the Hippocratic oath—to do no harm. Sometimes that oath can be hard to follow, like when a patient is begging you to make them thinner, and they're already thin. Sometimes, no doubt, some of the patients seem to have a frivolous sense of beauty or are unwilling to accept they're growing older. But I try to guide them gently, following the oath, avoiding any violation of the promise I swore to uphold, passed down from the time of the ancient Greeks.

It wasn't so easy to know what to do with Paco's request. I could tell he was a criminal, given the look of the guards and his threat to kill me. I could tell—since he was trying to change his appearance, completely—he was trying to run away from the law. I could tell that if he was a narco, which was the most likely explanation for his behavior, he'd probably killed dozens of people climbing to his position as a boss. I had no idea he was the Lord of the Heavens. I would find that out only later. But he had a presence, a way of commanding, that let me know he was a big shot who would fully be willing to kill me, and others.

By the Hippocratic oath, if I helped him change his appearance to run away from the law, then wasn't I becoming complicit in his crimes and in his harm to others? Performing the surgery would break the rule and put the blood of his hands indirectly on mine.

And if I didn't stand up to him, wouldn't I just be placing my life above others? Wouldn't I be saying, in effect, that my life was worth more than the many lives of the people he'd undoubtedly killed, and would kill in the future?

At the same time, it was hard to see how performing surgery on him was really any different from doing so on any other patient coming into my clinic and asking for a change of appearance. What he chose to do with his life—whether to kill, or not—wasn't an act I, myself, was committing. And, while it could be wrong to aid a criminal, the law of self-preservation is valid, too: sometimes it's necessary to do harm for the greater good. My life was my life. It wasn't worth nothing. And the more I lived, the more I might help others. It may seem impossible, but as I went through preparation for the surgery on Paco, I went through all these ideas as I scrubbed my hands and put on my surgical gloves, as I put on my clean medical scrubs, and as the assistants prepped the surgery room. Nothing was cast in stone. At any moment, I could pull out of the situation and say no.

Paco lay on the surgery table with the LED lights focused on his face, where I would begin. I told one of my two assistants, Jaime, to administer the sedative Dormicum intravenously to begin the process of anesthesia. I told him to be careful not to give too much of the sedative. The risk was too great, otherwise, that something could happen to Paco, that his heart could stop during surgery, and the consequences of the death of a narco were obvious.

Paco overheard the conversation, and he said to Jaime, "Give me double whatever the doctor said. I'm not going to let you torture me."

"The Dormicum is powerful," I said to Paco. My other assistant, Marina, cleaned surgical instruments and placed them by my side. "If too much is administered, you could die."

"I don't give a shit," Paco said. "If I die, nobody killed me. The only person who can kill the great Paco is Paco," he said, using his real name.

I signaled to Jaime not to listen to him, but I can't be sure Jaime understood my signal, or whether he refused to disobey Paco, or whether he followed my instructions. Paco went under, and I began the surgery.

We worked for eight hours. The two guards with the AK-47s came in, and they stood in corners of the room, one by the door, the other by the respirator. They'd dismissed the secretary, Veronica, and told her if she contacted anyone in the police, or told anyone, at all, what was happening, they'd go to her house and kill her.

The shape of Paco's nose was wide, like a fistful of lead. I narrowed his nose and shortened it, raising the tip. I opened his eyes wider and lifted his eyebrows. I reduced the widow's peak at his hairline and pulled his skin tight around his ears, so he looked ten years younger.

The respirator hummed, pumping into his body, but after four hours of surgery the sound paused, and I could tell the machine was somehow cut off.

"What's going on with the ventilator?" I asked Jaime, calmly, but extremely firmly.

"I'm not sure," Jaime said, and he checked the machine. An electrical outlet was near one of the guards, and Jaime found the machine unplugged. It was extremely strange that the machine could have become unplugged. I couldn't help but think one of the guards had removed the plug, or had kicked it with his feet. It was bad enough I was operating on a killer, but I could no longer be certain the two guards present weren't trying to kill Paco. What if they'd received orders to make him die during the surgery? What if they'd been bought off, by some rival narcos, to kill Paco and make it look like an accident?

I told one of the guards to put the plug of the respirator in, and he didn't respond. I couldn't tell if this was because he didn't want to hear me, or if he'd simply begun to doze off during the surgery.

A patient can last no more than three or four minutes without the respirator before permanent brain damage sets in. I told Jaime, sharply, to plug in the respirator. He bent beneath the AK-47 of one of the guards and reached to plug it in.

"What are you doing?" the guard said. "Are you trying to kill the jefe?" The guard seemed to snap out of his stupor. He pulled the plug out of Jaime's hand and plugged it in himself.

Beyond Paco asking for extra anesthetic, this was the second strange thing that had happened since the beginning of the surgery, but I decided to focus on the task at hand. I shifted the shape of the skin around Paco's abdomen and thighs. In the eighth hour, as we neared the end of surgery, I could hear the vital sign of his heart slowing. I asked Marina to check if the intravenous tube with the Dormicum was dripping at the appropriate flow rate. She said the drip chamber was open a little wide, and I told her to cut off administration of the fluid. The heartbeat slowed further. It flatlined. With his face in bandages, Paco closed his mouth and eyes, pushing against the clamps that held them open in their proper place. He looked like a phantom, up at me. I ordered Jaime to administer Flumazenil as an antagonist drug to counteract the effect of the Dormicum. I considered defibrillation to revitalize normal heart functioning.

"What's happening?" the guard near the door said.

"His heart has stopped, temporarily," I said. "We'll get it going again soon." I shouted this last bit between teeth as an order to Jaime to prepare the defibrillator.

"No one kills the jefe," the guard by the door said. "Only the jefe can kill himself." His heart wouldn't revive, and the guard by the door took a nearby pillow and placed it over the face of Paco and pressed the pillow into his face. The guard seemed to act to kill Paco, to suffocate him, though the patient was already dead.

"The jefe told me that if he was suffering I had to put the pillow on him to keep the pain out," the guard said.

I've been a surgeon for thirteen years, and I couldn't make any sense of all these strange actions. Had Paco been trying to kill himself when he asked for the extra Dormicum, and when he ordered the guards to put a pillow on his face? Was he constructing an elaborate suicide, to end his life but without disgrace? Had the guards tried to kill Paco in the pay of another, rival group of narcos? Had I failed, completely, to oversee the operation correctly? And was I responsible for his death? The only thing I knew was that Paco was definitely dead, and what it meant for me, I wasn't sure.

**THE DISPOSAL OF** the body was fast. I didn't have any say in the matter. The two guards took out a camera and took photos of Paco lying on the surgery table, his body already losing whatever pallor he'd had. It seemed an odd trophy shot, almost like the photos of Muammar Gaddafi or Saddam Hussein minutes after they were killed. There's something about the final photo of major tyrants—grainy, fuzzy, and stark—which reminds people, when it comes out in the tabloids, that they committed horrible crimes when they were alive. The guards' photography might imply they were truly on the payroll of other narcos, but there was no smiling, no cheering, as they took these shots. Nor was there any crying, nor wrenching of hair, which would show deep loyalty to the Lord of the Heavens. They stayed as neutral as the mirrors on their sunglasses, as professional as hired hit men, pulling out a body bag that they wrapped Paco up in, after they documented he was dead.

As quickly as they'd come, more than ten hours ago, they disappeared.

In some crazy way, the ease with which his body was disposed of, the fact all traces of him were gone—minus pieces of tiny flesh and blood that stuck to the scalpels and other surgical instruments—relieved me. It was like a nightmare that was over, and now I could awake.

But just like a nightmare, which never quite leaves the sleeper alone as they stay up, walking around in the middle of the night, Paco's sudden appearance and disappearance wasn't so easily sewn up.

I decided there was no way I could sleep in my apartment the night of the surgery. I debated whether I should call the police, but for the same reason I'd performed the surgery to begin with—a desire to live—I decided this avenue was impossible. I decided to keep everything hushed up, to say nothing, and I made Jaime and Marina swear they, too, would say nothing.

I went to my girlfriend's apartment. She's forty, and I'm forty-two. She's a Mexican banker, and she often works late hours. She has a reputation, in her office, for being a tough boss. She directs a group of twenty beneath her, in the bond department. My girlfriend is shapely, her breasts are large, she wears high heels, and she has a high voice, all stereotypically feminine, but these outwardly soft signs mask that she's a perfectionist who needs things done her way. When I came into her apartment, she'd just returned from work, and it was ten at night.

We often barely said hello to each other, when I came over to her place. If she came in from work first, she was likely to give me a peck on the cheek. If I came in first, I was likely to say a big hello, but then to disappear to take a shower before saying more. I couldn't tell her right away, therefore, what had happened during my day. I thought if I told her she might get scared and insist I call the cops. Or, I thought, she might suddenly worry about her own safety. I wanted everything to be normal, for everything that had happened that day to disappear.

We'd been going out for three years, sometimes breaking apart then getting back together. It was hard for either of us to know what we wanted. I'd take off for Seattle for a couple months, and she wouldn't come with me, or she'd go off to Turkey and not even tell me she was on vacation. We revolved like two atoms in the depths of outer space, attached but with barely enough energy to stay together, without the necessary warmth from the sun.

A week ago, I'd told her I wanted to have a baby. I admit the idea must have seemed like it came from out of nowhere. I told her this because my father had died a couple months before; my sister was in the process of divorcing; I felt everything in my life pulling apart, and I wanted something to come together. I wanted love—a love I seemed incapable of sparking in my girlfriend. She told me, immediately, she didn't want a child. She told me she didn't want to break up, but that she didn't know what she wanted next.

So I told her nothing about my day, as I came in. I slept in the bed beside her, feeling the space between us, wanting to come closer, but feeling her repelling me.

THE NEXT DAY, the police came to my clinic. They asked if Jaime and Marina worked for me. In an odd way, I was glad the police came, because neither of my assistants had come into work, and I was worried about what had happened to them.

"Do you know these people?" a police officer said, showing a photo of Jaime and Marina, their heads sticking out of two steel drums filled with concrete. Their faces were puffy with lacerations on their cheeks, as if they'd been tortured. "We found their bodies in the main pond of Chapultepec Park," the police officer said. "Do you have any idea why they might have been killed?"

I decided I couldn't screw around anymore, hiding what had happened the day before. I told the police exactly what had happened. They thanked me for my time and told me they might need to take me in for further questioning, but at the moment I wasn't under suspicion for the murder of my two assistants. They told me a full investigation would be made of the surgery I'd performed on Paco, that any evidence of negligence during the operation would be looked into, and that I'd remain under surveillance. They told me I wasn't permitted to leave the country.

The DEA came an hour later and did further questioning, informing me who Paco was and that they'd been on his trail, coming in closer and closer, the last two weeks. "Don't worry," one of the agents said. "We know you don't have any ties to Paco. We'll do what we can to get the local police off your case. The embassy has been informed of your situation."

The embassy may have been informed of my situation, but the question was, what was my situation? Was there someone out there who would be trying to hunt me down, as they had so quickly hunted Jaime and Marina? I told the DEA I wanted immediate protection. I told them I needed someone to be with me all the time, protecting me. I told them I wanted out of the country, fast.

"No can do about getting you out of the country fast," one of the DEA officers said, "but we promise to put someone on duty to watch what happens to you. We'll make sure nothing crazy happens. It has all the signs of an inside job—the guards wanted to get him. I don't think they'll have any interest in you."

"Then why'd they kill Jaime and Marina?" I said.

"Perhaps because they tried to talk about what happened. You did the right thing keeping silent. As long as you stay quiet, you should be fine."


THREE DAYS LATER, the news was in all the tabloids. I went with my girlfriend to the Parque Lincoln, near her apartment, to take her golden retriever for a walk. I'd canceled all my appointments. I'd closed the clinic. It was seven at night, late July, in the rainy season, and the sky was overcast. We walked through the park, and as I threw the ball, and as her dog, Maya, returned the ball faithfully, dropping it at my feet, I thought this was all I'd ever really wanted, the simple order of throwing a ball and having a dog bring it back, wagging its tail, showing the love and affection between a pet and its master. I'd never been able to have that kind of clarity in my personal life. I'd been married, briefly, to a woman in Seattle, and then divorced. I had few friends in Mexico City, but I'd been in the city ten years. Life was nothing like paddling hard from one end of a long bay, efficiently, to the other. It was nothing like throwing a ball and having a dog bring it back.

After a while of me throwing the ball, my girlfriend went up to Maya and took the ball from her. She told Maya to bring it to her, instead of to me. "He's not your daddy," she said. "I'm your mother, bring the ball to me." It seemed a cruel dig at my request, the other day, to have a child with her. She was saying I wasn't a parent; that she was the only parent.

I knew I was being sensitive, and potentially reading too much into everything, but I didn't want to play with Maya anymore.

Across the park, in front of a large birdcage a couple stories high, I was positive I could see a man who looked just like Jaime, even though he was dead. I told my girlfriend I'd be right back. I told her to please be patient but that I had to run across the park. I still hadn't told her what had happened to me, the other day.

I rushed across the park to where the man stood in front of the birdcage, wearing the same shirt as Jaime. I went up close and said, "Hey, Jaime!"

The man turned around, completely different from Jaime. It was a father holding a bag of peanuts, and his son came running around the base of the cage, laughing and shouting at the birds inside.

The boy's screams attracted a peacock inside the cage, resplendent in all the turquoise and blue that nature can conjure up to impress. The bird came toward the boy, the father, and me and opened its wide feathers, forming a big fan, so wondrous it stunned us all into silence. The pattern on the tail of the peacock looked like a thousand eyes staring at me, judging me. The bird shook its tail, and the eyes waved back and forth, evaluating me.

And it was then that I knew what I had to do. I ran back across the park toward my girlfriend. She was still holding the ball in her hand. She'd stopped throwing the ball at Maya. She seemed to watch me run back from the cage.

"I know I've been cold and silent the last few days," I said, when I got to her, panting a bit from the run, though feeling invigorated from the dash. "A few days ago, an unknown man came into my clinic, a narco, and he asked me to completely change his body. I did my best to do what he wanted. He died during surgery, and now I feel I'm being hunted. I don't know if I'm safe."

"Really? What a horrible, crazy thing," she said. "You should have told me," she said, softly. "Come here. Let me give you a hug." She came close and pressed her large breasts against my chest. It was the first warmth I'd felt in days, maybe even in months and years. I wasn't sure if things would be better between us, for the long run. I wasn't sure if everything would work out with the police. I could see a DEA agent in the distance, watching us, keeping us safe. I could feel her warm chest pressing into mine, feeling wider than the menacing tail of the peacock, and though Jaime and Marina were dead, filling me with confusion and mourning, for a second, wrapped in the arms of my girlfriend, I was the happiest I'd been in ages.

# THE SHARPSHOOTER

I had been down in Mexico City for two years, working with the DEA and CIA on covert activities to break up drug production and smuggling, when my buddy Charlie was shot. Charlie looked as young as I did, twenty-four, hair buzzed short, much taller than me, and a crack sharpshooter, just like me. Growing up, you would not have expected me to be some kind of crack sharpshooting hero-to-be, because I had dyslexia. I struggled to read at a fast enough pace to pass basic tests. But, through willpower, I learned you can do just about anything you put your mind to—including graduating from college with ROTC.

Before I came down to Mexico, I remember signing up for a class at Wichita State University. It was a class I really wanted to take, on contemporary American literature, but two weeks into the course I got orders from my superior officer that I was going to have weekly training at the same time as the class, and that I had to give it up. I was pissed off, for a second, that the commander on base hadn't thought enough to give us the schedule for training before the classes at the U. began, but orders are orders. I wanted to do what I was told—I had grown up without much money—and I wanted to get a college education, to progress with my life. If they had told me to walk backward to training, I would have done it.

"Jeremiah," my father told me, after I had learned about the scheduling conflict, "if they want you to sit, sit. If they want you to shit on command, shit on command. If they want you to roll over, roll over."

My father had been in the military for four years in Vietnam. Before he got his cancer, perhaps from all that Agent Orange over there, he told me, "The proudest thing I ever did was serve in the military. It made me into a man, out of a lazy sack of potatoes. It taught me order, discipline, and how to serve my country." He said he had absolutely no problem shooting gooks as he was told. He said there were people who knew better than those of us at the bottom of the heap, and sometimes you should just listen to them. He said all that second-guessing about the wars in Vietnam, Iraq, and Afghanistan was done by a bunch of crybabies who needed to toughen up and take one for the team.

"All those liberals," he said, "are always saying President Bush was fucking up, not showing the caskets of soldiers when they came home to Dover Air Force Base. Well what the hell do they expect him to do? Put those bodies on TV?" He was a big fan of Rush Limbaugh. If liberals said they wanted Hillary Clinton for prez, then they must want some kind of lesbian sex, he said, 'cause lord knows Bill wasn't giving her any. He'd rant about Obama coming from some Muslim country like Indonesia. "And now he wants us to believe, after he's tampered with his frickin' birth certificate, that he's not an alien."

Under those circumstances, I was first a Cub Scout and then a Boy Scout. I worked my way up to Eagle Scout. In high school, I occasionally walked around the halls in my Boy Scout uniform with merit badges pinned to my sash. When my father would say some of those things, from Rush, it would disappoint me. I agreed with some of the things my father would say, but I've always been a stickler for facts. Facts are what win battles, I thought. Facts are what win wars.

I used to stay up at night, as a kid, reading Time-Life books my father had about the battles of Iwo Jima and the landing of our troops on D-Day. I was impressed by the way Eisenhower had planned for that invasion, not letting any of the enemy know about the buildup of Marine amphibious ships, and keeping everyone on a need-to-know basis. I memorized those signs from the books that said LOOSE LIPS MIGHT SINK SHIPS and CARELESS TALK COSTS LIVES. And one of the phrases I learned is that when you confront the enemy, and when you do something wrong in battle, you have to admit it to *regain the mission.*

What I'm getting at is that even though the army exonerated me for what happened six days before I finished my tour in Mexico, the record needs to be set straight. The chips have to fall where they may.

Charlie and I had done everything together for four years when the incident happened, April 26. Stateside, before going down to Mexico, we went through our ROTC training together. Some Marines say the training we get in army ROTC is cushy, but beyond the extra studying with books, and strategy sessions to be leaders—able to explain to the troops, clearly, what our mission is—we go through the same rope courses and rubbing of our faces in dirt. I remember, once, after carrying sixty-pound packs of rocks, running in the hot Kansas sun, with the atrociously humid heat of 114 degrees in the month of August, I was lagging behind Charlie pretty bad, a hundred feet back. We were supposed to be jogging together, as a group. There were thirteen in our training platoon. I was extra-dehydrated. I had failed to obey orders and to drink two quarts before we'd started running. We were out on the WSU golf course, next to the main university campus, and I saw the golfers hiding from the heat under their golf carts, getting out of the carts only to barely lob balls down the fairway. I was tempted to lie down on the patchy grass of the fairway. It was so hot, even the grass was dying. I wanted to sit and say, "This is it. I can't go on. I can't take it anymore."

I had struggled through all the test-taking for years, with my

dyslexia. The office of student services, on campus, had told me I had
a right to take exams with twice the amount of time, and at first I,
regrettably, requested that amount of time. But I told myself it was
OK if it was necessary to complete the mission, and I slowly weaned
myself off that extra time. I wanted to be a full soldier, complete
and proud, just like everyone else, and I learned I could be. Usually I
carried my pack, not only keeping up with the group but leading it,
yet my legs cramped up bad this day. Charlie could have just left me
there to sit on the grass, but he risked his standing in the eyes of the
other soldiers—being seen as someone who had a friend that might
be going soft—and came back and lifted me off the ground. He carried my pack in front, his in back, and let me hop next to him. We
got back a full half hour late to the gym, where all the others were
waiting. But Charlie insisted on carrying me to the end of training.

—⋘◯⋙—

The soldier, Charlie, watched his buddy, Jeremiah, through binoculars at the Central de Abasto market. For five weeks they had been
ordered to direct a sting operation at the market. The place was full
of fish stalls, small vendors selling slabs of tuna, shrimp by the kilo,
lobsters, oysters, cheap sardines, and tiny fish to cook up and fry in
the inexpensive restaurants of Mexico City. The air stank of fish. The
stalls were elevated on concrete platforms, where trucks came and
unloaded their catch, trucked in from the Gulf Coast on ice. Hundreds of trucks arrived in the first light of dawn, an army that drove
from the coast during the night, to bring fresh fish to the whole of
the nation's capital, Mexico City. It was precisely all the trucks that
made it perfect for smuggling cocaine. Smuggling boats on the coast
mingled with other fishing boats near Veracruz, and the trucks at
the fish market were so full of blocks of ice and fish, there were a million places to hide kilo bricks of coke.

The Mexican authorities were corrupt, and Charlie had been
bought off, too, but Jeremiah didn't know anything about their cor-

ruption. The Mexican authorities pretended they hadn't authorized the operation. They'd said, in front of Jeremiah, gringos should stick to the north where the action was. They insisted all the big cartels were operating and fighting in the north, along the border, or in Sinaloa along the Pacific Coast. It was well known that many of the Mexican authorities didn't want to see what they didn't want to see, so the cocaine, pot, and meth ended up passing through the border into the U.S. and coming by hidden rail cars and in small boats into Texas, or attached to tourists as they flew into New York. The ingenuity of the smugglers was never-ending. The drugs didn't always come on small planes into the deserts of California or into Florida. They came in the bowels of mules, in latex bags in their intestines. They came in boxes stuffed into beehives, they came inside panels of old cars and in trucks as they went over the Mexican border. Everyone was a suspect, and Jeremiah had been trained, during his ROTC classes in Wichita, and then in his Special Forces training, to understand the enemy could be anywhere. So when the U.S. government gave the go-ahead for the sting operation, Jeremiah felt the mission must be getting close to some real drug-busting if the Mexican authorities wouldn't authorize the mission. They must be cutting close to the bone.

Charlie watched as his longtime partner, his buddy Jeremiah, whom he'd gone to Special Operations Group training with, appeared in the distance with a briefcase of cash, to meet his counterpart, the drug dealer Francisco Sosa. Through the binoculars, seeing Sosa live for the first time, Charlie was impressed by Sosa's formality. Often the drug dealers dressed in Hawaiian shirts that draped over their fat bellies, over slacks that fell to white alligator-skin shoes. The look was clichéd and gave them away. But Mr. Sosa wore a dark, worn-out suit and a frumpy panama hat, which made him look like he was the owner of a large area of fish stalls and truly from the coast, just as he was supposed to be. Through the binoculars, Charlie saw Jeremiah shake hands with Mr. Sosa. Sosa looked left and right, as if making sure no one was watching. He looked convinced the man with the briefcase meant business. He shook hands with Jeremiah again, and took him inside a fish stall.

Charlie watched the whole event from the inside of a fish truck with some dark windows and listening equipment, across the wide parking lot of the market. The outside of the truck looked like a run-down Isuzu delivery truck, one of the miniature vehicles that plied the streets of Mexico City. He switched to an image inside the fish market where Jeremiah talked with Sosa, transmitted by a camera they had put in the market a week ago.

Sosa said, "I promise you the product is fresh and of the highest quality." He never referred to the cocaine as coke, but always as "the product." It was known this was the best way to avoid any recordings being used in court, though the judges were mostly bought down in Mexico.

"Can you give me a taste of it, now?" Jeremiah said.

"We can give you a taste of whatever you need. I assure you the product is fresh."

Sosa told his assistants to bring some of the product. He looked around, to see if he was being followed into the back room of the fish-market stall. The image was clear. The head of a giant swordfish poked a long snout from behind Sosa, so the sword seemed to come out of his hat. Charlie zoomed the camera in on Sosa's hands. There was a brick of the product, a kilo of white cocaine, wrapped in layers and layers of plastic with tape. Sosa cut open the block his assistants had brought him. The outside of the package was brown with dark red blood on top, from the guts of fish the package had been sent in. Sosa stuck in the tip of his penknife, with white mother-of-pearl on the handle, and cut at the dense white brick until a few pieces came off in his hands. He gave the brick to Jeremiah to hold, to feel the weight. He lifted the blade of his penknife up to Jeremiah's face and gave the knife to Jeremiah. Jeremiah picked at the area Sosa had cut. He stuck his finger inside the brick and pulled it out with powder still clinging. He put the finger to his lip and tasted the powder and it numbed and tasted rich and real.

"My people will expect the shipment in three weeks," Jeremiah said. "Two hundred bricks. No more, no less. On time. To Houston. You know the place. Everything you asked for is here." He handed over the briefcase.

Sosa took the briefcase and handed it to his assistants. They took the briefcase to a different back room to count. They came back and told their jefe it was all clear. Sosa shook Jeremiah's hand. "It's a pleasure doing business with you." Jeremiah left and kept walking. He took a taxi, as predetermined by the operation, to a safe house.

Charlie sat in the truck and gave a thumbs-up to three DEA and CIA officials in the vehicle. They slapped each other on the back. This was the first test to see if the shipment would work, to be sure they had the real guys. The next time, they would arrest Sosa. With the recordings, they could begin to nail Sosa in the States, or they'd take him out, if necessary, in Mexico.

Later that night, Charlie called his corrupt Mexican counterparts to tell them Jeremiah had delivered the money and that the product would be shipped to their contacts in Houston. It was a perfect scam. The money had come from the U.S. government. The U.S. government thought it was paying for the first phase of a real sting operation. Only next time, when they went in to make the final bust, Sosa mysteriously would not appear. He would be tipped off. Charlie would pocket a million and a half of the current six-million-dollar shipment to Houston, and then retire. Jeremiah had no clue he was being duped by his best friend.

—⊶⟪◯⟫⊷—

This is how it happened. This is how you end up shooting your own buddy.

Three weeks before what they call the "incident" in the military report—which wasn't an incident but a shootout clusterfuck—I

went for drinks with Charlie. It was the day after the first Sosa connection. Charlie wanted to go drinking and whoring, and while I
tended to avoid that kind of crap, to remain as upright a soldier as I
could, after posing as the decoy with Sosa, which I had been selected
for by picking straws with the other guys in the group, I felt I deserved some booze and pussy.

We started out having a martini at the Condesa DF hotel, a
super-fancy place that always seemed out of my budget, where the
pool on the roof shines aquamarine, in cool hues, up to the pul-
sating sky of el DF at night. There were fancy women who went to
the hotel, women who wore designer dresses and who walked with
imported Italian leather shoes, and me and Charlie sat in one of
the white couches with a view of the skyline and of the hemlines of
those women as they went by, and it felt like life was good, downing
the vodka in shot after shot with a whole bottle Charlie insisted on
buying.

"Ain't this the life?" Charlie said. He was chewing on some ice,
and he popped in a cocktail shrimp from a plate of twenty he had ordered. I thought of the simple bars of Wichita, where the women all
look like aging sorority girls by the time they're twenty-five, where
the only plan is to get married, find a solid job, and raise the kids, if
you don't get caught up in a divorce too soon and they make you pay
alimony.

"I've learned a thing or two over here," Charlie said.

"Like what?" I said.

"I've learned black and white can be the same color, if you look
at them long enough."

"How's that?" I said. I was into reading martial arts books and
strategy by Sun Tzu about the art of war, and I understood how you
could take the power of your enemy and absorb it to fight back at
them, but I didn't understand what he was getting at.

"Well, you know how here—if some Mexican says they're coming to dinner, they may or may not come?"

"Yeah, I hate that," I said.

"Well, at some point, I came to realize maybe I was the one with too rigid an expectation the person *should* come."

"But they should," I said. "Don't give me that crap you're going all culturally relative on me. I hate that relativism. Some things are right. Some things shouldn't be done."

"Okay, okay. Different example. Here, if I call some woman up on a date, and I go out with her and she doesn't like the evening, then she tells me she had a good time. She smiles at me and says I'll look forward to your call. She's giving me the turn-on but she really means the turn-off."

"What's so good about that?" I said.

"Because no one has to do what they don't want to. They just do what feels right and worry about everyone else's feelings later."

"It sounds like you haven't thought that one fully through yet," I said.

Charlie went over to the pool, where a woman in a long, silk dress with flowers printed on the fabric was standing alone. I watched him from my seat in the leather couch. "Hey, señorita," Charlie said. "How about grabbing one of your woman friends and going out with me and my buddy?"

The woman smiled politely at Charlie, and looked down at her shoes.

"Aren't you interested in going out with a handsome stud like me?"

Charlie looked as out of place in the hotel as if you had just dropped him out of an army helicopter onto the roof. He was handsome and tall, but his whole body language was stiff. He gestured too much. He waved his hands in the air, trying to persuade the woman she should go with him. He looked like a soldier trying to buy a camel in a foreign land, and these women weren't camels.

"Excuse me," the woman said to him. She was speaking in English, because Charlie had been speaking in English to her. None of us spoke much Spanish. "I would really like to be able to go out with you, sir, but I'm afraid I'm busy tonight."

"Aren't I good enough?" Charlie said. "Don't I look good enough? Don't I look like the kind of guy you would wanna bring back to your mamacita to show off?"

The woman winced. She was standing by the edge of the pool, next to a ladder that went in and out of the water, and she started to grip the ladder tightly like she needed something to help her out. She started to step away, trying to walk slowly so she wouldn't seem impolite.

"Oh, now, don't go away, little honey . . ." Charlie said. "Don't you do that."

One of the men a couple booths away, the manager—a tall Mexican wearing a tailored suit, with a black shirt made of silk and expensive leather shoes, a five o'clock shadow neatly cut in the way of the fashion of the day, and bald in a manly way—came over and said to Charlie, "I'm sorry, sir, but it seems the woman isn't interested."

"'Cause she thinks she's too rich or too fancy," Charlie said, shaking his head. "That's what they think, around here." He said this turning back to me, but then, speaking so loud he was almost shouting it to the entire rooftop, continued, "It's all about class, class, class in this fuckin' country. Everyone thinks they were born from some rich Spanish king or queen. Like they're all fucking *güeros*." He was using the word for "whitey"—a güero. He was saying everyone wanted to be a whitey.

"I think it's time to hold your liquor better, soldier," I said to Charlie. "It's time for you to get in line for roll call."

"That's your problem, Jeremiah. You're always thinking the only path to take is the one of a soldier. There are other paths, too," he said.

In the heat of the moment, I let the comment slide. I didn't think all that much about what he was saying. I wanted to stop my buddy from getting into a fistfight in a fancy hotel with the other Mexican guy, before he called the bouncers.

"Come on, soldier," I said. I pulled Charlie's arm.

"She likes me. I'm telling you she likes me. Black is white. I'm telling you."

By that time, the woman had moved quickly to the far side of the rooftop patio. The water from the pool cast strange shadows against everyone's faces. I saw a darkness, and sneer, on Charlie's face I had never seen quite the same way, though he often liked to get into bar fights. I knew the first rule we were taught about being in another country: *Always learn the local traditions and culture. Get the other culture on your side. Use the strength of the enemy village and government to engage in counterinsurgency.*

They pulled Charlie off the rooftop—two bouncers—and held his arms behind his back. The bouncers were dressed in crisp white suits, similar to the one of the rooftop manager. They escorted us toward the door. I spoke to the two bouncers in as much broken Spanish as I could. "Please tell your manager and the señorita we are sorry," I said. "We are sorry and we didn't mean any disrespect."

"The fuck I didn't," Charlie said. "I meant every word I said in there. These fancy Mexicans think they're better than everyone." When they got us to the front door he said, "Come on, let's go find ourselves some place that's got some real women to fuck."

Outside, he insisted on grabbing his car. He wouldn't give me the keys. He was so worked up, he was going to drive. He was drunk and on his way to getting drunker.

The rest of the night is more or less a blur. We drove to the Zona Rosa, where the prostitutes hang out. We chose two women. They wore tight miniskirts, the way none of the local women ever did. One had long black hair that cascaded down to her knees. She had on a red skirt, and she let most of her breasts show out of a loose, leopard-patterned camisole. She oohed and aahed at the car as we drove by. "I want that one," Charlie said. "I want her to give me a fuckin' blowjob."

I had no interest in really getting it on with any of these women, but I realized my mission for the evening was going to be to keep Charlie out of any serious trouble and that he'd need me along for the ride. In the military, when you go swimming, when you are out in the bush, you know you always need to have one buddy who's going to keep your ass safe. That's the person you can count on, no matter what. It doesn't matter what they say or what they do, you stick to them like a fly on shit. You are their eyes and ears. You hump them home, if necessary.

I chose the prostitute I thought was the prettiest, but who wouldn't get in the way. I chose a petite thing that looked like she was a good daughter, just trying to make a buck. We went to a bar called the Cuatro Aces, and we sat around with these women getting one drink after another.

"You see," Charlie said to me later in the night, leaning in close to hug his gal, "these women know a good man when they see one." The woman he was with pulled a cherry out of her drink and put it in Charlie's mouth.

We went to some hotel and grabbed a pair of rooms, and the walls were so thin I could hear Charlie in the next room yelling, "Come on lady, ride 'em cowboy! Ride it!"

"Don't you want to make love?" the woman I was with asked me. "Come on, let me make you happy. Let me give you a party." It was two in the morning, and I couldn't get out of my mind that we had a ride down to Cuernavaca we were going to have to make the next day, with a couple of Mexican military officers, at 1500 hours, but the booze was pulling at my mind. I'd had a bunch of vodka and tequila. I couldn't help but hear Charlie in the other room saying, "Yes, yes, more, more. Give it to me. Give it to me. Give it to me, little lady. Give it to me."

I may be a soldier, but I'm not a saint. I didn't like paying for my loving, or for whatever sleeping with a prostitute meant. Call it the relief of manly urges. I had no illusions that the women giving us the blowjobs and sex liked it. I knew they were just trying to make some money. *Know the real face of the enemy. Don't be fooled by the smiles locals will give you,* I remembered from my training. I let the woman get on top of me and ride for a bit. My head was swimming. I remembered the tension of going in to see Sosa with the briefcase. It was just "the mission," but it had been a tense one. I tried to let out some of the tension. I got on top, and with the booze flowing through me, I felt more like an animal, spurred by the sounds of Charlie in the other room, and I thrust hard until I came.

That night was the beginning of something new with Charlie, something that seemed odd to me, after knowing him and living with him in the next-door bunk from base to base and operation site to site for a few years. A couple days later, I saw him with a gold Rolex. He didn't wear the Rolex when we were with the other soldiers, but he put it on when we went out for a drink.

"What's up with the new watch?" I said. "You get it at one of those pawn shops in el Centro?" I had been walking around the center of Mexico City, where there are plenty of shops where they buy and sell gold by weight. I figured he must have gotten a deal at one of those places.

"Nah. Not at a pawn shop," Charlie said. "My whole life my dad used to buy things at those pawn shops. This one's for real." He pulled it off his wrist and held it in front of his face like he was holding the Promised Land.

"Must have been expensive," I said. "How'd you get it?" Our salaries were shit in the army. People always thought we made good money, because we were Special Forces, but we didn't.

Charlie looked at me and said, "How the hell do you think I got it? Saving up money. I earned it."

But I knew a new watch like that cost thousands, and he was suddenly spending more on a lot of things. He kept going back night after night to that same prostitute we met in the Zona Rosa. I went back with him once, since he was my buddy and I wanted to let him know I was with him, but I couldn't keep up his pace—either with money or with desire—and I let him just tell me stories of conquering love when he came back to the small base where we lived.

He started buying fancier clothes, too. He told me he was sending money back to his mother, in Wichita, and the day we were going to meet Sosa for the second time, he had a bag all packed, with some of those nice clothes, next to the foot of our bunk, and he said he was going to go on a nice vacation to Cancún once the operation was over, when we were going to be given a couple days of R&R. The whole thing seemed odd to me, extravagant, and I couldn't figure out where he was getting the money.

—◄◄◄◄(( ))►►►—

Three weeks after the first contact with Sosa in the Central de Abasto, Jeremiah lay on top of a roof looking over the parking lot and the area where the delivery trucks came with fish, where a football field's length of stalls spread one after the other, and where men carried fish in and out of trucks. It was early morning, and the first light of sunrise was hitting the clouds. Looking through the scope of his M86 sniper rifle, trained on the same storefront across the way where he had met Sosa before with the briefcase, to give him the money, he was so focused on his targets he didn't notice the fiery struggle of dawn. Above his shoulder, crouched on the roof behind him, the head of the Special Operations Group, Colonel John P. Saunders, had come to direct the final sting operation. Saunders had been brought in, unexpectedly, three days ago, and the rumor was he was brought in because the operation might be compromised. He was a veteran of foreign battles, head of a counterterrorism group that had operated in Iraq for three years and then in Afghanistan. He was known as a powerful son of a bitch who didn't take whining from his soldiers. With gray hair cut close, patches for valor and leadership pasted across his battle fatigues, he looked like a puma ready to spring off the roof, watching in the same direction as his soldier below him, Jeremiah. His right hand formed a fist, and his knuckles pressed into the roof tar.

Across the way, and walking up a staircase to meet Sosa, Charlie carried a briefcase identical to the one brought by Jeremiah before. They had all picked straws, again, to see who would carry the case this time. It was dangerous being the one who delivered, if anything went wrong. Professional buyers used different mules to bring the cash all the time. It was a game of musical chairs. Everyone had to have trust, but everyone had to know that at any moment both sides could disappear, vanishing in the night. The world of drug deals was like a mirage, water that came in the desert like an oasis and then went.

It had fallen to Charlie to deliver the cash this time. Below Jeremiah, where he looked through the scope, the same Isuzu truck with the listening equipment was in the parking lot, with four men. Six other men were also stationed, with short-range Uzi machine guns, dressed in plain clothes, pretending to be workers on the fish docks. Charlie was protected and surrounded. The plan was to have Sosa taken out with one shot when he came to meet Charlie. Jeremiah would aim with precision and shoot. One shot, to the temple, and Sosa would fall. Sosa would likely be outside for only a second before he would want to retreat into the back room, where fighting would be more difficult. So they wouldn't wait to shoot. In the immediate mayhem, Charlie would jump down in front of the concrete platform where the delivery trucks unloaded, to protect himself. He was wearing a bulletproof vest under his loose plaid shirt. While Charlie crouched beneath the concrete barrier, the other six men with guns on the platform would deal with any return fire. It was the most likely way to get Sosa, with a sniper bullet. It was quick, simple, and efficient and sent the right message: this cartel was going to be eliminated. Colonel Saunders had announced the plan to his group three days ago, when he took over direct command. "In the second raid, once we know they have delivered the packages to Houston, we will eliminate Sosa. We will let them know operations in this area are forbidden and will cease to continue. Are there any questions?" Colonel Saunders had asked the group.

"Why not just bring in Sosa alive?" Jeremiah had said, during the briefing. "Get more intelligence. Make an example of him, publicly."

"And just how, Second Lieutenant Young," Colonel Saunders said, "do you think we are going to grab a guy like Sosa alive without more manpower down there to do the job, putting them at risk? And what the hell do you think is the probability a Mexican court will not be bought off, or that our own courts in the U.S., if they ever get jurisdiction for the case, and if we can get him extradited to the U.S., won't give some crap that the evidence we've provided is tainted, that we have somehow failed to protect Sosa's rights, while thousands of young Americans are poisoned in their bodies, through the scourge of drugs, because of this man, destroying the manhood of our country and increasing drug use in the ghetto? This operation is going to be clean and efficient, and legal within the authority vested in this group. It is my final decision, and it will be done this way."

Jeremiah had looked forward, standing at attention, chin flat and eyes looking into the distance, seeking not to see anything other than the command he had just heard, after receiving the dress-down and final order.

On the rooftop now, he felt the presence of Colonel Saunders next to him, tense, chewing gum, surveying the target area. Jeremiah squinted into the scope of the gun. He followed the crosshairs just in front of Charlie as he walked up the concrete stairs to the delivery platform. The scope made everything clearer than in normal reality, Jeremiah felt. It showed a man as he was, as a physical body, as a plane in space rather than a mind. Through the scope he always felt he was finally in control, that he was master of his defects, that he knew why God had put him on this planet, making it harder for him to read in order to give him another gift instead, the gift of being a supreme shooter, slow and steady, one of the few who could breathe calmly in and out, so calmly the gun barely moved, maintaining only the will of his targeting, until he followed orders and took out the necessary target. In shooting he felt the certainty he was completing his mission. He had taken out thirty-nine targets during his two years, so far, in Mexico. He had shot from rooftops in Juárez and rooftops in Guadalajara, and out of hotel rooms in Acapulco. He had watched men with briefcases scatter onto the pavement. He had missed only twice. All other times, it was one bullet, one carefully placed projectile, preferably in the base of the skull area, where the flesh was softer, or higher up, between the eyes, if necessary, or in the chest as a last resort, where there were more bones to protect the heart. The bleeding was longer there before death.

Through the scope, he could see Charlie up on the platform, mouth pursed, eyes looking around for Sosa. Six men came out to meet him. Two approached to give him a handshake. They looked oddly relaxed as they gave him the shake. Not tense and distant the way they usually interacted with the client. Charlie stood on the platform, and he seemed to ask for Sosa. He pointed to the interior, from where Sosa had come out the last time, and raised his hand in the air, questioning. He waited and waited. The other men with him milled about, looking left and right to see if anyone was coming. The pause was getting longer and longer. It was far too long to be normal. Looking through the scope, Jeremiah ran his finger up against the trigger. Soon, Sosa would appear. Soon he would shoot and it would be over.

The men on the platform suddenly crouched down, their knees pointing forward in the direction of the Isuzu, and they began firing with all their intensity at the vehicle. The truck was no more than forty yards away.

The bullets hit the truck and the windshield crashed in. The driver inside, a Mexican in on the surveillance group, who was used to blending in with the locals, was instantly killed. The bullets came more and more, against the rear of the truck where the four DEA and CIA operatives listened in.

The men in plain clothes, in the team on the platform, came running from the fish stalls. They were a mix of Mexican military. The Mexican military had been brought in on the raid at the last second. If things got violent, it was going to be necessary to have their approval and participation, and they had finally chosen to be in on the mission.

Jeremiah shot at the men on the platform who were shooting at the Isuzu truck. He aimed, with the precision of a mathematician, and killed one man, with long hair and a black leather jacket, who was firing at the truck. He looked to the left and took out a man wearing baggy jeans and a black T-shirt with a skull. He heard the sound of bullets going back and forth, at the Isuzu truck, pounding harder and harder into the truck and at the gas tank, until the tank gave way and the truck exploded.

Through the scope he could see Charlie had dropped down to the front of the concrete platform where he was supposed to jump once Sosa was shot. But Sosa had never come.

"Take him out. He's a mole," Saunders said. He put his hand on Jeremiah's shoulders.

"Who?" Jeremiah said.

"You know who. You can sense it, solider. He has betrayed this entire group. He has betrayed his country. I received intelligence last evening that he tipped them off and that Sosa wouldn't come. Sosa hasn't come. It's confirmed true. And now you'll get rid of the cancer within the unit before it spreads. Take him out."

"Sir," Jeremiah said. "Sir, this is not how we deal with such situations, sir." He couldn't believe his buddy had betrayed him. He couldn't believe he had betrayed the unit. He could not believe he had betrayed his country. He could not believe he would do such a thing. "Sir, is that a direct order, sir?"

"Yes, it is."

And though in his conscious mind, if he had had time, he would have reflected harder on the fact that he had the right to disobey an order he knew directly to be against the law of his country, he felt the hand of the colonel press hard between his shoulder blades. He saw, out of the corner of his eye, the truck in flames. He had heard, on the group radio, the cries of the men in the Isuzu truck. He saw the men firing back and forth on the platform. He saw Charlie run along the base of the platform, running away from the scene with the briefcase, toward the taxis. He knew, looking through the scope, that if he wanted to, he could shoot the target between his head and shoulder, at the back of his brain, completing the order just as he was told. But he chose not to. He knew he could not do that. He could not kill someone in his group, even if he had betrayed the group and led to the deaths of others. He moved the scope ahead of Charlie, running. Yet he could not do nothing at all, with the colonel there, ordering him, even if his order was unacceptable. He would shoot in front of Charlie to scare him, to let him know he had been found out, to complete, in some form, the order of the colonel, while disobeying him. He had to do so. This was his dilemma. It was a direct order. He aimed wide, to the left, in front of Charlie's feet as they twisted and hurried across the pavement. The bullet sped forward. The gun recoiled. And then it all happened in what felt like a long moment. There in front of him, through the scope, to his surprise, the bullet caught the tips of Charlie's toes. It hadn't totally missed. It had grazed one of his tennis shoes. Charlie bent forward and down, suddenly arrested, as if suddenly realizing he had feet that he had taken for granted while fleeing. He dropped the briefcase and looked for who was shooting, up at the rooftops. He looked in the direction of Jeremiah. He turned back down and reached first for his foot and then for the briefcase on the ground. He hobbled forward with his left foot slightly wounded. And in that moment of arrested running forward, a pause in his running toward the taxis, one of the

men on the platform, who had been fighting for Sosa's cartel, found
Charlie was running away and turned to Charlie and fired at him
and shot Charlie in the head and in the neck. It was that moment of
pause, surely, which led to his death, Jeremiah thought. Charlie lay
on the pavement of the Central de Abasto, his head caught in a pot-
hole with the sloppy residue of the fish market, bleeding into a mix
of water used to hose off the fish stalls, fish oil from scattered fish
bones, and the oil of the idling trucks. His body lay twisted, his hand
reaching toward the briefcase, his eyes looking up at the sky, blank
now, no longer quivering as they had just done, dead, as Jeremiah
looked at him through the scope.

—«««(()»»»—

Had it all been in my mind? Was Charlie really gone? My buddy
gone? Certainly his suitcase, which was at the bottom of our bunk,
was gone when I got back to base. I sat on the bunk bed, thinking of
Charlie, shocked and crying. Could Charlie have really been guilty,
as the colonel said? There was the watch and the sudden money. But
I needed proof, much more proof than that.

What I knew is that the colonel had gone crazy. Such a direct
order to shoot Charlie could only have come from battle fatigue,
from too many tours in Afghanistan and Iraq before being sent to
the relative calm of the "pasture" of Mexico. But six months later,
stateside, out of the heat of the moment in the field, I wasn't so sure
the order had come from battle fatigue. I had seen headlines in the
newspapers that confirmed what I had seen on my own: drone
strikes in Pakistan and Afghanistan, taking out people who had
never been judged in a court of law. American citizens shot by the
drones. Those were true terrorists, true enemies, and before the incident with Charlie, I had never thought about them too much. Yet
now I could see, placed within a command environment of choosing
who lives and who dies, and deciding that even American citizens
could be shot from the sky, and placed in situation after situation

where millions of dollars of cash are given out to buy the loyalty of men who are thieves, like the president of Afghanistan, Hamid Karzai—how far of a step was it from those actions, approved every day by my government, to an order that crossed the line, like the one from Colonel Saunders asking me to kill our own man, simply because he had double-crossed us? Yes, in Saunders's heart of hearts, he must have known somehow that what he had ordered me to do was too much, a crossing into the land of some character like Mr. Kurtz in that novel by Joseph Conrad that I read once called *Heart of Darkness*. Coming home, I began to read up more and more, even at the slower pace of my dyslexia, to make sense of what had happened to me down in Mexico.

This morning it is Memorial Day, and a full year has passed since I left Mexico. I told the other men in my unit, after the battle where Charlie died, what the colonel had ordered me to do. None of the men would believe me, or they chose not to hear. The army wrote up a report about the "incident," as they called it, and they said that after a case of accidental "friendly fire"—as they call such shots from us when we hit our own—the soldier, Charlie Reynolds, was lightly wounded and then taken out by the members of the Sosa Cartel. The description is completely accurate as to what happened, physically, and yet it is completely false. The colonel had me removed from the unit. He said I had done great service to my country but that I was getting tired and needed a rest. The army gave me a Silver Star Medal for the many kills I had made as a sharpshooter, and sent me home.

Back home in Wichita, I got to thinking about truth and lies. I thought about My Country 'Tis of Thee Sweet Land of Liberty and shooting and taking out those thirty-nine people in Mexico, by my hand, by my own will, by my own following of commands and orders, by my own volition, by my own feelings of honor and duty, and so on and so forth, and what all that meant. How, exactly, did killing some drug dealers help to raise the American flag high? Where was one drug user who was using drugs less because of any one of those men I had killed? The drugs would come as long as the people wanted them. Remove one drug dealer and another will mushroom up. And another. And another. Every person smoking a joint, every person snorting coke or injecting or snorting heroin, knows what they are doing, knows they are tied into the drug trade, and yet they are not going to stop doing what they are doing. The feeling of getting high is too powerful, too good. The liquid train of drugs will forever come into the country as long as people want to party, as long as people are sad, as long as people feel they have nowhere to turn in their hour of need, when God and Jesus and nothing above will seem to quiet the pain within.

I began to deeply question what I had been a part of. I began to ride down the wide avenues of my city of Wichita, so neat and clean, each road wide enough to have a military parade, the roads paved and graded, and the box stores of Walmart and Best Buy and one soulless mall after another spreading out in an infinite plain of vapid consumption, while there was no money, I had been told, to send me to college without me joining the ROTC. I was not complaining. I was not whining. I was not saying the government should give me a handout. I was not saying that I had never wanted to be an Eagle Scout or a Boy Scout. But what kind of country, I began to wonder, makes it easier for you to get an education if you are willing to kill than if you want to talk about peace?

After Mexico, I couldn't stand living with my father. That was no longer an option. I took an apartment for myself. I lay in bed reading, thinking, and recalling the faces of all thirty-nine of the men that I took out with single bullets. I began to drink hard. I drank Jack Daniel's first, and then moved on to cheaper schnapps. For the better part of six months I drank. And then I saw a homeless vet walking down the street, carrying all his possessions in a shopping cart, wandering from here to nowhere, as I'm sure you've seen so many times before. Before I had gone down to Mexico, I had looked at those homeless vets as failures, as aberrations, guys without discipline who just couldn't hold it together. Not like me. I was a real solider. A kick-ass soldier. I was America's finest. I was bred to be the best. Yada, yada. Just like on the army recruitment billboard that I saw every day in my neighborhood that towered above the street, and over the vets who wandered to the vet thrift store to get some clothes. I saw that homeless vet, and I was tempted to give him my alcohol. I no longer judged him. I went home and poured out all the booze into the toilet. Who dares to judge a homeless vet like that on the street, or to even feel pity for him, until he has been in battle?

This morning, I saw the front page of the newspaper. There was a glowing, patriotic photo of a soldier at Dover Air Force Base prepping an empty dress-uniform to be placed inside the casket of a fallen soldier. The message of the photo was that America takes care of its own. We make sure we treat our soldiers right.

I hopped in the truck my father had said he didn't need anymore. It was an old, beat-up Chevy pickup, with dents on the back from being used on a farm outside of Wichita, moving equipment. I didn't know where I was going to go, at first. I drove around the endless desert of strip malls, along the flat, wide avenues of the city, passing an International House of Pancakes then a Staples, a McDonald's, a Target, a Hog Wild BBQ, a pawn shop and then another pawn shop and then another. I got out of the car at the A-OK Pawn Shop holding my medal for my tour of duty in Mexico in my hand, and walked into the shop and put it on the counter and asked, "How much for this?"

"This? You sure you want to sell this?"

"Yes, I'm sure. How much?"

"Truth be told," the man at the counter said, "the value is more in what it means than in what you can sell it for. I can't really get all that much money for a medal. You'd be better off going to a specialty collector than trying to sell it in a pawn shop."

I looked around at the interior of the store, old electric guitars from dreams of making it big in a band, old tools from mechanics who couldn't find jobs anymore in construction during the recession, or who had been laid off from the airplane factories because of Chinese competition. I saw weed whackers that looked like they may or may not be able to run anymore, things discarded from garages stuffed with too much junk. I saw merchandise that looked like it had been sold by small-time drug dealers—high-end speakers way too scuffed-up to have ever been owned by someone who had real money from a legal job. I saw videos and DVDs, row upon row of movies no longer wanted, that had been seen, digested, and found not worthy of holding on to. I saw people overweight at the checkout counter buying things on credit cards. I saw a man with a dark tan, with a long mustache falling from side to side and a part down the middle, who looked like the peak of his life had been serving in the military and now he was smoking two packs a day and trying to hold down a job to feed his family. I saw all this as I looked around the A-OK Pawn Shop, with wedding rings that were being sold after marriages had gone sour, diamonds that no longer shined.

A young, disillusioned man could look at this forever, bitter, seeing things he wanted to see reflected back at him, seeing his own reflection in objects. And then it was that I saw my own true reflection, in a mirror between the section of the store devoted to tools and the section devoted to jewelry. I looked up behind the man working at the jewelry section, who had told me my medal might not be worth as much as everyone thought, and I caught the reflection of myself. There was a young man looking too tired, too dejected for his age, his short hair no longer looking buzzed, no longer neat and orderly, no longer standing on the drill field at attention. I saw the bags of sleeplessness around the lower edges of his eyes, and the brown pupils that seemed so dark they swallowed into the iris. What was I doing in this pawn shop? How did I get here? I picked up the medal from the counter where I had left it while I wandered around the store. It was time for me to find that core of humanity inside me, again. It was time to erase the image I had seen of myself in the mirror. I picked up an old acoustic guitar, hidden beneath the electric guitars. It was old and used, but there was still life in it. I strummed on the guitar. I didn't know how to strum well, but I kept picking at the guitar for a while, until the man in the store came over and said to me, "You seem to play pretty well."

I went up to the counter and bought the guitar and went outside and put it carefully in the back of the pickup. I drove out to Charlie's grave, on the edge of town, at the small plot where he had been buried a little over a year ago. There was his tombstone, with plastic flowers still fresh. The military wouldn't give him a burial. They had simply sent the body home.

"Charlie, you fucked up," I said, "you wanted too much, you got greedy. But they did you wrong." I looked down at the grave. "I did you wrong." I left the guitar on his grave, and I went home knowing I was going to go back to school. There were other ways to "Be All That You Can Be." If I had made it as far as winning a medal as a soldier, I was going to be far more as a civilian.

# THE PAINTING PROFESSOR

In Puebla, the professor was losing his mind. After the bullets of the
night before had quieted down, he went outside of his compound to
inspect the walls of the fortress of his studio. The studio had been a
factory, once. Fifteen feet high, thick walls bordered the compound,
and there were small watchtowers on each corner where the guards
who had once protected the factory could take aim and fire, if necessary. More likely, they hadn't been protecting the factory from theft,
but rather keeping out unionized workers in the old days, the professor had thought, when he'd first bought the place.

He was a professor of painting in Mexico City, and he had bought
the studio in the city of Puebla, an hour and a half away, in the late
'70s, when traffic was less bad and it didn't take so long to get out
of town to his private painting retreat. The factory had been a sock
production facility. The interior of the compound had three buildings. One still had the old, rusted metal molds, like upside-down
Christmas socks, which threads were wrapped around. It was a bit
of a mystery what the metal figures were for, but they looked like
a garden of statues to the professor, like pinwheels floating in the
air in the first building. He had left the space alone as a monument
to what the compound had originally been. In the second building,

he had stored his paintings for thirty-five years and used the wide, industrial open space as a studio. Old fiberglass patched the tin of the roof here and there, letting in a tired light. It was like his brain, he thought, fragments of light coming in and bending, diffused. His thoughts were this way, no longer clear and focused the way they once had been. He was in his mid-sixties. For a man who had been so alert only three years ago, the increasing dullness of his mind, the feeling he was no longer who he had only just been, came to him regularly—and more than usual now, as he looked up at the bullet holes in the front wall of his compound. He would have to do something about the holes. He would have to climb up a ladder and patch them up and paint them over with the creamy, pink adobe he had selected for the outside of his home. He had chosen the color because it was innocuous, keeping the world at bay, he'd hoped, shutting out the world enough so he could be left alone inside his artistic compound, but now, it seemed, the gang warfare in the neighborhood wasn't going to leave him alone.

Where had his mind gone? he wondered, looking up at the wall where the chunk of plaster was missing, high up, just where a stray bullet had wandered, divotting a piece of the old adobe. Stephen Hawking, the physicist, said there were infinite black holes in the universe. But the holes were supposed to be out there, somewhere up in the heavens. He pointed up at the sky, moving his finger up from where he had picked at the wall, cursing the empty space of plaster. So many holes. They were supposed to be affecting the minds of others, and now he couldn't deny the accumulation of the last three years, the feeling in the morning that he couldn't grasp the newspaper firmly, the feeling he would begin an article and then his mind would wander and he would put the paper down and find he was just staring into space, lost in reverie, but with no beauty to the reverie, just a focus of the mind on things that were too small, like dust motes floating in the air.

His second wife was inside. His first wife had been more than dutiful to him. His first wife had given him two beautiful daughters, even if the younger one found it difficult to find work, after being laid off as a flight attendant. His first wife had watched him rise in the painting world, evolving from a young, modern painter who painted with bright, bold colors, with patterns that had made him a figure in the Mexican art scene of the early '70s, into a painter that had moved on to scenes with abstract backgrounds with shades and folds so subtle they felt as detailed in their brushstrokes as the fabric in a painting by Caravaggio. Most abstract painters relied on quick, violent brushstrokes, but he'd moved the compositions forward with the elaborate shadings of light and dark, integrating the techniques of Old World masters he had found in Italy, into modern fantasy spaces as wide and open as the skies of the universe. That technique wasn't the part his first wife had to be tolerant of. Those were the things that had made him somewhat famous—a painter's painter. It was his drinking. He was a brooder. He looked for the shadow under every rock. He delighted in pointing out the darkness of the sky to the audiences of Mexico, rendered in such precision and with so much powerful energy that even those who thought he should be painting political art—which he despised—had to admit his brilliance. The students had loved him and clamored to be in his small painting studio, where he let in only six students every year. But there were times when he wouldn't show up in class for weeks, when the demons in his mind would take over, when he would simply sit in his room and drink. And then there had been the multiple affairs he had had with his students.

Which is how he had arrived at his second wife, a very mediocre painter, one he would normally never have taken into his own studio, but whom he was so attracted to he couldn't say no. He had slept with at least a dozen of his former students by the time he met her. His second wife was good to him, she took care of him, and especially now that his mind was less reliable.

A shopkeeper from next door came out to look at the professor looking up at the bullet holes in the wall. "It's getting worse," the shopkeeper said. "Last night there were eight of them. I watched them from the window of the store. I had the lights off and I could see them, spraying gunfire one at the other. Didn't you see them?"

"Oh yes, I saw them," Professor Mauricio Sanchez said. When the gunshots had started, at first he had thought it was more of the nightmares, which seemed to echo through his mind too frequently, these days. But then he'd realized it wasn't the case. He'd told his wife, Ana, to stay in bed, to close her eyes and pretend not to hear. Then he'd climbed up the strange, twisting staircase of the third building of the compound, which he had renovated, where he'd created a house of lofts and spaces that felt like the winding layout of a medieval Spanish town.

From the rooftop patio he'd peeked over the rim of the wall, the mercury lights in the distance barely giving much sense of the shooters below. The gang members crouched behind cars on both sides of the road that went out of town. He had bought the factory because it was cheap, and it was far from the beautiful, Colonial center of Puebla. The men shot in rapid bursts. He could barely see the car just below him, in front of the compound wall of his studio, but he had a clear view of the cars across the way, where bullets blew through the glass of an old white Ford station wagon. The glass popped and fell within. At least one man was killed. The bullets went past the car into the front of a local hardware store, blowing holes in the glass behind the security bars that were meant to keep out criminals. After the spraying of bullets back and forth, like the roar of infected lions screaming at each other, one of the cars suddenly drove off, tires tearing against the wet pavement, where water had collected from the summer rains. The cancer was gone, for the moment. It was like one of the increasingly frequent headaches that came and went inside Mauricio's brain. They came and rattled. They banged at his temple. And just like the psychiatrists that couldn't give him any medicine that would completely control the headaches, there was no law and order, no police that came—or that would come—to solve the growing violence in his neighborhood.

—–◦((◦)))◦–—

Last night, in front of that fucking professor's house, that was one fuck of a gun battle I was in, man. That old man, he's been in the neighborhood forever. He's been here since before I was born. This neighborhood is a nothing place, man. This neighborhood is just on the road out of town. I don't know why the fuck he would ever have wanted to come here. I saw the professor last night, looking down at us while we was shooting, and I thought, Why does that guy get to sit up there so nice and comfortable-looking? He was pretending we couldn't see him. He kept peeking over the edge of the roof of his building. I mean what the fuck does he think, that we're just a bunch of cattle down here that can't see nothing? I could have shot that motherfucker to kingdom come last night. I thought about it, too, just to put him in his place. That's why I shot a few bullets up high on the wall, to let him know we can take him out anytime. But I got so much more important things going on than that old cabrón, you know what I mean?

Me and my compadres, we never asked for the shit to go down last night, you know what I mean? Yeah, we started selling some drugs in a new area. I admit it. So what? A guy's got to make a living.

I've been selling small packets for four years now, next Saturday. Four years, and I'm still alive. 'Cause I've got what it takes to move up the ladder. Not like a bunch of these sad-asses around the neighborhood. Chucho is the one who hooked me up. He came around four years ago to the little store, around the corner, where my father used to work before they fired him. I was sixteen, then. My father had told me to come help him move some gas tanks onto one of them delivery trucks. My papi never asked me for nothin' unless he needed it, so I went and gave him a hand, and he said he was goin' to give me twenty pesos if I helped him move the gas canisters. Those things are big. Too big for him. And I was trying to pick up change however I could.

So when I was loading up the canisters, that's when Chucho, who was driving the truck, asked me if I wanted some more regular work, if I wanted to make some real money. He gave me a nod to let me know he was talking about more than fucking twenty pesos. And I was interested, so I went in closer to him and he said, "Sometimes we've got some things we need distributed around the neighborhood, you know what I mean? I know you. I know all about you. I've heard from your father and others you're a real man. They tell me no one can scare you."

So that's how I started. Delivering small packages, in the gas truck. That's how we moved around town. The old men, like Chucho, they'd sit in the truck while I'd unload the big gas canisters from the back. Those forty-liter tanks hurt like a motherfucker when you take them off the truck. But I'd take them off. I acted like a regular gas man, and then, every once in a while, I'd drop off a package. You know what I mean? A secret package. No one had to tell me what was in them. No one did, at first, but I knew they were drugs. That's how we moved some of the product around the city. It was small shit at first, like that, and then I started moving up.

And one time I delivered gas to the professor's house. We had to do some real gas deliveries, too, and he opened them big-ass doors that keep his compound closed. I walked in there, rolling one of those 40L gas tanks on the base, along the ground, the way you have to after you've pulled the thing off the truck. And I noticed he didn't even notice me. It's like that professor, he was just lost in his thinking. He was lost in all those weird pieces of metal that looked like socks hangin' upside down.

It was strange in there. I couldn't understand why there was so much space for one guy just making some paintings. We had heard about him. A painting professor from el DF. I like painting and all. I had my car airbrushed. Had my friend do it. But I couldn't see no paintings around when I went inside. He had some cool shit in his house. There was some old ceramics and he had a big paper-mache doll of La Catrina—she was all bones and she was a big old skeleton rattling around with a sun hat on her head. I kinda dug that. But I noticed the professor thought I was just some boy. One of the people who just worked for him. Like his muchacha, Carmen. Everyone knows Carmen in the neighborhood. She says nice things about the professor. She says he's a bit weird but that he treats her right. But I didn't feel that one bit. He didn't even notice me. Gave me a two-peso tip, which was the normal tip everyone gave, and I kept thinking—with all that big compound, with all that space, couldn't he have found another peso or two? What's he so hard up about?

—◄◄◄◄◄(()))))►—

The day he had planned was unraveling. In the morning, after he'd pulled out the ladder and climbed up to the divots from the bullets, and had filled them with some of the adobe he'd found in bags stored in the wide factory space where he also stored his paintings—so many paintings, many under cloth, work from his earlier days that he held on to out of sentimentality, or because they were experiments which he hadn't sold and would be valuable to collectors someday—his muchacha, Carmen, had called to tell him she was feeling sick and she wouldn't be able to make it to clean the house. It wasn't like Carmen to call in sick. She had a mother who had cancer, but even though she needed to help her mother, if she could, she was almost always present. It was one of the things that amazed Mauricio, the way people with the least made the most effort to help others. Some might say it was because they needed money the most and couldn't afford to lose their job, and there was some truth in that, but he felt, without wanting to overly romanticize the poor, that in the case of Carmen, she was simply more giving. He had turned to Buddhism the last few years, because of his older daughter, and because of a half-Japanese, half-Mexican student he'd once taught, who had died tragically in an accident in Japan. He was drawn to the asceticism of the Buddhism he'd learned from the parents of the student. The discipline, the long sitting on a tatami mat focusing and training the mind, had appealed to him. He would sit and think about decoupling from the material world into the spiritual world. And he felt Carmen did this without having to do all of those elaborate meditations. She wanted less, and expected less, and so she seemed happier than those who wanted more, like Mauricio, who, even though he claimed he painted only because he wanted to paint, and even though that was his main reason for painting, his desire to have some fame also was something he couldn't do without.

He wasn't sure why he needed the attention. He realized, even though he was now an adult man with a gray, rough-cut beard, the need for attention from his second wife and from his former student lovers, and from his children and even from his first wife, made him a little childish. But he liked to give, if he could, so when Carmen called in sick and said she might have to go to the clínica, he didn't hesitate for a second and he took her to the hospital.

The clínica was ten minutes away by car—not too far, but Carmen didn't have a car. He took Carmen up to the third floor and waited with her in the lobby thirty minutes until a doctor could see her. The waiting room was crowded, and once she had gone off with a nurse to have a number of tests to see why she was feeling so low in energy, he felt his bladder full, pressing and demanding he take care of it. He felt his body more and more. He had given up drinking four years ago, when he'd understood it was taking over his life. It had seemed better, at first, even though he struggled with the temptation all the time. The only way he could give up the booze was going cold turkey. And, although stopping drinking brought him back on the right track, he found he had this restless energy, a need to constantly move, and with his bladder full, he couldn't hold himself in the lobby anymore and he went off wandering. He found the bathroom on the third floor and it was locked. A sign indicated it was being renovated and was indefinitely closed. He needed to go badly, and he tried to remember just where the hell there was another bathroom in the building. He entered an elevator and wandered down to the first floor where he had once donated blood. In Mexico, you had to donate blood anytime someone you knew needed surgery. He had given blood six months ago, and he remembered there was a bathroom down there. His memory sluiced in and out, sometimes knowing exactly where a bathroom was but then incapable, anymore, of remembering just what he'd eaten for breakfast the day before. Down a hallway he traipsed. He felt his feet shuffle, without the full control of his mind. He felt the weight of his belly, which he hadn't had until the last two years, a byproduct of giving up drinking. He had gone from skinny to fat, a potbelly that must have come as a side effect of the pills the psychiatrist gave him to try to calm his nerves. The blood-donation clinic was just ahead, the place where people waited, and then behind the waiting area the rooms where they took you to give blood. The donation area was closed off, forbidden for people who weren't giving blood, but that's where he had last gone to the bathroom in the hospital, so he opened a door with a sign that said for nurses and patients only. He walked back into an assault of bright fluorescent lights. The halls were suddenly tight like the innards of an endless spaceship, all lit up, far too incandescent. He wondered where the toilet had been. Where had he gone to pee, before? He saw some nurses and patients at the end of the halls, disappearing as he approached wanting to ask for help to direct him, though he didn't want to be found out to have left Carmen.

Before he could find the bathroom, he opened a door to where he thought he should go, and he entered a room full of complex machines, whirring, with IV needles plugged into the arms of three people donating. This is where he had found himself the last time he'd donated. The machines clicked in powerful ways, letting all the patients know the plasma separators were in control of their bodies, and as he looked at the three patients who seemed like blobs feeding the machines, he suddenly made out the face of one patient and realized it was the man who had been shooting at his studio building the night before. It was one of the men who had been firing wildly. The man's forehead was wide and his black hair greased back. His jaw was tight and triangular. He had the peach fuzz of a mustache he seemed to choose not to shave. He was scowling, it seemed to Mauricio, at Mauricio and at the world. Mauricio didn't mean to stare but his eyes—which were used to taking in all visual details— looked at the mole on the left side of the young man's face, at the premature wrinkles on his forehead, at the wannabe rich gangster fake Gucci glasses perched on his head. This was one of the people taking over his neighborhood and threatening him. He had seen the kid crouched behind the white Ford station wagon the night before, looking up at him as the kid shot in his direction. It had felt like he was intentionally shooting in his direction. And now he stood face to face with this thug.

"What are you staring at, old man?" the gangster said. "Haven't you ever seen someone give blood?"

"Yes, of course," Mauricio said. "I was just looking for the bathroom."

"Well, I'm not the bathroom. Even though you might think I'm the toilet. You don't remember me delivering gas to you, once, four years ago, do you?"

He tried to remember all the people who had brought him gas, and he could only remember the round face of the man with thick grime on his fingers who had delivered gas the last year, or two. The gas-men came like men from the engine room of a ship, essential for you to move your boat forward in the ocean, and then they disappeared. Sometimes a new engineer popped up on deck, and then was replaced by someone else. The number of gas-men who had come and gone in his adult life melded. He knew he always smiled at them. He knew he always gave them a tip and thanked them; he knew he called out in frustration, sometimes, when his gas ran out and he couldn't find a gas deliveryman. It was strange that—for someone so important, without whom he wouldn't be able to cook or heat his tea in the morning—he couldn't remember any of the gas-men except the one from the present.

"I know about your two daughters," the gangster said. "I know one of them used to be an airplane flight attendant. I know the other takes yoga classes in the center of town when she comes to visit you. I know you rarely go outside your compound. I know a lot about you, señor, and you don't know a thing about me, do you? You think you own the world in there, inside your castle, looking down at us shooting below. You think your daughters are more beautiful than us. But I've got news for you. I sold a small package of coke to your younger daughter. Oh yes, she's a lot more wild than you think. That one who goes biking all the time. That one who you think is fucking up not working anymore. She's lonelier than you, inside your castle."

Was it possible this punk could really know so much about him? "How do you know these things? Who are you?"

"I'm like the ghost of the barrio. I'm everywhere and nowhere. I lurk in the shadows. You've seen me all the time in the neighborhood. You just haven't wanted to admit I'm there. But I'm there. Just like that paper-mache statue of La Catrina you have in your kitchen—that bag of bones you've forgotten about. And if you say anything to the cops, I'm going to come and get you."

He was lying, Mauricio thought. He was saying crazy things about his daughters just to torment him. Nothing he said was real. It was all made up. How could he possibly know his daughter had been a flight attendant? How could he possibly know his other daughter liked to do yoga? How could he possibly know he had a statue of La Catrina that he had looked at so many times he'd almost forgotten it was present in his kitchen? And then he realized the boy was no longer a boy. It was the boy who had been around the corner, the one who worked for the small grocery store a block away, but now

all grown up. It was the same boy, only he was older now and shooting bullets.

"Get out of here, old man, and forget you ever saw anything last
night, or I'll come and kill you."

It was a threat, like so many other threats to him now: his heart,
his lungs, his mind. His mind hadn't been behaving. His mind had
been making up dark nightmares and secrets. His mind must be
making up this one, too, he thought. This whole conversation was
happening in his mind. It wasn't a real conversation. He would shut
out the hallucination. He would go. He would find the bathroom. He
would go back up to Carmen. He looked away from the bad dream
and it merged back into the machines, and the clicking and whirring
sounds of blood being sucked in and out, donations being made to
save lives of people hidden in back surgery rooms. He felt the texture of the fabric of the earth fold like a drapery around him. The
demons were running and running through his brain.

—«««( )»»»—

That old man, when he came into where I was giving blood so they
could fix up my compadre, Angelito, he looked like he had just seen
some guy trying to rape his daughter. He looked at me like I was the
scum of this earth. There he is, thinking he's some kind of clean-cut,
perfect professor, and what's he think he's so fancy for? That house,
it's just a sock factory. My papi said my grandfather used to work
there, fourteen-hour days, sometimes seven days a week. My grandfather, I never knew him. He died before my time, bless his soul, but
my papi told me he was one hard motherfucking man. He busted
his balls, working in that factory. And then, one day, this guy—the
professor—he come into the town and he bought the whole place
up like he thinks he's some kind of king, and he locks himself in
there, all hidden away. And it's like it's his harem, or something, but
they say he never keeps no women in there long-term except his
wife and two daughters. He's just some hidden king working on his

paintings. And I asked my papi, once, how can I see those paintings? I like paintings. I wanna see 'em, and my papi told me there's no way to see the paintings there, you got to go to some museums in Mexico City. And I'm like, what's he keepin' them hidden for so far away, you know what I mean?

So one day I was in Mexico City, and I'm in some bus full of people, holding on to the roof with my hands pressed against the ceiling, trying not to fall onto all the other people, 'cause there was a woman with a baby behind me, and we was all swaying like animals stuck together in that bus, with no air to breathe, but my face it gets pressed against a window where the doors are in the back and I look out the window and I see a photo with a poster of some painting by the professor and it says there's a show by Mauricio Sanchez. So I thinks to myself, let me off the bus. Let me off this bus.

I pop out at the next stop, when some guys jump on and off. There's no official stops for the peseros. I squeeze by the baby cryin' and I think to myself I'm going to go see what the old man's art is all about, 'cause I never forgot the time I went into his house to give him that gas, and I thought, that's what someone should do, you know. That's what someone should do to move up the ladder. That's what all of them rich people do. They look at art. And I thought, I want to be someone, you know. So I go up to that museum on the big Avenida Reforma. And it's not like any other building I've ever seen. There's strange statues in front of the building that look like chopped-up metal from a construction site, and the glass on the museum is black and reflecting, keeping the world out, like it's some kind of rich man's glass tomb, and I walk up to the front door and when I get to the door I tug at it, and it's locked, and I think, man I just missed the bus because I was so stupid I thought I should go see this museum, but I know the place ain't for me. Them museums, they say they're for free, but then the guards look at you once you get in there. That's what happened to me. I realized the door wasn't locked, it was just I was opening the wrong side, which made me feel like, why don't they tell you which side to use, and when I gets in there one of the guards he looks me up and down and he tells me it's gonna cost me forty pesos just to look around that building and I say, I just wanna look at the paintings of that professor, Mauricio Sanchez, 'cause he owns this strange fortress-like building in my neighborhood, and they say well, that's fine but it's gonna cost you forty pesos. And I tell them I don't have forty pesos to give them to go into the museum. I just spent three pesos taking the bus, and if I had forty pesos I woulda taken a small taxi. And the guard he tells me I can come back on Sunday when it's free if I want to. And I tell him I'm not going to be in el DF on Sunday. I was just doing a quick in-and-out from Puebla. So he wouldn't let me in without the money. So the only thing I saw was that poster of the professor's paintings.

I slunk outa there and had to wait a bit more to get the bus and when the bus came I felt like a fool for having gotten off to go to the museum, before, so I just walked all the way to where I had to meet these guys to deliver a package. That wasn't a package of drugs, but I was delivering something important—I don't know what that was—in an envelope someone had given me to deliver.

And the whole incident, it got me thinking about the professor more and those museums they build that are kinda like the professor's studio, with big doors on them that shut tight. So I thought it was kinda funny when one day I was doing my rounds, making sure all the clients had their stash, making sure the guys below me was delivering, 'cause that's what I spend most of my time doing now, checking up that others aren't fucking up, that they're getting the product to the customers. Lemme tell you, I'm just as good a fucking businessman as them bankers in those big towers. The only difference is they've got the connections from their papis to get there.

And so, one day, I'm like checking up on my crew and I see the professor's daughter, and she's buying a little bag of coke from one of my guys. And I'm like, ain't life funny—me I was trying to get into that museum and here's the professor's daughter coming to *me* to get what *she* needs. That's the daughter who's the airline flight attendant. She was telling my man that she didn't quite have all the money with her, that she was going to have it for him next time, and asking him if he could just hold her over. And sometimes we'll do that just to make sure the customer don't stop using, know what I mean? So we'll let 'em get away with not paying for a little bag as long as they pay the next time. But I told my compadre, when I seen that daughter, I said to him and to her, right in front of her face, "If you want some of this, you're gonna have to pay interest. You know what I mean? We could go somewhere and we could have some nice romantic dinner, but that's the only way you're gonna get some of this for free."

She gave me this nasty look like she didn't need me. Her black hair was cut kinda messy and she looked pale like she hadn't found her makeup, and her mascara was put on too thick, like maybe she'd been crying. And I thought, man, I'd like to do her. I would like a piece of the professor's daughter. 'Cause even though she had this messy look, she was as white and pale as they come, and kinda sexy wearing a tight skirt, the way no one does in my barrio—whiter than a güera I ain't never tasted in bed before.

And she says to me, "What kind of woman do you think I am? You think I'm some kind of woman who sleeps around for drugs? You think I need your drugs that bad?"

And so, I says to her, "Well, I didn't see me coming up to you. Looks like you crawled up here to this place all on your own."

And she just spit on the ground in front of me like she was some kind of boss-queen. She bent her head down to spit, and while she did it I could see her shirt open up a little and I looked down into her chest where her breasts were, and I ain't never seen no breasts that up-close so white and clean. I could almost see her nipples. So I said, "Sooner or later you're gonna find out everything cost somethin'. Your daddy's been spoilin' you. He's been making you think mangoes fall from the sky. But to get the green mango and turn it orange, without spoiling, you've gotta pick it up off the ground when it falls."

She still gave me some disgusted look like I was just some parasite telling her she'd been sucking at the teat too much of her daddy. I knew she'd go around and find nobody else was gonna give her that coke for free for long. Maybe once. Maybe twice there'd be someone that would give her a packet for free to get her as their customer. But not for long. And I was right. One day, 'bout a month later, I saw her come up to my compadre and she was asking for me and where I am, and I showed up from behind, a back room where I'd been listening to my compay, and when she saw me she said she was still laid off from being a flight attendant and she didn't have any money and could I give her some for free for a couple of days, and I said, "I told you that's gonna cost something." So she said she'd meet me for dinner at this restaurant I told her where to meet me at. And that night I had the first white pussy I ever had in my life. And I can tell you, she didn't seem like she was minding it so much. She looked like she was a nymphomaniac. Some of them rich girls, they'll pretend they don't have a penny and then they'll fuck your brains out. I know she didn't have the money, but she looked like she was OK with it, rocking on top of me in the hotel.

—《《〔 〕》》—

The professor stood in his studio space in front of a large canvas mounted on its easel—where he had planned on painting earlier in the day before he had to take Carmen to the hospital—and no new painting would come to him. He had been stuck on this painting and series for over six months now. He would put paint on the canvases, and he wouldn't like what he saw, so he would paint over them. Or he would just stand in front of the canvases and nothing new would come to him. Six months ago, he had finally been able to return to his painting, after giving up directorship of the painting department at the university. The stress of running the program, the numerous faculty he had to direct, the meetings with the administration, the setting of standards, the managing of students, had all worn on him for six years and he had had almost no time to do what he was meant to do—paint. It was like having his purpose removed from him, turning him into a body, a vessel instead of a spirit. Halfway through his time chairing the department, he had felt little edges of his mind bend from the stress. He had attributed it, at first, to giving up the drinking, to the effects of trying to go on the straight path. Maybe he needed the juice to keep himself whole. But that was preposterous, he knew, and so he'd continued forward with the Buddhism and with the meditation, trying to heal himself more, which had helped for a while, but the stress built and built. He wasn't meant to be an administrator, even though he was good at it. The university had wanted him to continue directing the program, until they realized his behavior was becoming more erratic. One day, he walked into the university and students heard a howling in his office and they didn't know what was going on. He had locked himself in his office chanting Buddhist prayers and the chanting had risen in sound until it became a full-blown guttural howl, like a sheep trying to find its lamb.

He resigned quickly. His older daughter took over his painting classes and he moved permanently to Puebla where he thought he could return to being the great painter everyone expected him to be. He had a show lined up in a year. People were expecting great things from him at his gallery in Monterrey. He would have a show at the main museum up there. But six months had passed and nothing but crap would come to the paintings.

Staring at the canvas, in the descending light of the evening as it bent through the fiberglass patches in the roof and slapped against the canvas in harsh dots of light, the light reflected off the white canvas like emergency lights in bright oranges and reds. He watched the light move across the canvas, lost in the sundial. He saw a flash of Carmen coming out of the hospital. He saw a flash of the insolent smile of the gangster in the blood donation room, hooked up to the plasma separator. He saw blood everywhere, sluicing in and out of the machine, and blood on the ground across the street that he had touched earlier in the day with his fingers. The coagulated blood had stuck to his index finger when he'd dragged it through the mud. The images swirled, flashed. He heard a high-pitched buzzing in his ear and then a *gong, gong, gong,* and he threw the canvas onto the ground and was surprised by the sound of the wood frame clattering against the concrete floor.

He walked into his younger daughter's room, which she had been using more and more since she was laid off, and since he had moved to Puebla full-time after finishing up directing the painting department. The words of the gangster in the hospital kept coming to him, that his daughter was snorting coke. Had he failed as a parent, too? Was he not there for his daughters? He had wanted to be there for them, always. Often, the painting had taken precedence. Often, his first wife had to do much of the real, day-to-day raising of the children, while he had worked hard in the studio painting and showing his work.

But he had felt certain he was there for his daughters when they needed him. He would meditate on the floor with his elder daughter. The two daughters looked nothing alike. The elder daughter was plump and happy in her roundness, radiating light off her smile. The other daughter had black hair and pale skin and had inherited his fervent energy, his need to be absorbed in a project at all times. She had finished school and tried to be a chef, but that didn't work out, so she had become a flight attendant. Her eyes often looked sad to him, especially since she had lost her job.

But perhaps, he now remembered, the look in her eyes had begun earlier, ten years ago, on her twenty-first birthday. That was when he was still married to his first wife, Cristina. A party had been organized at the studio compound in Puebla for his younger daughter. It was the custom of his family to get together, every year, in Puebla for her birthday. The party had started at three, but he had arrived at nine at night, after sleeping in the apartment with one of his female students, whom he had been seeing for six months. His hair was messy from the encounter in bed. He had completely forgotten about the birthday of his daughter. When he arrived at the back of the studio house, at the long patio decorated with his good taste in Mexican pottery that looked like Greek amphorae, traditional Talavera tiles from Puebla, and the trickling fountain, he expected to simply find his good taste reflected back at him, but there, running along the patio, was a table with the tablecloth bent wildly upward at the corners onto the table, as if the process of beginning to clean a big mess had begun. The table was covered with plates dirty with the remains of discarded food, the knives and forks filthy, wine stains covering the tablecloth, and the wax of burnt candles spreading all the way into the fabric.

Everyone had left the party except his two daughters and his first wife, Cristina.

His wife looked at him quickly, then continued cleaning. His elder daughter said, "Papá, where have you been? You missed the party." She looked at him, genuinely baffled he could have forgotten such an important thing.

"Maybe he was sleeping with some other woman," his younger daughter said. "Maybe he was sleeping with her back in the house in el DF."

Her mother, Cristina, told her to shush. Her mother said, in a high voice, she would have no such wild talk in front of everyone. "Quiet, Alicia. What kind of horrible thing are you making up?"

"But it's right in front of your eyes, Mamá. It's right in front of all our eyes. He's been fucking these women for years. He's been fucking them right in front of our nose, and thinking we can't even see.

And there he stands, after forgetting my birthday, and he pretends he doesn't even know what we're talking about. Look at him, with his shoulders hunched, like I'm making things up. Look at him running away, into his studio, he's too cowardly to even admit what he's done."

That was the end of his first marriage. That was the beginning of the sad look on his younger daughter's face. She had found out about the affairs, he had learned later, from the muchacha who cleaned the house in el DF and from former students who eventually spoke to his elder daughter.

Inside his younger daughter's room, he didn't want to pry, but he began to look at the surface of her desk and then, after he had made the determination to look inside, her desk drawers. He pushed away pencils and pastels and oils. She had decided to paint since she couldn't find any work. She was painting flowers, lately, and they were three-dimensionally well rendered and with bright colors, but they looked as cold as plastic. He couldn't lie to his daughter about her work, so he told her nothing about them, and since he said nothing she must have known what he was really thinking. He searched inside her closet, inside her shoes. He had no reason to believe anything would be inside them, but he couldn't help but pick up the leather shoes, sniffing the smell of the dry sweat inside like a crazy animal looking for water in the desert. He looked under the bed mattress, and there he found two small plastic baggies, the size of an inch, no more, one with the residue of white powder, and the image of the gangster came back to him telling him his daughter was lonely and unhappy and that she had been buying coke from him, and he went back into the closet looking for the upper reaches of the shelf where he had an old box from his father with a gun his father had received when he was in the Mexican Army. The professor kept the weapon in good condition. He'd had it oiled and maintained regularly, not only to honor his father but because the neighborhood was changing.

He pulled the gun down with the box and put the box on his daughter's desk and he wanted to swallow the plastic bags and the gun and make them all disappear and he picked up the gun and waved it in the air and hopped on one leg like a warrior and the snaps in his mind were snapping away and he wanted a drink, but he wasn't going to go for a drink, and he bleated and moaned, but no one was in the house with him. His wife had left, back up to Mexico City, after the shootings the night before. She was scared and he had told her she should go.

He was alone in his castle. He heard the *gong, gong, gong,* in his brain and he was being called to action. His head felt hollow, and then suddenly full again, like a pile of mercury liquid had been poured into his brain and was sloshing around. But the *gong, gong, gong* was a knocking at the door. And how had it become so dark? Only fifteen minutes ago, it seemed, the orange light had been moving across the canvas. He pretended the banging and knocking at the door hadn't happened. It might be the police. Maybe it was the police coming to speak to him. When he'd come home from the hospital, when his wife went back up to Mexico City, he had called the cops and told them they needed to do something about the increasing violence in his neighborhood. He had used all of his connections to speak to an assistant and then to the boss of an assistant, on up the chain of command until he'd spoken to the local chief of police of Puebla. Mauricio was known in the city as "the painter." People who knew nothing about art still knew his name in the city, even though he was reclusive, and he had told the chief something had to be done. Things could not continue like this in his neighborhood. The bullets were climbing up the wall. Next time he would peek over the wall and one of the bullets would hit him. There were young children, young men, dying in the neighborhood and no one cared. The chief had said yes, yes, something would be done, police would be sent, but no one had come. But maybe now the police were at the door. The knocking was louder and more insistent and he went through his painting studio and continued through the building with the metal molds of socks and out again to the large front doors that kept the world out.

When he got to the doors he tried to gather his thoughts, to shut the creeping mercury off, and he said in a feeble voice that felt to him like a loud voice, "Who is there? Are you the police? Have you finally come? What took you so long? Who is there?"

The knocking didn't stop. It was a persistent bang against the door, but the person banging wouldn't announce who he was. He could open the peephole, but he didn't want to see who it was, he wanted to turn back and run into the house. He felt his father's gun in his hand. The gun felt heavy and pulled down to the ground, the barrel of the handgun pointed at his feet. He needed to look more like a warrior, he thought, so he struggled and lifted the gun into the air and waved it over his head in silent pantomime, wanting to scream, and then he opened the rusted metal box which covered the primitive hole through the thick wood door. On the other side he saw nothing. Not a thing. It must all have been in his head. He must be having hallucinations again. He had to see if it was all just in his head, so he opened the door and looked outside, and he saw emptiness. Absolutely nothing, at all. He left the door open in his shock and scurried back into his compound, forgetting he had left the door ajar, and he went into the kitchen and sat at the kitchen table, an old wood table, and for the first time in years he noticed the paper-mache statue of La Catrina. She was supposed to be a symbol of life after death, but the whiteness of her paper-mache bones came to him now, and he could feel his own mortality coming, and he sat staring at the folds of her rib cage and at her scrawny body, which felt like the withering interior of his body, and in the doorway to the kitchen he felt a presence and he looked over and saw the silhouette of the boy who had turned into a man whom he had seen earlier in the hospital.

"I told you not to call the cops," the man-boy said. "I told you that if you did I was going to come here."

"Was that you banging at the door?"

"What are you talking about, old man? You even left the door open. I've never seen you do that, but you left it open."

"What are you going to do to me?"

"You're the one who made the choice to call the cops."

"But they haven't come."

"It doesn't matter. And it won't matter. They won't come. We own the cops. Don't you see? My boss's boss. He owns the cops. That's how I know you called them. But we can't have you making noise. It gets messy."

"Are you going to shoot me?"

"You need to show me one of your paintings, first. I tried to see them, once, in the museum in Mexico City, but they wouldn't let me in. So you're going to give me a private showing."

"I'll show you one of the paintings now."

He took the gangster into the studio. He took him in front of the white canvas that he wasn't able to progress on. He picked the canvas up from the floor and put it on the easel. The light switches were far away, in the corner, and he told the gangster to stand in front of the easel with the canvas while he would turn the lights on. The gangster did as he was told. He stood in front of the white canvas. The room was still dark; the professor hadn't turned on the lights.

"Do you see the canvas? Do you see the whiteness there? That is my troubled mind. No one will want to buy this painting."

"Then that's not the painting I want to see," the gangster said. "I want to see the painting you have that is worth the most money. I want to see the painting that is your most valuable and beautiful one. I want to see the painting that you have been keeping from me and my compays all of this time, hidden in your fortress."

The professor threw on the switch and the bright mercury lights started out dull at first and then they screamed with whiteness so hard he could barely see. He pulled the gun out of his pocket, which he had been hiding. He walked up to the gangster, with the gun pointed at the gangster's head.

"Go ahead and shoot," the gangster said. "I know you don't have the guts to shoot me or anyone else. That's why you're a professor. You don't have the raw power and beauty and evil inside necessary to shoot another person. It takes a lot of power to do that, to just shoot a man at his face. That's why the new guys they just shoot the AK-47s, because they're too scared to shoot a handgun into another man's face."

The professor could feel the gonging again, the knocking at his temple.

"Why did you sell the coke to my daughter?" he said.

"Because she was a client. Because she wanted to buy, and we don't ask questions. But she didn't always pay, you know. One time she slept with me and I banged her white pussy and I gave her some coke for free."

The gangster reached into his pocket, and he threw some keys in the direction of the professor, hard, making the professor want to protect himself. The gangster fell on the ground and rolled and pulled out a gun, and the professor shot once, twice, a third time into the chest of the gangster while a bullet came out of the gangster's gun, missing the professor, hitting the tin of the roof, breaking a hole through to the dark night outside. The gangster's body lay, spread wide on the floor, the peach fuzz on his face covered with sweat, the hair gel perfectly combed back like he had just looked into the mirror. How could he have shot this man? How? The gun dropped from the hand of the professor and he lay over the body of the gangster and cried. He held the body in his arms and rocked back and forth weeping. He took blood from the chest of the body and went up to the white canvas staring at him like the blank walls of his mind and he smeared the blood on the canvas and rubbed it into the white surface and scratched the blood deeper and deeper into the white paint until the white and the blood dug into his nails. He wanted no part of the blood, but the blood was now stuck hard into his skin, and even after he cleaned his hands he would never be able to clean the blood.

FOR A YEAR, in the neighboring town over from Puebla of Cholula, the professor climbed the remains of one of the highest pyramids in the world, the Tlachihualtepetl. The pyramid was built by the native Indians and then the church built a sanctuary to the Virgen de los Remedios on top. He did not believe in Christianity, or no more so than he believed that all the gods were the same, but people went to the church to find remedies and he supposed he did the same. From the top of the pyramid, where there is a balcony that gives a view out over the plain that runs until it reaches the base of the giant volcano of El Popo, and in the other direction to the peak of Orizaba, he looked out at the vastness of nature and at the people who dotted the ground. What difference did it make that he had killed one person out of the multitudes, when that person was a gangster? What difference did it make when so many—over seventy thousand— were dying in the drug war? That is what some of his friends told him. The police said he had acted in self-defense and they refused to judge him. There was an investigation. The case was clear, the gangster's weapon was found in the studio, and the shopkeeper had seen the shootout with the gangster the night before. No one blamed the professor. But he blamed himself.

He had practiced meditation before with his elder daughter, but never with his younger. It was exactly one year, to the day, since the shooting—June 15. He asked his younger daughter to come with him up to the top of the pyramid. He thought it would help both of them to heal on this one-year anniversary. The two daughters came with him. All three of the family walked with yoga mats, and they lay the mats on the ground at the top of the pyramid, on the balcony, in a place they could look out at the width of the valley, with green spreading into the distance until it slowly curved into a darker hue up the majestic mountains. A year ago, El Popo had exploded, but the volcano was calmer now, the lava contained, though there were recent signs of abnormal activity. The professor had been painting for a year, and he would have a show in Monterrey that his gallery owner said would be seen as brilliant. The professor sat on the ground and felt the rays of the sun falling peacefully on his chubby cheeks. He was plumping out more. He was returning to a state of near contentment. His younger daughter sat next to him and she imitated the movements of the elder daughter, folding her legs one on top of the other. All three of them faced the sun, closed their eyes, and held their palms gently in their laps, imitating the pose of the Buddha. The professor felt the presence of his younger daughter beside him. "I have been blind," he said. "I have been so blind. I was blind to the man I shot. And I was blind to you. I could never see the suffering my affairs with the students had on you, growing up." He reached over, with his eyes closed, and touched his younger daughter gently, and she held his hand for a second, her hand warm, then it fell to the side, cold.

He opened and closed his eyes, and he could not get out of his sight the color red. It was the color of blood and his personal weight to bear. He asked for forgiveness from the heavens. He asked for his daughters to always be beside him. He asked for their love and understanding, and for the power to pay enough attention to them. He asked for his home to no longer be a fortress, to open his art up to the world. He had understood this from the gangster before he was killed. He asked for his mind to be stable. He asked for all of this, silently, and then he turned up to the sky radiating hard and pure light on him, light of judgment and forgiveness, and though he would have to ask for this forgiveness every day for the rest of his life, and though there was much for him to work on, he felt a bubbling lightness inside, a lightness perhaps too strong, too giddy, perhaps unstable, again, perhaps a delusion, his mind sluicing in and out, and he knew the universe was good, and with medication coursing through him his mouth opened partway and formed a vacant, distant smile, and it was not easy to see the trees in the distance.

# THE AMERICAN JOURNALIST

For twenty years I have been a bounty hunter. Not a guy tracking down bodies, but a journalist based in Mexico City tracking down stories. I've seen it all, drug kingpins strafing bodies with machine guns, firing bullets out of a Hummer while the narcos they're firing at shoot back, until both cars go up in flames. I've seen the nastiest prostitutes working the streets of La Zona Rosa at night, giving blowjobs for a simple sniff of glue. I've seen mothers claiming the Virgin of Guadalupe came to them in a dream, delivering their child immaculately, without sex with their husbands. I've seen swimsuit contestants dive off the cliffs of Cabo San Lucas in Mr. Universe–type contests. I've seen child acrobats beg for money on the streets of Mexico City, at the streetlights, while their fathers swallow flames and show off how resistant their skin can be to glass as they press their backs into broken beer bottles on the hot pavement. I've seen mothers with babies strapped to their shoulders walk a hundred miles to protest the lack of food back home, to politicians who wouldn't give them the time of day. You name it, I've seen it down in Mexico during my time as the main correspondent for the *Houston Chronicle*. And while I was a Marine once, who huffed and puffed carrying a hundred pounds of rocks on my back, in my youth, running through whatever foreign lands they sent me to, I've seen shit down here in Mexico that would make you weep.

The editors of the paper wouldn't let me file the story about Ernesto. I think because it didn't fit into any of the neat categories I've just described. The papers are fine with stories of poverty or violence, as long as it all fits into a neat bow. A story that fits what we already think is golden. Ever notice that all the roadside bomb stories in Afghanistan are A-OK? Or the stories about drones that have gone astray, killing a few collateral-damage villagers? Stories that make you feel safe, glad you're secure and cozy in the U.S., rather than in some godforsaken place like rural Afghanistan or caught up in the drug war in Mexico, those stories are all right, as long as everyone plays their role correctly. But Ernesto was a bit of an odd tale.

First, there was how he looked. Tall, with a big, hairy beard, a white guy with forehead wrinkles who looked like a nightclub bouncer, but he was an insurance agent who worked to save his company a lot of dough in big cases, and he was also a member of a punk rock band. The punk rock part is what ruined it for my editors. What's an insurance company guy doing in a punk rock band? Ernesto collected fine art. He would hang out with some of the top visual artists in Mexico City. He had some of the best oil paintings in his apartment, and he liked conceptual art, like a thousand gold necklaces grouped together, hanging from the ceiling in the shape of a phallus.

Bottom line: Ernesto didn't fit the image of a brown Mexican caught up in the violence of Mexico. Which is why they killed the story I sent about Ernesto when he was murdered two days ago. It didn't help that I was with Ernesto when he was shot. The editors told me I was his friend. They said I was writing a biased story from the gut. They told me to take a few days off and then get back to writing "real stories."

I MET ERNESTO a couple of years ago in the port of Veracruz. Some big tanker ship had banged into the pier at one of the enormous port facilities. The case seemed open and shut: a storm had pushed the boat sideways until it smashed into the pier, causing a few million dollars of damage to the pier and sinking a fifty-million-dollar boat. I was already in Veracruz, covering a story about dead bodies showing up from drug violence in the city, and editors always like it if you can get two stories in one location, and they love it even more if there's a story about a natural disaster. Natural disasters fill readers with awe that after all the science we've developed, after all the robots and moon landings, we're still at the mercy of the heavens. Any immense natural disaster story is good, but one in which a complex, expensive machine gets destroyed is even better. It hits home at our vulnerability. So I went over to the port to get the story, as extra gravy, during my time in Veracruz.

Ernesto had on a button-down shirt, to give off a look of professionalism, but he was a professional in action, too, his collar wide open, his sleeves rolled up showing off his hairy arms, a clipboard in his hand, and wearing a hardhat. He had half a dozen divers in the water beneath the pier, checking exactly how the hull of the boat hit the dock. He gathered photos. He collected evidence. He proved there was doubt the ship had actually smashed and drowned because of the storm. It could have been due to a drunk captain. The angle of the impact against the dock wasn't congruent with the angle of the prevailing winds and the damage from the storm. In the end, he saved his insurance company fifty million dollars, and only the dock was paid for under the policy.

If Ernesto had to hire undercover cops to go through garbage in the dumpster behind a bank to prove his case, he would happily do so. He always wore sunglasses, aviator-shaped and large, with a mirrored cover to make it impossible to see his eyes and what he was thinking or calculating.

I'm not sure he ever planted evidence to suit his cause, but I wouldn't put it past him. I kept in touch with him because he was the kind of guy who could give you the kind of dirt, the kind of background information you sometimes needed to finish a story, to give it the color of the panties found from a lover inside the room of a politician, or whatever else the editors in Houston thought could "sex up the story."

But over time, what I liked about him most was that he would always invite me to the performances of his band, and I'd go.

I wouldn't say his music was punk, per se. It was rock, but with the kind of hammering repetition and rough voice that came out of punk. The drummer of his band had stripes carved on the side of his hair, giving him the look of an attacking tiger. The bass guitarist was round in shape, cutting hard on the rhythm, a fairly well known visual artist. And Ernesto would stand ramrod straight, in a dark nightclub with his mirrored shades on, in the seedy joints he and his pals chose to perform in, where there were sometimes prostitutes. The crowd was upper-middle-class friends from their high school days. The music was a release, a reminder of my own old high school days, a way out of the pressure of the "real" stories of one more child caught in the crossfire in a place like Ciudad Juárez.

I WAS WRITING a story about collectors in Mexico. Carlos Slim is widely known as the richest man in the world, worth personally seventy-five billion dollars. He owns the main telephone company in Mexico, Telcel, a monopoly he was given. He owns bakeries and malls and a chain of fast-food diners. He owns so many things, you can go to malls down here and every single type of shop in the place belongs to him. He's also a collector of art, and he just built a large museum, called the Soumaya, that's so tacky, in many respects—the typography for the name of the museum is the same as the typography for the name of his fast-food restaurant chain, and he has one of the restaurants in the basement of the museum, beneath multimillion-dollar paintings by Van Dyck and Rubens. Slim let his son-in-law design the building, so it ended up a complete disaster of nepotism, a structure with no natural light inside, which makes it almost impossible to see the otherwise fairly good collection. In one of the galleries, there's a silver model of the architectural design of the museum, which rests in a leather case made by Bulgari—part of the whole self-congratulatory monument.

Ernesto told me he knew another collector in Cuernavaca who he was willing to introduce me to. It was a politician, a local governor, who collected life-size dolls of *Star Wars* characters and Superman, all made by a Japanese company called Hot Toys. I had vaguely heard about these kinds of collectibles. I knew there were people who paid a lot for these toys on eBay. But I had no idea just how rare and valuable these kinds of dolls could be. Ernesto told me the governor was paying fifteen to twenty thousand dollars a month on these toys. Some of the individual dolls, with details as precise as the acne scars on a character like Han Solo, were going for as much as ten grand. It was the kind of story that seemed like it could go over well with the editors back home: goofy collections with pop culture dolls that everyone in the U.S. would know about, with the added twist this was all happening in Mexico. My hope was to try to get in the angle about corruption in Mexican politics, the idea that who the hell knew where all the money for this kind of collection was coming from?

I asked Ernesto if the politician was independently wealthy, if he'd had money before he became a politician.

"His money's all new," Ernesto said.

So I asked Ernesto to introduce this politician to me the next time he went down to Cuernavaca.

A month later, Ernesto called out of the blue. He and his buddies were going to be doing a concert in Cuernavaca, so he invited me down. He set up an appointment with the politician for us to see the doll collection, in the afternoon, the day of the concert.

Some people like to hide their wealth when they know they've acquired it illegally, but others can't help themselves, and they need an audience. That's how a bunch of corrupt guys ultimately get caught. In Mexico there are guys, sometimes, driving three-hundred-thousand-dollar Ferraris around Mexico City, and when you see one you know the guy stole his money, somehow.

I went to the house of the governor with Ernesto, and the governor's maid opened a large wood door, from the sixteenth century. The house was just up the block from the Robert Brady Museum, the home of an American collector who established himself in Mexico in the 1960s, and who was a major friend of the collector Peggy Guggenheim. Brady did a painting of Guggenheim once, with her sunglasses on, holding her three white Maltese poodles. Brady had Frida Kahlo and Diego Rivera paintings mixed in with sculptures of clay penises he'd found around the world. My point is, even the good collectors have some weird taste, a mix of good taste with the bad. It's the rare collector who doesn't have some secret fetish lurking in the background.

Ernesto and I went into the home of the governor, and after we made it past the Spanish Colonial door, we entered a stone courtyard where monks used to roam, when they were living behind the main cathedral, and the courtyard was filled with life-size statues of Princess Leia, robots like R2-D2 and C-3PO, and a perfect replica of Sigourney Weaver panting with her sweaty shirt in *Alien* as she tried to escape from the deathly spaceship. There were figures from *Blade Runner* and of the Transformers. Each doll was handcrafted in Japan in limited edition, sent by airplane to Mexico City, and then brought to Cuernavaca.

"Nice dolls," I said to the governor. "How long have you been collecting them?"

"They're not dolls," he told me. "They're life-size action figures." He slapped the back of a figure shaped like Darth Vader, minutes before Vader fights Luke Skywalker almost to the death.

The governor looked a bit like a life-size character himself, his hair combed up and back Elvis Presley–style. His cheeks were scarred from what looked like bad skin as a child. He had on a kelly green Polo shirt, with the large figure of a polo rider on a horse. This kind of shirt, with the Polo insignia blown up to be three inches high, is well known as the kind of clothing a certain type of narco likes to wear.

The violence in Cuernavaca had been getting much worse, lately. There were military checkpoints throughout the city. Rival narco groups were fighting in the streets. Not all the time, like up in the north near Juárez, but more and more. The son of a famous poet was killed, but in his case by the police, after some police working for some of the local drug gangs saw the son catching a glimpse of them. Rather than leave potential witnesses alone, the police just knocked off the son of the poet and his friends. They were found dead in a car.

It was strange to see these action figures from dramatic, violent scenes when all around Cuernavaca you didn't need action dolls to feel the tense moments of Hollywood; you could just go out your front door and into the main streets of the city.

"Come here," the governor said. "I'll show you one of my favorite parts of the house." He took us into the basement, down ancient stone steps with Roman arches overhead, where cobwebs were growing in the corners. I expected him to want to show us his wine collection. Some of these politicians love wine, and they like to show off how—supposedly—sophisticated they are.

He came to a large wood door with metal plating, with spikes coming out the plating and with iron bars in the center of the door. The door looked like the entrance to an old debtors' prison. The governor pulled out a metal key about a half-foot long, and he twisted an ancient lock open. He opened the door and brought us into the

dank space. There were old wheel-racks of the kind they used to torture the early Christian saints; there were metal pincers hanging on
the walls, which he explained were used to pinch the genitalia of
bandits and free thinkers during the days of the Inquisition. There
were hoists to lower prisoners onto hot, burning embers until they
cried out in confession. There were handcuffs with chains attached
to the walls where prisoners were whipped, until they fell with the
weight of their body in exhaustion to the ground, to the point of suf-
focation. Some cheap flickering lights wavered back and forth, giving the whole place the look of a haunted house. There were some
life-size action torture dolls of prisoners attached to the walls, suffering as a branding iron was placed onto their naked flesh. The doll
figures had ripped burlap and old cotton clothing, their hair splayed
wildly back, their mouths open in terror, as they were abused.

"Pretty realistic collection, eh?" the governor said.

"It's cool," Ernesto said.

"Cool" was definitely not the word I would have used. The place
was giving me the creeps. The governor walked in front of us, and
left us to inspect the room a little closer, and suddenly I heard the
main door close, and the governor locked the door.

"You get a better feel for the whole terror of the place if you're
forced to stay in there, for a while," he said, and laughed. "I'll be back
at some point," he said, and he left.

I tried the door, and it was definitely locked. I tried to see Ernesto's eyes, beneath his mirrored sunglasses, but all I got was a blank,
mirrored expression. Only his pursed lips, between his beard, gave a
sense he didn't think this was in any way funny.


AFTER AN HOUR of being locked up, the governor came down to the
dungeon and opened up the big wood door. For an hour, I'd gone
through all the possible reasons the governor could have locked us
in there. One option was that he was just one of those incorrigible

gamers, one of those guys who loved to make the world of his magic and make-believe real. This is, more or less, what Renaissance fairs are all about, where people dress up like knights in shining armor to fight other knights, to get the love of a thin woman dressed like a damsel in distress. I did a story, once, about Mexican game-addicts, and the governor was showing some of those tendencies—life-size dolls, the grandiose way he showed us his basement with instruments of torture. It had all the signs of someone in way too deep with his hobbies.

Another possibility I'd run through was that the governor was sadistic and any minute he was going to come down, personally, dressed in black leather to whip and torture us. This was more the Quentin Tarantino scenario, like in his movie *Pulp Fiction,* where the Gimp is kept in the basement for ages until turning into some kind of animal.

A final option was that Ernesto had something to do with this treatment. I asked him point-blank: "Do you owe him any money? Is he usually like this?"

"It's the opposite," Ernesto said. "If anyone owes any money here, he owes me a few thousand. I sold him a painting a month ago, by a pop artist in Mexico City, and he hasn't paid me yet. But the painting is only five thousand dollars. He should be able to come up with that amount, easily."

"What's the painting like?" I asked.

"It's a pink, airbrush version of Darth Vader in a gay pride parade."

"Is the governor gay?"

"He might be. But I don't think so. I don't even think he knows what a gay pride parade is. I think he just saw the painting and loved the fact it had Darth Vader in it. As you can see, he's a bit obsessed."

So, while Ernesto and I stood in the haunted house of horrors, I couldn't come up with the reason we were being kept in such a "nice" place.

The governor came down the steps, his feet dragging against the flagstones to the dungeon, and I could hear a few other men behind him, some yelling from the top of the steps to others at the bottom to be sure to protect the jefe, to stand in front of him.

The door opened and two guards came and took ahold of Ernesto and me. The governor came in.

"So, have you figured out why you're here, yet?" he asked.

I felt like giving a sarcastic answer, that the reason I was here was to write a story about his goofy, life-size action doll collection. Oh, the places writing fun stories for the editors back home will get you. But I've learned, over the years, to keep my sarcastic side in check and to play dumb.

"No idea," I said.

"None at all?" the governor asked.

Given his mocking tone, I tried to think further through the potential options for the fun treatment we were being given.

"How about if I refresh your memory," the governor said. "A year ago, you wrote an investigative piece about allegations of new drug trafficking in Cuernavaca. You wrote about the marriage of my niece to an important businessman, who had just opened a large apartment complex with a golf course, and you raised suspicions that the owners of the golf course—El Paraíso—were involved in laundering drug money. Does this ring any bells?"

It did, of course.

"That article was completely false, and you will write a retraction. You are going to turn in your resignation to your newspaper, and they are going to write an article saying you have been dismissed, completely, for improper conduct. The article will appear on the front page of your newspaper."

I was used to hearing about these kinds of requests, for local journalists, on a daily basis. There were dozens and dozens of journalists killed trying to cover the drug war. There were more than dozens told to shut up what they were writing, or they would be killed. The situation for local journalists was horrible, and getting even more so all the time. It was something that we foreign journalists talked about regularly when we got together, informally, at a bar in Mexico City every Friday. The noose of the violence was closing on anyone who wanted to expose the truth. But, so far, almost all foreign journalists had been left alone. And there was a fine line that we all knew, usually, not to cross. Don't give any specific details of the hideouts of the drug kingpins. Don't go into too many details about the people being pulled off buses and shot at gunpoint. Keep the articles from a mid-level distance, about the general trends in the drug wars, about the general territorial battle. As long as the focus was kept a little further back, you could get the broad story out while avoiding putting your own life at risk. But it seemed, in naming the governor's niece in passing, I had put the focus in too close. And—who knew?—maybe he had some financial interest in the El Paraíso golf club.

"I'm sorry if you were offended, in any way, by the article," I said. "I had no idea your niece was mentioned." I looked at the guards holding Uzi submachine guns.

"The question isn't whether I was offended but that you're spreading lies," the governor said. "Do you stand by your story?"

I have learned that if you are going to be in this business, you can be polite, you can weasel around a bit to get the bad guys you report on off your back, you can tell a few white lies to be able to keep reporting the truth; but there are some moments when you have to stand up to the bullies. If you don't, they'll push you right over.

"Yes, I do," I said.

"Yes, you 'do' what?" the governor said. "You stand by your lies?"

"Yes, I do stand by the story."

One of the guards twisted my arm behind my back.

"You see this guy—Ernesto," the governor said. "He never should have brought you here. I don't know what he was thinking. Maybe he was thinking he's some kind of special smartass. Maybe he was thinking he knows more than he knows about everything. Here's the deal. You are going to leave this place, and you are going to retract the story, and you're going to quit being a journalist, and if I see you write one more story, then I'm going to send some people to your apartment in La Condesa and I'm going to have you taken out. You have one week to leave the country." He had his men take us upstairs, and they pushed us out the door. I'd never seen Ernesto, such a big guy, look scared before, but leaving the governor's house in Cuernavaca, he took off his shades and he didn't look so big or tough anymore.

BACK IN MEXICO City, I got to thinking about my twenty years of writing stories in Mexico. What had it all been for? After all the stories about every kind of human interest I could find, had I made any difference to the world? Had I done anything to help the people around me, or was I just documenting the freak show and the river of human misery? I'm fifty-two years old. I look younger than my years, with big muscles, with the build, still, of a Marine, but my head is bald and no one can deny the passage of time. I could call the editors in Houston and tell them it was time for the ship to come in. I could ask for an editing job that would be cushier than writing the day-to-day ins and outs of a country on the brink of descending into chaos. If you live in Mexico City, you can have a fine, perfectly nice life. I have a fairly comfortable apartment with modern furniture. If you stay away from the riskier stories, you can do all right as a foreign correspondent. The big papers like the *New York Times* rotate their staff in and out of countries, so you don't get too comfortable in any one place, so you don't lose your edge and hunger as a reporter looking for stories. They do it to eliminate too much bias, as you get too close to the "natives." Maybe it was time to pack it all in. If I left, I didn't have to call it caving in to a piss-ant, small-time politician in Cuernavaca. I could call it coming to a "lifetime decision" after some "reflection." But that was a bunch of bullshit. If I left, it would prove I was becoming soft and that I hadn't given a damn about real journalism, about really standing up for the truth, since the first day I'd arrived in Mexico City, twenty years before.

I decided to ignore the threat from the governor. It's not that he was all bluff, but a lot of these evil guys, lurking in the shadows, just try to scare you and then—like a dog barking—they move on. It didn't make much sense for them to try to take out a foreign journalist, especially an American one. It could lead to too many investigations by the CIA and the State Department.

Seven days had passed and I went to a new, fancy bar in Mexico City called La Romita. There's an old, art deco staircase that sweeps up a couple of floors to the main area. The bar is grandiose, with black and white checkered tiles, bartenders whipping up exotic drinks of mezcal mixed with guava juice that they flambé. The customers are trendy, dressed in the latest foreign jeans that go for $250 a pair in the Meatpacking District of NYC. Women come and go in strapless concoctions that show off their Acapulco tans. Men wear leather motorcycle jackets, or the latest glasses and shoes imported from Italy. This is the crowd of young hipsters that live off the bank accounts of their mothers and fathers, the elite-in-waiting of Mexico who, while they're young, party hard, proving how cool they are by how much money they can spend, while beggars lurk on the streets outside.

Ernesto's band has an underground, decadent touch, and they were invited to play in the bar, so I chose to go see what was up in the club. I wanted Ernesto to know I wasn't going to leave Mexico. I wanted to let him know he shouldn't worry—any more than me, pretending I wasn't visibly worried—about what had happened in the dungeon the week before.

The ceiling of La Romita is two stories high, with a glass roof that opens to the sky. A wide balcony faces the street, hovering above the uneven sidewalks below. A couple hundred clients were packed into the space, some standing on the staircase that floats to the upper floor, dressed in their finest clothes, one woman with a Gucci cream-colored dress.

As the band got louder and louder, Ernesto standing ramrod straight, the crowd was into the decadence of seeing a punk-sounding rock band in such an elegant space. Ernesto spewed out his somewhat filthy lyrics, and people ordered fine martinis with Bombay Sapphire gin.

The gunshots came from out of nowhere. Maybe the guy who shot Ernesto was up on the top balcony of the bar, shooting down at him. Maybe he was mixed into the crowd. Three shots came fast, and by the sound—so powerful it cut into the amplified guitars—it must have been a 9mm weapon, something as big as a Glock 9.

The crowd recoiled. People shouted and fell to the floor. The bartender, next to me, couldn't see what was happening, at first. He seemed to think it was all part of the show, of the craziness of the packed bar. He lit another flambéed cocktail, and then, when he figured out what was happening, he doused the flame, dropping the drink on the floor.


I FILED THE story, that night, to the editors. I told them, at last, about the threat I'd received from the governor a week before. I hadn't wanted to tell them, because I was afraid they would pull me back home. I didn't want to leave where I'd been living the last twenty years.

I called up the editors and told them, "You've got to publish this story. The significance is that the violence is now coming to Mexico City. It's finally infiltrating the capital. This is going to be the next wave of the violence."

"Then get out of there," they said.

"But there's no reason for me to leave, yet," I said. "It's not that dangerous for me, yet."

"Well, either it's dangerous or it's not. And if it's not, then this story isn't something new. Look, Shawn, you've been down there too long. You've been down there twenty years. Maybe it's time to come back to Houston. We could find you a position at the foreign desk, or you could take time off to write a book, for a while. You could take the time you need to get back to some real stories."

It was two in the morning. Normally, this was the time when I would finish up going over a last-minute major piece with the editors, before they put the story to bed. But for the first time I could remember, when I said the story should run, they said no.

I went outside my apartment, taking my dog to the Parque México, which runs in a big oval shape, with tall palm trees, where there was once a racetrack, decades ago. I walked around the park. It was so late, none of the usual people walking their dogs were in the park. I took out a cigarette, and I looked up at the palm fronds waving in dark silhouettes against the lit-up sky, over the giant valley of Mexico City. It was time to pack it in. It was time to move on. I was no longer strong enough, anymore. I was no longer a bounty hunter.

# EVERYTHING ELSE IS
# GOING TO BE FINE

To live in Mexico City you have to pretend there aren't many dangers. There are the occasional bullets, of course, which most of you "gringos" read about in the papers. I put the word gringos in quotation marks because I know better than to make that kind of slur, but the honest truth is that's the way we think about you guys to the north. We have all sorts of guesses as to why we call you gringos. One of the reasons, supposedly, is that you guys wore green uniforms when you came down and took what are now Texas, Arizona, and New Mexico during the Mexican-American War. So we called you "green-gos." But that doesn't make much sense to anyone who speaks English, which I do. Take the origin as you like it, when we call you a gringo we mean it as a slur.

I know what it's like to speak to you about these things because I work for an American company, run by the U.S. gov't., called U.S. Wheat. I've been working at the company for four years now. It's not ideal. It's a place I found some work, with a degree in biology, when the economic crisis started in 2008. The goal of U.S. Wheat is to make sure everyone in the world—from the Philippines to the tip of Tierra del Fuego—eats as much wheat grown in America as they can. And by "America" I'm using that all-encompassing word by which you guys call the U.S. (even though there are other Americas, like South America, and even though we, in Mexico, think about Mexico as being in North America, which you guys think is in Central America. Don't even get the Canadians going on whether they think they're Americans).

In the office, I never tell my boss I'm gay.

He's two hundred and fifty pounds and from Kansas. He wears a crisp, white cotton shirt, ironed by his *muchacha*—the maid that most upper-middle-class Mexicans have—and he pits out, leaving big sweat stains under his arms. He moves as an imposing presence through the office, speaking to us only when he has something he wants us to do. "You'll have to go to Colombia at the end of April for the Wheat Conference," he'll say. And, even though I already have ten other trips planned around then for work, I'll have to jiggle them around to fit in the trip to Colombia.

No one else at the office knows I'm gay, either. There are four of us. It's a tight space. One of the four is our secretary, and if I told even one of them, they'd all know right away.

IF YOU LOOKED at me, the first thing you would think isn't: he's gay; you'd think: he's a runner. I'm skinny. I'm five feet seven. My chin is fairly triangular at the bottom. I guess I've been told my face is a bit boyish. I have soft brown eyes, with somewhat long eyelashes. My hair is straight and dirty blond, combed with a part on the side, and a bit long like a boy's, though I'm thirty-seven. It's hard to know what we look like to others, but I would say I look like a runner. Someone else might notice my thin legs. They might notice I always rush around, never really stopping, always in some kind of motion. Even when I'm sitting, my hands are moving, or my mouth is moving. I don't like long pauses between sentences. I like to speak fast, even in English.

So I'm always doing something: sending off a link to a YouTube video, like of a thirteen-year-old girl singing about what it feels like to suck at the tit of her mother. That song is called "La Tetita." It's campy, with this Peruvian girl dressed up in traditional mountain clothing and a tight blouse, swaying back and forth like a little girl, singing out in this high voice, "De día y de noche, la tetita"—*All night and all day, the titty.* I just think that's hilarious. So I send that around to a few of my friends.

Or I go to el Cabaret. I like to go to the Cabaret. It's a theater in the neighborhood of Coyoacán where they perform all sorts of outlandish, raucous theater. Men dress up as women. People sing in drag. They do political spoofs, making fun of the president, or whatever. I go with a small group of my gay friends who, like me, are out to each other at night but not to our coworkers or to our parents or to most people during the day.

SIX MONTHS AGO, I was out running on one of the elevated freeways that stretch across Mexico City. When I'm heading into a marathon, I'll do a twenty-mile run. I run six miles every day, and then I'll do a twenty-miler at the end of training. It's almost impossible to run in normal places in the city. There are a few running tracks and a couple big parks, like Chapultepec, but those get pretty confining when you want to do twenty miles. There are oncoming buses and cars everywhere in the city, and no one follows the traffic rules in any case, so I run up on the elevated freeways. It's illegal to be up there. But, unlike in the U.S., no one ever comes to force you out of the way. There's a Wild West attitude in Mexico, so if you do things like you know what you're doing, most people just let you do what you want. So I run along the side of the freeway, elevated sometimes more than ten stories in the air. Up there I feel free, like no one knows who I am. I look out over the wide valley of Mexico City, with hundreds of thousands of concrete houses below, stretching for miles into the distance until they roll up the ring of mountains far away. The sky is dramatic, with big gray clouds that come and go, indifferent to the activities of the human beings below. There are more and more skyscrapers in Mexico City. In the center there are few, because of the prevalence of earthquakes. Most are up on a hillside called Santa Fe, and only one big tower, of Ixe Banco, stands in the center. The building is fifty-five stories tall, but it looks minuscule and alone beneath the clouds, standing ostracized, smaller than the power of the choices nature makes.

I wonder, sometimes, looking at the clouds, why God made me gay. It's a question that comes to me every time I run, looking at the immensity of the force of nature and at the Catholic churches that dot the floor of the jammed urban valley below. Call it what you will, a gift, a curse, I'll tell you what they call it here: *maricón*. Faggot.

Six months ago, on the segundo piso—the elevated highway—a van pulled up beside me and drove slowly, neck and neck, as I ran forward as steadily as I could in my mental running zone.

The van was a Ford Aerostar—thirty years old—with the paint peeling, white tinged yellow from the Mexican sun. One of the guys on the passenger side rolled down his window. He was drunk and he held a bottle of tequila.

"Where you running to, faggot?" he yelled out the window.

I ignored him. I've discovered silence is the best way to confront that kind of comment.

"Eh, *maricón*! I'm speaking to you! Where are you running to in your faggoty clothing?" I had on my usual electric-blue nylon running jacket with fast-looking white stripes running down the back. I was wearing my black running tights, which hug me like a second layer of skin. My shoes had neon yellow soles and silver reflective mesh. It was standard gear for any runner.

"He must be a faggot," the man yelled, "because he doesn't answer me." The driver, on the other side, seemed to look into his side mirror to see if any cops were behind him.

He sped up, pulled over in front of me in the lane I was running in, and halted. Four men jumped out of the van. They were all drunk. They spoke with slurred words to each other.

"Grab the motherfucker," the guy who'd been shouting out the window said. "Hijo de puta," he said, which means son of a whore. "Just tell me you're a faggot. Just tell it to me. Just admit it. Look at your fagotty-ass haircut and the way you run."

I didn't break my normal run as I approached them. I thought I could just ignore them and pass through. In Mexico, a lot of times, you have to bluff. You have to pretend you don't hear or see things, because if you do the whole world will come crashing in on you like a tidal wave. It was only when I got closer to them, and I could see they weren't going to let me go, that I started to sprint to the left to get away from them, but the drunk guy who'd yelled at me out of the van lunged and caught the back of my right leg. He pulled my foot out, suddenly, into the air like a ballerina in an arabesque. Then he pulled my other leg out from under me, and I fell with my chin onto the pavement. I struggled as much as I could. I'm small, and a bit scrawny, but I'm tough.

"Just let me go," I said to the guys, firmly, with my face against the ground. "This is going to be a problem for you if you keep holding on to me."

"You've got to be kidding me. A problem for me, if I keep holding on to *you*?" the guy who'd had the tequila bottle said. The others laughed in unison, with me squirming like a worm on the ground.

They kicked me in the ribs. They kicked my face. They kicked me until I went unconscious, and flopped me like a U over the guardrail as a warning sign to any other faggot who might come along. When I finally came to, I felt a wave of nausea, the shock of vertigo, and I looked down from the second floor of the highway at the pavement far below, cars rushing into the remote, aloof distance of the city.

THE NEXT TIME I saw my family, I did not tell my father what had happened on the highway. I did not tell my sister. I didn't tell the one of my two brothers who was present. I didn't tell my grandmother who was there. I believe I am close to my sister and to my father and my brother and my grandmother, but I have never told them I am gay.

The reason for us all getting together was to celebrate the upcoming wedding of my sister, which would take place in a few months. She had told me over the phone she was getting married, and I was really pleased for her, because I like the guy she'd been going out with. When my father heard the news, he immediately organized a brunch at one of our favorite restaurants in the center of the city.

My sister hadn't arrived yet for the brunch. My father and I waited at the crowded restaurant to get a seat. It's an old Colonial building, like many in the center of Mexico City, which reminds you of the conquest of Mexico by the Spanish, when Ferdinand and Isabella, the Catholic king and queen, took Spain back from the Muslims and sent Columbus forth to the New World to bring "civilization." The staircases in the restaurant, of ancient cedar wood, have yellow Sevillian tiles between each step that commemorate the taking of the Mexican people under the "protective wing" of the Church.

My father didn't ask further about my black eye when I told him it was "nothing." It's not that he wasn't concerned, it's that he knows when he's approaching too close into my private life. Sometimes, I imagine he must have known I was gay. It's simply not possible he couldn't know. But we kept complete silence about the matter. I never volunteered if I was going out with someone. I'd simply keep the conversation light, or about something—anything—other than what my sexuality was. As we waited for my sister to arrive with her new fiancé, my father said we would have to go looking for a bouquet of hideous plastic flowers, that afternoon, to give my sister. It was a running joke in the family to give a kitsch gift to celebrate marriages. It was our way of showing deep love. And I knew I would never get one of those kitsch gifts.

My grandmother was the only one who didn't follow this protocol of dancing around who I was. Halfway through the meal, later, she turned to me, just after we'd toasted my sister and her fiancé, and she said, "And when are you going to get married, Miguelito? You've been a bachelor for too long. Tell us who you're going out with these days?"

I shrugged my shoulders and said, "I guess I just haven't met the right one."

She gave me a look like I needed to hurry up. She took my hands in hers, which were old and soft with age, her wedding ring still on her hand, though she had been a widow for twenty-seven years. "A man without a wife is nothing," she said. "Without a wife a man is like a lost sock fallen to the ground."

I HAVE BEEN living with a roommate for three years now, and he doesn't know I'm gay. He's home most of the time, and I'm rarely home, traveling the world—especially the Caribbean and South America—promoting U.S. Wheat. He likes to bring friends back to our apartment and to open one beer after another, speaking with his buddies into the night. He's as hetero as they come. He's the kind of guy who plays poker with his friends late into the morning, and wears his jeans a bit baggy, hanging down so his underwear shows. It lets you know he has a lot of hair down there. It lets you know he's a bit stinky.

I take showers every day. I have almost no hair on my body. I like to make sure the bottles in my part of the medicine cabinet are in order. I like to make my bed. I like to cook, when I can, though I'm usually on the road. I don't bring friends over. I don't think they'd like the space. It feels too dominated by my roommate. But I stick with my roommate because he never asks me anything. He just says,

"Hey," when I come in the door. He respects my space. I respect his. Everything is properly compartmentalized, and I save on rent.

**"IF I COULD** have love without sex, that would be my ideal," I tell Raúl. We are on our second date, three months ago. Raúl is smart. He's a stock trader for Banco Santander. He's older than me, by a few years, and his hair sits like a gray mop on his head. His leather jacket is a size and a half too large for him, and he slouches in his chair, outside at an Italian café in Polanco, a rich neighborhood of Mexico City, yet in a no-man's-land part of the neighborhood. This café is known to almost no one. No one fashionable would ever come here or know the place exists. The sign of the café burns with metallic, fluorescent light. We're the only ones sitting outside, and the café is about to close.

"Why would you want love without sex?" Raúl says. He seems to ask the question more to the evening air than to me.

"Because I've never been that interested in penetration, you know? I just want to be hugged. I just want someone to hold me."

"You mean you don't want to be on bottom?"

"I don't want to be on top *or* on bottom. I don't want sex. I want love." Like with most people, Raúl and I lasted no more than a few weeks. We never had sex. Eventually, he got tired of waiting and he moved on.

**WHEN I WAS** thirteen, it happened in back of the cathedral in Cuernavaca where my grandmother used to take me. My parents didn't care about going to church. They went once in a while, and they've been divorced for fifteen years now. But my grandmother took me, regularly, to church, and I became involved. It was the thirteenth of December, and there was a humid chill in the air, though it was a bright, cloudless day.

The cathedral of Cuernavaca is one of the biggest in Mexico. There's a large patio connected to the main worshipping area. Beneath the portico, around the patio, there are paintings of old frescoes, worn out, with row upon row of the hierarchy of the Church. The priests are scrunched so close together in the paintings, it's hard to tell one from the other. The priests stand over the nuns on the map of the hierarchy. The paintings let you know there's a code of obedience, who is master and who is not.

Padre Francisco took me into his office, after he'd finished the 8 a.m. mass. I was dressed in the long frock of a choirboy. He had never touched me before, but I had heard he'd touched others, and I had remained silent about the rumors I'd heard. He was a major figure in the church, at the time. He told me to put down the large candle he had asked me to carry into his office. He closed the door behind us, and the room was dark except for the big candle, which I had placed on his mahogany desk, where he'd told me to. His cheeks were white with powder, which he seemed to have put on to cover some of the popped capillaries on his face. His glasses were thick, with bifocals and a sharp metallic frame.

When I put the candle down, I felt his body suddenly behind me. I felt the weight of his black vestment, a flowing robe as thick as it looked, the heavy cotton brushing against me. He put his claws on my shoulders and squeezed. "Come now, Miguelito," he said. He ran a hand down the side of my ribs. "The Heavenly Father calls you into his arms," he said. He put his lips, old with the juice of wine, against my ear and whispered, "In the name of the Father I pronounce you my son." He lifted my robe and stuck his finger in my asshole. He stuck his penis in me and pushed back and forth, rapidly, for a few minutes, as I lay over the desk with the candle next to my head nearly burning my hair. I didn't say anything. I knew not to say anything. It happened another dozen times, and then he moved on to another.

THREE DAYS AGO, a friend of mine from the Cabaret, Arturo, asked me if I wanted to go to the Vazquez Hermanos Circus with him. The Vazquez Hermanos Circus is one of the five biggest circuses in Mexico. There are more than four hundred smaller circuses that tour around the country. Arturo regularly plays the role of a clown at the Cabaret, and he used to work for the Vazquez Hermanos Circus. After fifteen years of touring with the circus, he gave it up. He loved making the children laugh. He loved handing out balloons to the kids, or play-fighting with the other clowns and watching the whole audience fall back in the aisles with laughter. But the rigors of picking up and traveling after every performance—the circus took six hours to put up, with its three rings, and two hours to take down—wore him out, and he eventually gave up the life on the road.

"The other thing that got to me," he told me once, "is that when you're a clown no one knows who you really are. They expect you to always be funny. I got tired of people looking at me and assuming the person I was, inside, was the mask."

Arturo has been a longtime theater partner with me. We go to shows at the Teatro Auditorio Nacional together. Sometimes I get him free tickets, since he doesn't have much money. When the Vazquez Circus came to town, he had two comp tickets, so he asked me to come with him. Arturo can make those sad clown faces, in pantomime, if you don't do what he wants, and I can't resist that look, so I decided to drop what I was doing—preparing for my next U.S. Wheat trip to Nicaragua—to go with him.

During the performance, I watched the tightrope walkers sway back and forth as they passed above the arena. I watched the trapeze artists barely grab onto the hands of the receiving man on the other side. I saw a Bengal tiger put his jaws around the neck of the lion tamer. The audience oohed and aahed, on the edge of their seat, wondering if each performer would survive. I was on the edge of my seat, too, but nothing in the show could come close to the fear I experienced after the regular performance.

On our way out of the ring, I saw a bunch of schoolchildren, tightly grouped together. I saw some priests accompanying them, and it reminded me of the way Padre Francisco used to shepherd us to events around the city of Cuernavaca. Arturo must have seen my reaction because he said to me, "What's wrong? You look pale as a ghost."

I found myself unable to stop looking at one priest in particular. He looked so much like Padre Francisco, though he was much younger than Padre Francisco had been. His metallic glasses were the same, now thirty years out of date. He must have been from the countryside, or he wouldn't have been wearing that kind of glasses anymore.

I pulled my shoulder away from Arturo, who had patted me on the arm to try to comfort me. "It's nothing," I said.

Arturo looked at me intently, as if trying to make sure I was truly OK. He tried to distract me. "Let's go to the back of the circus. I want to introduce you to my friends."

As the audience rushed out of the main tent, Arturo took me back toward the trucks, waiting behind the three-poled, big, movable arena. Dozens of men were already rushing about, putting the hippopotamuses, tigers, elephants, and camels into their cages, giving them straw and snapping the faces of the animals away from the bars if they tried to poke their noses out too far.

"Come back here, further," Arturo said. "I want you to meet the man who taught me everything I know about acting. He's the one who convinced me to be a clown."

We approached an old, wood trailer, with its red paint beginning to peel off. On the outside center of the trailer a large poster of a clown laughing uproariously was plastered to the wood. The mouth of the clown was open with melodramatic joy, and no sound came out of his mouth, but the promise of laughter was implied.

Arturo opened the trailer. I looked around, seeing no one at first, and Arturo pointed toward the floor at a dwarf still dressed in the costume of a clown, with a bowler hat with polka dots, and clown-red cheeks, his lips drawn with makeup in an upward swoop on both sides, a tear penciled in black and white coming down off his left eye. His Rudolph-the-red-nosed-reindeer nose had already come off. But in all other ways he still looked like he had just come from the stage.

When the dwarf saw Arturo he began to pull a long handkerchief out of his short pants. He pulled and pulled, and one handkerchief led to another, all connected in a long line; he pantomimed struggling to get to the end of the handkerchief, and the cloth came further and further, coiling into his hands and down to the floor. He pulled, and he pulled, and it seemed the handkerchief would never end. Arturo pantomimed back, in silent laughter, slapping his knees, throwing his head and chest back uproariously, laughing so the whole audience could see. It was a sign of mutual respect, a sign Arturo had learned well from his master, the dwarf. When it seemed the string of handkerchiefs could come out no longer, the dwarf gave one last harsh tug and pulled out a stuffed rabbit that seemed as big as the pant space around his legs.

Just then, a cold draft of air came from behind me, and I turned to see who was at the door. A man with a baseball cap with the logo of Ed Hardy—with a skull on the cap and a bloody dagger through the skull, in the style of a tattoo, with shiny rhinestones like white diamonds studded all over the cap—had punched open the door. He strode into the trailer, moving slowly with his hands patting the sides of his jeans like he was itching to pull out a gun. He wore a red leather jacket, unzipped most of the way to show a white undershirt below. His hair beneath the cap, to the sides, was gelled back, combed too neatly. The cap sat large on his head and cocked to the side.

"Hey, you! Midget," he said. "Where's your boss."

The dwarf dropped the rabbit to the floor, gently. He seemed calm. He seemed like this wasn't the first tense moment he had experienced in his life.

"The manager is out now," the dwarf said.

"No, he's not," the young man said. "Who the fuck is that behind you?" And, for the first time, I noticed a man counting money in the back of the trailer. The man at the end wore a suit. I realized, now, he had been the ringmaster during the performance.

The young gangster grabbed the hand of the dwarf and lifted him in the air, so he dangled with his legs kicking. The gangster went to the back of the trailer to the ringmaster. "You're late on your fucking payments," he said.

"Business has been slow," the ringmaster said.

"Liar. The tents are full. I saw it myself, today. And the jefe doesn't care if your business has been slow. I'm taking the midget as payment, for now. The jefe says he wants a midget. He says he wants someone to dance for him. He says he's bored." The gangster pulled out a gun. He dropped the dwarf to the floor. "Get up," he told the dwarf. "Stand up. Or are you too short? Dance for me. Dance for me, you ugly piece of shit. Dance for me and maybe you'll grow."

The dwarf looked at the gun. He stood up from the floor and began to dance.

The gangster looked over at Arturo and me. "And you, faggot!" he shouted, pointing his gun at me. "What the hell are you looking at, you fucking pansy? Does this make you sick? Does all of this dancing make you sick? Take off your pants. Take your pants off and dance with the midget."

I took my pants off and moved next to the dwarf. The ringmaster made no sounds of protest. Arturo said, "No," but the gangster shot at the floor in front of him and the sound of the gun burst through my eardrums.

"Get in front of the midget," the gangster said. I walked in front of the dwarf. "Now, you! Midget. Pretend to fuck the faggot. Show him who's on top. Get up on a stool and show us you can make him your whore."

The dwarf got up on a stool and pretended to press his body against me like he was making love. And maybe it was the sight of the priest, earlier, coming out of the circus tent, but I felt, once more, the presence of Padre Francisco, and I bent forward crying.

The gangster leaned back, roaring. "Oh, I knew it. I knew you were a maricón! This is too much." He wiped tears of laughter from his eyes. He took the dwarf and went to the door. "If any of you says a word about this, if any of you says anything, you're dead."

He pointed his hand in the air like a pistol and fired; then he left with the dwarf.

THIS MORNING, I went up to the elevated highway to run. I needed time to think. I needed to make sense of what had happened to me at the circus. Arturo was looking frantically for his friend, the dwarf. The ringmaster had told him to keep quiet about the whole affair. He'd told Arturo he would make the payment soon, and that the dwarf would be returned then. He begged Arturo not to go to the police. "Just shut up about the whole thing," he said. "Shut up about it and everything will turn out best. If you get the police involved they'll come after me. They'll say I did something wrong. They always screw up everything."

The ringmaster was asking for silence in a country that is always asking for silence. This morning, before I went running, I picked up the newspaper, and I saw a headline about the new president, Enrique Peña Nieto. The president told the press they were writing too many negative things about the country. They were writing about too much crime instead of all the wonderful, positive things taking place in the country. "Write about the real news," the president said. "Don't write about the junk."

Arturo told me he wouldn't stay silent about his friend. After the circus, I had accompanied him to the police, at the nearest station. We went in to file an urgent report of a kidnapping. We told the police officer exactly what had happened—minus me standing without my pants and the dwarf pretending to have sex with me.

"When do you think you will have some information?" Arturo said. "When can we expect to hear something? I don't want this case to become just like one of the others. I want you to do something about this man. He's like a father to me."

"You can rest assured we will look into the matter fully," the police officer said. He took the printout of the case and put it on a stack of others. There must have been twenty-five cases sitting in the tray above his desk. He seemed in no rush to touch any of them. He asked his secretary for some tea. "Give me some extra sugar," he said, and he squeezed at her bottom.

Arturo and I had spent the last two days driving around the city looking for any sign of the man with the baseball cap and the red leather jacket. If we could find him, Arturo said, we would tell some other police officers where he was located. Or we would free his friend the dwarf and not even bother with the police. "That's the only way to get anything done in this country now," Arturo said. "If you see your own bicycle has been stolen, you have to steal it back."

I was petrified, of course, as to what would happen to Arturo's friend. The more hours after a crime begins in Mexico, the less chance it will ever be solved. The case slips into a collective amnesia. The whole country is weighed down with the guilt of disappeared people who were loved but forgotten.

But as I ran, what concerned me most wasn't, I have to admit, the dwarf. What concerned me most were my own efforts at amnesia. I had never told anyone of Padre Francisco. I had never shared my inner secret. And the wound that was festering within me wasn't only the wound of being abused by him. In my mind, the questions that I had turned over and over, and that I turned over and over again as I ran, were: Was I responsible for my abuse? Had I somehow led Padre Francisco on? Had I enticed him? Or, was I gay because he had somehow made me that way?

And yet, as I ran along the upper floor of the highway, it came to me that for far too long I had been conflating the two—Padre Francisco and me. I had been assuming there was some relationship between the two, when there was none. I realized this as I thought about the dwarf being forced to entertain the gangster, and as I thought over the whole incident at the circus. The gangster had forced the dwarf to perform for him. The gangster had put a gun in front of him. What choice did the dwarf have? If he didn't dance, he would have been dead meat. The gangster had ridiculed the dwarf for being a dwarf, but he didn't *become* a dwarf because of the cruelty of being put on exhibition. He was a dwarf and had always been a dwarf. And he would die a dwarf. The cruelty of the gangster had nothing to do with who the dwarf, fundamentally, was.

Likewise, I had intertwined the two. I had confused my sexuality with the abuse of Padre Francisco. I had assumed I was somehow responsible for what he had done to me, and though I knew it shouldn't be the case, I felt guilt for being gay. I felt that being gay was a sin. I felt that my sexuality—who I was at my core—was wrong. But if the dwarf was no more responsible for himself than being born who he was, then why should I torment myself for who I am?

Slowly, methodically, I worked through these ideas as I ran along the pavement. It might seem I should have come to these conclusions years ago. It might seem these ideas were so simple that surely I would have understood them before. But until the violence of the moment of being forced to dance with the dwarf, of being forced to be his victim, playing out the role, in some way, that I had once played out with Padre Francisco—yet as a full grown adult who could now think about what he had just experienced—I could not come to these conclusions.

I ran along the upper roof of the city, and I could see layers of

clouds upon clouds, just as the mind is layered in all of its confusion.
I saw the twinning of lampposts as they came out of the sides of the
pavement, climbing up with hard metal, splitting forcefully into two
lights that lead against and away from each other. I saw a crow attack
a smaller bird and dive at it and try to humiliate the other bird, forc-
ing it away from its hidden nest beneath the highway. I looked down
at the traffic on the lower floor, rushing back and forth, cars coming
in and out, and I realized the cars stop for no one, you have to break
your own path forward through the traffic.

THIS MORNING, AFTER running, after taking a shower to clean every inch
of my body, I put on my crispest white cotton shirt. I took out an
old iron and unwrinkled the fabric. I put on a tie, although I never
wear a tie to the office—only when I go out on the road to sell and
promote U.S. Wheat. I put on a blue blazer, a pair of smooth khaki
pants, and I polished my shoes. I didn't have to go into the office,
today. Technically, I was off because I was headed out on the road
tomorrow.

I put my running shoes in the closet. I had been running away
from myself for years.

When I arrived at the office, I asked my boss, the secretary, and
my other coworker for a meeting at eleven. They looked at me, surprised to see me in the office and so dressed up. My boss looked me
up and down. He said, "What's up with the spiffy clothes? You going
to communion today?" He said the last words in a sarcastic tone. He
knew I almost never went to church. "How about at eleven-fifteen?"
he said. He always had to have the last word.

"I can't do it then," I said. "It has to be at eleven." I was tired of
him always pushing us around in the office. It was all the same to
him—11:00 or 11:15—so I told him it had to be at eleven.

At eleven we all gathered around the conference room table.
The boss had a box of Cracker Jack with him. He didn't care for local,

Mexican snacks, and he bought junk food at the U.S. embassy commissary.

When they were all gathered, I closed my eyes and I saw an image of Arturo's friend, the dwarf. I saw him encouraging me, pulling his handkerchief longer and longer until I laughed. I saw an image, in my mind, of Padre Francisco behind me, and I took the handkerchief and I tied up Padre Francisco with the dwarf's cloth, binding his hands and feet, wrapping the cloth, of bright yellow and blue handkerchiefs, around Padre Francisco's eyes. I did not open my eyes, at first. I kept them closed as I spoke. "I have something I want to tell you. For thirty-seven years I have denied who I am. I have been in the closet my whole life." I paused. My voice had started out quavering, a bit, but now it was strong. "I am gay," I said. I opened my eyes and looked firmly at my boss. His mouth was paused, in midair, with bits of snack floating in mid-arc. And then he continued chewing and said, "You need to get me that presentation to go to Colombia. You're late on that. Everything else is going to be fine."

# THE PRISON BREAKOUT

This morning, I took the first steps to help a prisoner in a maximum-security prison in Mexico make a breakout. I brought in a metal file in the base of my briefcase. I have a black, simple nylon bag, which I have worn for years, as I speak to death row inmates. Usually I carry the bag in the U.S., bringing files to support and represent death row cases in the U.S. I have been living in Mexico City for twenty-two years now. I am a U.S. national. I am also a writer. I was down in Mexico City for five years, writing away, trying to have an intellectual life, reading books seriously, and living the cheaper life that is possible in Mexico, writing some fiction but then basically getting more and more involved in tracking down nonfiction stories for magazines and putting together a book of essays about all of the humanity that I found swirling about me in Mexico. That wasn't going to pay the bills alone, so I took a job working for the U.S. government, looking into the background of death row inmates in the U.S. who are Mexican. Before any of the cases is finally exhausted someone has to, by law, check to see if there are any mitigating circumstances that might help in favor of the death row inmate. Someone has to go into the town of the inmate, or wherever they come from, and speak to the family members and to the people who grew up with the inmate, to see what kind of circumstances the prisoner grew up in, and to see if there is any background information which the court should know about that might help to explain how the prisoner became such a deadly individual.

This is strange work, in that I am constantly surrounded by people who know they raised a killer, a true killer; and I myself, while I have a lot of sympathy for these killers, do not deny that in 97 percent of the cases the man in prison is someone who genuinely did murder someone. But the more you get into this business, tracking down information about the people behind bars, you can't help but notice many of the cases do not stack up. Many times, it's clear someone behind bars simply could not have been the person who committed the crime he's been convicted of.

For years and years, when I came across those cases, I simply presented my findings to the court. I did my research as best I could. My job has not been to reopen cases, and I don't generally see my job that way. As I said, in most cases the man is guilty. But guilty or not, you can say I am hired to see the humanity of the prisoners as they work their way through the U.S. justice system, until most of them, after they exhaust all possibilities, are finally put to death.

My work, which is paid for, is for the criminal justice system in the U.S. I am not paid to help or to work with prisoners in Mexico. Down in Mexico, they don't have the death penalty. But they do happily put prisoners behind bars.

The case of Jésus Martinez, in Mexico, is a case I would normally never have been caught up in, precisely because there is no one to investigate cases like Martinez's in Mexico. There are no court-appointed researchers in Mexico to find mitigating circumstances about someone put in the slammer for life. Finding an "impartial judge" is even harder in Mexico. There is not a jury system in Mexico the way we have in the U.S. There are not the checks and balances that can force a judge to hold back, to momentarily pause and consider which ways he may be wrong in his assumptions, or which ways the police may have taken evidence improperly, or which ways witnesses may be lying. Instead, the judge is like a god down here, who processes case after case, slowly, with witnesses often rounded up by the police and told they'd better write down on paper what the police want or they're going to be beaten up. I don't want to crap on the system of justice in Mexico too much. No system is perfect, anywhere. Some systems don't even exist, in some countries—that is, in some countries, where there is, for example, shariah, the victim is lined up at a stake and stoned to death to enforce God's will. Mexico is nothing like that. And yet, even with a judge, a robe, and the occasional Latin word thrown in, it is certainly not a place where *I* would want to be charged with a crime.

In the case of Martinez, the main piece of evidence against him is that he is deaf and he knows sign language. Someone went into a bank and pointed to the teller, and without spoken words, using only his hands, directed the teller to give him all the money. He had an accomplice in the case, a man he used sign language with during the robbery. Everyone clearly saw two men using sign language. The teller behind the counter put money into the bag she was given, at a Bancomer bank, as slowly as possible. She followed the procedures she was given when she'd trained to become a teller. She put an ink bomb in the bag with the 500-peso notes the thief was taking. The ink bomb was supposed to explode, later, to mark the bills, so they could be tracked down by the cops. But as she was following the procedures, perfectly, and after she'd pressed the button beneath her counter to indicate a robbery was in progress, and just as the co-conspirator in the robbery was holding an elderly woman hostage in the back of the bank to let the tellers know they should hand over the money quickly and without fuss, the teller handed over the money in the bag the robber had given her, the bag was just in front of the face of the crook at the counter, and the ink bomb exploded in his face. In pandemonium, the second bank robber, holding his gun to the temple of the elderly woman, shot her dead. Both of the men committing the robbery signed back and forth it was time to flee. Apparently, according to someone watching the whole thing— there were fifty at the crime scene in the bank—the first robber signed to the other in sign language, "What the hell have you done? How could you have killed that woman?"

The second signed back, "I didn't mean to, but you scared me when you jumped back from the bag."

"Run, run," the first crook signed.

They ran out of the bank, to bicycles they had waiting. They were both dressed in black, wearing ski masks. The crime occurred in the part of Mexico City where the Avenida Isabel la Católica enters an area of printers' rows, where hundreds of little businesses print T-shirts, plastic mugs, and business cards, etc. The two rode off on small BMX bicycles, riding as fast as they could, the first crook holding the bag of money, a burlap sack that normally holds coffee beans and that was covered with ink stains and filled with worthless bills. They swerved in and out of the hundreds of small buyers who had come from around the city to order their little entrepreneurial projects in the printers' rows. The crooks disappeared behind the printing machines, into the cracks of Mexico City. The few, fat cops—otherwise known as *panzones*—ran after the crooks, one of the cops trying to shoot at the criminals as they escaped, but failing to shoot either of them. Back in the bank, people fell to the ground in fear. The old woman, a grandmotherly type, in a nicely ironed brown dress with a sash carefully tied around her waist, her gray hair neatly combed back in place, had crumpled to the ground, dead. Her family would never see the lovely abuelita again.

Needless to say, the case was a mess, as all cases are a mess, in that there was a genuine victim, a genuine tragedy at hand. A week later, Martinez was hauled in to the local police station by a local cop. He was a deaf man. He knew sign language. He had a BMX bicycle, which he liked to do tricks on. Never mind he didn't fit any of the other descriptions of either of the thieves. He was short when the men who'd committed the crime—everyone agreed, when I eventually interviewed them—were tall. Martinez didn't have any money when they found him. There was no evidence of any coffee bag and none of the 500-peso bills were discovered with him. His whole family agreed, independently, that he had been at a birthday party at the time of the crime—a party for him. He worked as a mime in a troupe, making money downtown doing street theater, when he wasn't working in the mechanics' garage where he worked the rest of his time. The man who ran the garage was questioned independently, by me, about the birthday party. Everyone agreed on the color of clothes Martinez had been wearing at the birthday party; where the party had been held; that friends of his, who he mimed with, had been at the party; what food they had eaten at the party; and the exact time of the party, because the performance troupe of a friend—a group of clowns—had been brought in to perform.

After all my time looking at death row cases in the U.S., and meeting families down in Mexico of the perpetrators of crimes, it was clear to me the case against Martinez was so flimsy, based solely on the fact he was deaf, that I couldn't believe he could ever have been convicted. But there he was, behind bars, in a maximum-security prison in Mexico City, placed in prison for the rest of his life, with no real chance of parole, for the killing of a lovely grandmother who I was certain he'd never met before in his life.

I HAVE BEEN thinking about what made me bring the metal file in to Martinez this morning. What made me act? What made me cross the line? I am normally an observer, not an actor. I sit on the edge of the world, like most writers, watching and taking in every detail, seeing more, perhaps, than any person should see.

Growing up in New York, I began to see lies at an early age. I remember, once, as a boy, watching my brother steal some candy from the store around the corner. He ran and ran with the few pieces he'd stolen from Mr. Horowitz's local grocery on Fourteenth Street and Eighth Avenue. He did it for the sport, more than anything. We didn't have much money, but we weren't so poor he needed to rob that candy. I watched from across the street as my brother came dashing out of the grocery, Mr. Horowitz running onto the street after him twisting and huffing and puffing through the cars, until he hung his head, hangdog on the sidewalk, with my brother running away through the alleyways of the West Village. My brother had taken that man's bread and butter, the fruits of his hard work, and I asked my brother, when he got home and he ate the candy slowly in his bedroom, why he'd done it.

"What? Done what? I didn't do nothing."

"But you stole Mr. Horowitz's candy. I saw you do it," I said. I was no older than seven. It was my first experience with a bald-faced lie, something I knew was wrong staring me in the face. I could have told on my brother. I could have gone to tell my parents, or a teacher, or even Mr. Horowitz.

I was shocked when my brother said, "Georgie did it." Georgie was a black boy who lived down the street. "Georgie took 'em. I didn't do nothin'."

And I didn't do nothing, either. I watched, I observed. I saw him make his racist accusation, pinning the blame on another boy, simply because he knew he was an easy target.

As I grew up, I saw the same thing, over and over. I saw the lies pile up. I'm fifty-two. I was born in 1961. I remember, as a kid, watching President Lyndon Johnson on our black and white TV telling us North Vietnam was a country of Communist invaders that wanted to destroy my country, and I watched the older brothers of my friends go off to Vietnam to protect my country from Communism, from the evil red carpet that was going to take over the world, but I never saw that red carpet come close to my shores, all I saw was the silent, faraway look of those boys as they came home, looking older in their faces, like men, when they were only twenty-two. And that was the big lie, the lie that let me know my country wasn't going to tell me the truth, and as a kid I watched the protests up at Columbia University, and I took the subway up there when I was just twelve, and I saw students screaming through megaphones, I heard them shouting, "Hey, Hey, Ho, Ho, President Nixon has got to go!" By then, they were protesting against Watergate and the bombing of Hanoi, and Nixon and Kissinger's plan to end the war with "Peace with Honor," words which even then I could tell had nothing to do with the photos of bombed-out bodies I saw on the front page of the *New York Times.*

My parents were hardworking Jews who'd immigrated to the U.S. as kids, just before the end of World War II, ferried through England from Germany. I knew that lie, too, when Hitler said he was going to cleanse Europe and make a Reich that would last a thousand years. I grew up with history books in the house, which told of President Wilson and the gassing of World War I, and of the League of Nations, and of the "War to End All Wars," and of Neville Chamberlain's "Peace in Our Time." And I saw the worn books of Yiddish writers that my father would read and finger over and over, which told of the pogroms my ancestors had fled from in Russia before they'd landed in Germany, before they fled to the U.S. The history was everywhere, the history of lies, and power and abuse, and I read those books in bed, sometimes long after my mother said I had to be asleep, with a flashlight under the sheets.

When I was older, I knew of other lies, the lies of another president, Ronald Reagan, as he sent money from the secret sale of weapons to the government of Iran, which he'd labeled the devils of Islamic tyranny, but he sold weapons to them anyway, to funnel money off to his secret war in Nicaragua against the Sandinistas. Those were the images I grew up with in college, photos of people dying in mass graves in Nicaragua and El Salvador, all funded by my government.

I am not telling all these things because it is any surprise to anyone hearing about this, I am telling this to give the context to why I took a metal file in to Martinez this morning. Because when I look back at all these pieces of news, at all these incidents, from the stealing of the candy by my brother to the wars and the lies of my politicians—the leaders of the country whose speeches and pro-nouncements flooded around me like syrup in the air, inescapable, everywhere—I realize that for years and years, my reaction was al-ways one of quiet outrage, of words of denouncement, of curiosity, of anger, of telling others in cafés and at my schools that I was upset, but doing nothing. I did nothing. I watched, and knew, and became more and more knowledgeable, and could see the wrong, and I told myself that what mattered was that at least I *knew*, at least I was aware, at least I was conscious unlike the others who didn't see, who weren't conscious, who didn't even take the first step to responsibility. Be-cause at least I *knew*. I was *informed*, unlike those other Joes.

And when I came down to Mexico City, at the age of thirty, twenty-two years ago—deciding to leave the world of my country behind in the U.S.—wasn't that a political statement, even though I said it was just because I liked Mexico City better than New York? Wasn't I really saying that I wasn't going to participate in the lies of my country anymore? Didn't that make me somehow cleaner and better than my fellow citizens, because I wasn't going to be tainted with the blood of America?

No, not me. I was a serious thinker, someone who could see things as they were. I read and I read, and I rented a cheap apart-ment in La Roma, a neighborhood that is now chic in Mexico City, but that wasn't chic at all when I came to Mexico City in 1991. There was a big earthquake in Mexico City in 1985, and the ground of La Roma is on the part of the city that is much looser, since the city was constructed on an old lake in the center of a valley, and the buildings shook and many fell apart in the quake, so the fear of living in such a neighborhood after so many had died meant that the neighbor-hood was undesirable. So I found a cheap apartment, and I began to live off the savings I had from working as a young journalist in the U.S. I wrote and I wrote, and I conjured up characters that I thought were pregnant with meaning. None of what I was writing was very good, but I was writing so earnestly, with so much belief that what I was writing mattered. Fiction is nothing like writing journalism, and I wasn't making much progress, but all the time I thought I was doing something that might show what I really felt, that might really change the world. Because isn't that what all those great writers, whom I admired so much, like Dostoyevsky, were trying to do, to change the world? Weren't they trying to reflect the pain and torture of our existence back at us so we might take pause and choose to change our ways and reorganize who we were and how we decided to act?

But my fiction wasn't any good. My characters had no life in them. They were puppets, extensions of my ideology. And after a while I realized that wasn't why Dostoyevsky and the others wrote, in any case. If they brought us to action, it wasn't because they were trying to get us to change our ways, it was a by-product of them simply creating life, and when we looked at life it made us see the need to make changes. If we saw the world as it truly is then it couldn't help but make us pause and reflect that we had to make personal changes, just as the characters always went in these nice arcs from ignorance to enlightenment, to epiphanies that caused them to change their ways.

And yet, as I spent days in my small apartment in La Roma, reading and reading, and writing and failing to write well, what I realized is that I had epiphanies up the wazoo. I was one walking, giant epiphany. I had seen the sickness of the world, right in front of me—how far did you really have to go?—looking out at the poverty in my neighborhood, at the poor men sweeping up the streets so the rich men could walk by and make it dirty, again. Did I really need to know more? Did any of us really need to know more? I began to realize the hard thing was to act. The hard thing was to take action, not to know, because knowing was the relatively easy part. I had *known* that my brother had stolen the candy, I had *known* the politicians were lying to us all as they waltzed into other countries and stole from those countries and killed their citizens. I had *known* I was an earnest young man wanting to be pure when I left my country, looking for adventure. It wasn't the knowing that was hard, it was the doing.

So I took a job doing more of what I thought needed to be done. I took the job to pay the bills, working for the U.S. government with the death row inmates. I took the job meeting the family members of the death row inmates, seeking out any "mitigating circumstances" that might influence their sentences. For, Christ!, wasn't the possibility of saving a life the biggest act of doing you could do? The words "mitigating circumstances" were the most Orwellian I could think of. Who doesn't have "mitigating circumstances" in life? I found the way most of these men grew up poor, and the small shacks where they grew up, and the places where chickens ran around on the street, and where there often isn't any running water, and hell, yes, there are mitigating circumstances, and I presented my findings to the court as ordered, in neat folders, neatly printed out on paper. And all of this was a form of doing, and yet I felt I was still an observer. I wouldn't have broken the law if the law had come looking for me, because I thought the best way to *do* is from within the system. You can't change the world unless you work within the world the way it is. I didn't want to be one of those guys throwing himself against the barricades in the French Revolution or in the revolts of 1968. I was a thinking man's doer. That's how I would do things. Let others throw the stones; I would do by working within "the system" and making it change.

Until Martinez. Martinez was different. When I saw Martinez, something clicked in me, and I knew I didn't want to be working within the system anymore. I was, for the first time in my life, about to become, as they say, "radicalized."

THE FIRST TIME I saw Martinez, two months ago, he was on the floor in the corner of his cell, smelling of feces that clung to his body. He was in the back, far right corner of the small area that pertained to him, and I thought he wasn't even present. "Watch out for the prisoner. Keep going forward," the warden of the prison told me.

"Where is he?" I asked.

"There. In front of you. To the right, on the ground."

I had been in so many Mexican jails before, nothing should have surprised me. They are nothing like an American jail. The prisoners often have to get their food from their family in the outside world. They sleep so many to a bunk, there is frequently someone sleeping on the concrete floor beneath two others in mattresses above. The prisoners do not always have time out in an exercise yard each day. They often have to bribe the guards who run the prison for basic necessities like toilet paper and chances to ask for their cases to be reviewed.

Given that Martinez was all alone in his cell, I knew it was almost inevitable his cell had been cleared out, just before I saw him, to give the appearance he had the whole place to himself. There was no real chance the whole place was just for him, since I had never seen such a solitary cell for a prisoner, and this most likely explained his crouching on the floor as if he had just been liberated of the presence of other prisoners. I had been told of the existence of Martinez by a friend who worked, independently, for the release of prisoners, funded on his own dime and based on money he raised himself. He had approached me because he knew about my work with death row inmates in the U.S., and I went to the prison in the south of Mexico City because I thought there might be an article here worth writing, not for the American press, but for a slick glossy magazine called *Gatopardo,* a bit like *Vanity Fair* but for Mexicans. The thought I might be exploiting Martinez if we put him in the magazine only vaguely crossed my mind. What I thought of, instead, was that this would be a good chance to get my foot in the door with a magazine that paid well, which reached a sophisticated audience, and that I might be able to do something to further the cause of prison reform with the elites of the country.

What I didn't expect with Martinez is that he would act out what he had experienced and what he felt, with such strength of facial expressions with so many movements, like a great mime, every bit as good as the French Marcel Marceau. I had little experience with mimes, and little experience with deaf people, and I expected that I would spend most of my time writing questions on a piece of paper, with Martinez writing his answers to my questions back on the same piece of paper. This definitely happened sometimes, but the first thing I didn't fully expect is that Martinez would be a perfectly good lip reader. Once the warden left me inside the cell and the guards closed the doors, and I was warned he was "very dangerous," I approached a table in the middle of the cell, which took up a good chunk of the space, and I sat down, leaving Martinez in the corner to decide how he wanted to respond to me. I had learned from other prisoners, in other jails, that it was often best not to approach them with too much haste or with too much directness, to let them get adjusted to me and to decide whether or not they wanted to communicate with me. Giving the prisoner the liberty of choosing how to react to me placed them in a position out of their normal routine, and allowed them to enter into a different dynamic with me than with the other prisoners and guards.

Martinez took his time in the corner as I sat at the table, Martinez deciding, it seemed to me, whether he even wanted to approach me. I had a piece of paper and a pencil out, ready to write to him. He looked me up and down, moving his head in a smooth, sweeping gesture. He wore a gabardine trilby hat, which tilted back rakishly on his head, which had been shaved until he was bald. He had on a white undershirt that left his shoulders bare, a pair of worn-out jeans, and a pair of even more worn-out flip-flops. His shirt was clean, which led me to believe the prison had washed it for him just for the interview. He walked back and forth in the prison cell, touching each wall in a repetitive movement, ignoring me, back and forth and back and forth as if a man in a play by Beckett, losing himself in the space, which seemed foreign to him now that the cell was empty of the belongings that were usually there, tapping his head, with the brim of his hat, against each wall before turning to take five paces to the other side.

This went on for five minutes, and I watched him, and then he abruptly sat down across from me in the other chair provided and he put all of the attention that had previously been focused blankly on each of the walls and stared straight into my eyes. It was a challenge to me, I felt. He sat perfectly motionless, with his back straight, his gaze level into my eyes, still not looking down at the paper. The challenge seemed to be: "Don't come here just to exploit me, to rob from me. Look at me for who I am." And then, after he had my full attention, he wrote as much on the paper. He picked up the pencil and wrote in Spanish, "They tell me you want my story so you can write an article. They tell me this is for an important magazine and that I should behave. What makes you think I want to speak to you? What makes you think you have the right to just walk in here and take my story to put it in a magazine? I am not some plaything, you know, some object of curiosity."

I began to write my answer, but he stopped me from writing and pointed at my lips and showed me I should talk. He used his hands to show me I should speak slowly enough so he could read my lips.

"OK. You've got me," I said. "I admit there is some element of exploitation in this. But how many other people have come, recently, to try to bring your story to the outside world? Without me, you will stay in this prison for the rest of your life."

"That's a threat," he wrote on the paper. "I don't need threats. I am threatened in here every day. Sometimes, when they don't want to do anything, they threaten to never let us get food again, or that we will have to sleep with that bucket of our shit, over in the corner,

forever. There is nothing you can threaten me with. I am prepared to
stay in here forever, if I have to."

"So what do you want?" I said. "To be a martyr?"

"I want you to take me seriously. I want you to promise you will
keep coming to this prison after you have written your story. I want
you to show me the article you write, before you publish it. If there
is something that strikes me as false, as a lie, I will cross that part of
your story out and I will ask you not to publish it."

"I can't let you tell me what to do," I said. "It's characteristic of a
lot of prisoners that they tell me a bunch of lies, and if I let you edit
my article then it might end up with a bunch of your fantasies." It
was, perhaps, bold of me to tell him this, but this was the truth. Prisoners loved to make up stories. I had almost never met a prisoner on
death row who didn't claim he was innocent.

"You think you're smarter than me. You think you're better
than me. How much do you really understand of the other prisoners you have worked with?"

This simple question was not really new to me. It was a question I had asked myself, before, but the question had never come to
me directly from a prisoner, and the force of the question, the im-
mediacy of it, within only minutes of meeting Martinez, made me
stand up and come out of my pose of knowingness. He was right in
his question, I could see. He had figured me out in only a matter of
minutes. I did feel I knew more than most of the prisoners I inves-
tigated. I even felt I knew more than most of the people I interacted
with. Arrogance had always been my Achilles' heel. I did not mean
to look arrogant, but the way I lifted my chin when I spoke, the way
I often paused between my sentences, listening to myself speak, as if
I had words that were particularly important to say, made me look
arrogant. It was not the image I intended to give off, but it was true
about me. My head, which was bald, made me look, in some ways,
like a mirror image of Martinez across from me. My head was bald
from older age and an effort to keep my skull from looking like

that of an old man; it was a way of me trying to remain appearing like someone who was cool. It gave me a suave, debonair look that I liked to use to my advantage at parties, to pick up younger women, sometimes feigning interest in what they told me, even if I wasn't interested, to woo them into a bedroom. I had always thought of myself as fair and righteous and just, even though I often doubted that about myself, and here was Martinez who had called me out on my worst inner feelings and habits in a matter of minutes. It was unnerving to see him across from me, reflecting me back to myself so powerfully and so easily.

"If you want me to leave," I said, "I will go now. I'm sorry if I have disturbed you today."

"That's better," he wrote. "I can see you are speaking to me sincerely now. No, go ahead, now that you have made the effort to come all the way to this prison, we can talk."

"How did you end up here?" I asked him, even though my friend in the agency had given me the basic blow-by-blow.

He stood up from the chair and began to mime what had happened to him. He showed me a party, where he was with his friends, laughing, as he blew out a birthday cake. He drew the candles on the cake in the air in front of me. He showed me a clock with the hands at three o'clock at the party, as he ate a piece of cake. Then he drew a line and shifted his arms back and forth, on a flat plane, to show me he was going to another scene. In that other scene there was a thief asking for money at a window with bars. He pulled out his pockets to show that the person was asking for money. He frowned and pouted, to let me know this wasn't him. He pretended to be a nice old lady. He pretended to be another man holding on to this nice old lady, twisting back and forth to do the face of the man with a gun and the face of the old lady. Then he pointed a gun with his fingers at the temple of the old lady and pulled the trigger and she fell to the ground. He lay on the ground, taking in the full pain of the lady, not moving for a good long while to let me know she was really dead.

When he finally got up from the ground he mimed tears coming from his eyes, to let me know the whole story was very, very sad.

I was mesmerized by the story he told with his body, by the way he swayed to and fro, arching his back to make me feel the story he was telling; and by the way he made his face extra expressive.

"You're an impressive mime," I told him when he came back to sit in front of me.

"Thank you," he wrote. "But I want you to understand I'm not being melodramatic. And I'm not doing this to entertain you or to impress you. I mime because that is how I express my feelings and because you are deaf impaired."

"Deaf impaired?" I said.

"Yes, you not only can't sign but you have no idea what it is like to be in my world. So by miming maybe I can hint at some of the things you miss in usual body language."

"Are you saying all deaf people can mime, or that they feel like mimes?"

"No, of course not," he wrote. "I am just saying that there are many things you might think you know that you might miss. If you come again, I will teach you some more."

He was, according to my friend, no older than thirty-three, but he knew he had things to teach me, someone nineteen years his senior. It was the first of five meetings over the next two months. I came as often as the warden of the prison would let me. They told me I could visit no more frequently than once every two weeks. The reason they gave was so as not to disturb the prisoners, but I sensed it was because every time I saw Martinez they would have to clear the others out of his cell, and Martinez wrote me as much on his paper the next time I saw him.

On the last visit, two weeks ago, he stopped writing on the paper and he looked me straight in the eyes, and he mouthed at me, insisting I watch his lips and try to read them as he always watched mine. There was something he clearly did not want to write on the paper, which I kept after each interview but that he must have believed the guards could see. "I want you to help me escape from here," he mouthed to me. "I do not belong here. You know this now, completely. You know every part of my story."

He had told me, by then, how he had grown up, who the members of his family were, what the hardscrabble ways of his growing up had been. He had poured out every part of his youth, all mimed in front of me as I sat transfixed, watching him act. He had given me all his story, and now what he was asking for was something in return.

I stopped and told him, "That is something I can't do. If I did that, then I would instantly end up in prison myself, and I wouldn't be able to help any of you on the inside." It was a perfectly logical answer. He wasn't the first prisoner to ask me to help him try to find a way to escape. Other prisoners had found enough confidence in me to ask the same question. But he was the first prisoner to make me think twice about my reply.

Going home, as I drove from the prison through the endless concrete small houses of Mexico City, and then as I paced in my small apartment back in the neighborhood of La Roma, I thought about a flame thrower I had seen the night before in the central plaza of Tlalpan in the south of the city. There, the evening before, I had seen a street performer light on fire a large circle with multiple torch endings and throw the circle around and around, larger than a hula hoop around his body, then on the ground in front of him, moving his body in and out of the flames. The risk of what the performer did, only to make a few pesos, trying to wow the crowd, had entranced me. The performer put his life on the line every night, and like many performers in the city, he probably performed at streetlights as well, doing his show, risking burning his hair, all to make a dime.

Did I have the same guts, not to make a dime, but to help a man who had been condemned to prison for life on completely phony charges? By now, I was more than convinced Martinez had never committed his crime. I had, in between prison visits, interviewed all the other people at his birthday party and the few people I could find who had been at the actual bank crime. It was clear he had never been at the scene of the crime. It was also clear the particular judge who had sentenced him had a particularly bad reputation for sending innocent people to prison.

How much was I willing to get inside the hoop of flame? I thought about my life in Mexico, how comfortable I felt in the country, how every day that I woke up I felt like there was a new surprise with something to teach me and to fill me with curiosity and awe. I thought about the risk I might lose all of that, the sense of place I had become attached to. I thought about the feeling that in this country, I was always alive. It was not that this country was completely better than mine. I wasn't interested, after a number of years, in comparing one country to the other. But what I felt was that here, people cared about me, and I cared about them. There was time to care. We were not separated by all of the barriers of private spaces and private homes, which carved out so much personal space in the United States that it often felt like we had bubbles keeping us from one another. In Mexico, those bubbles felt smaller, and often nonexistent. This had become my home. I had become a permanent resident of the place. To risk all of that, my right to live in the country, in order to bring some means of escape to Martinez, was risking it all. There was the very real risk that if caught, I could be brought in front of the same kind of despicable judge that had thrown Martinez in prison for life.

But for the first time in my life I knew I had to let more than my rational mind make decisions for me. I had to step into the ring of fire twirling around and around above my head and around my body. I had to risk it all, to take the action to see if I could make one big wrong right. I packed a metal file in the bottom of my briefcase on the next visit. I opened the stuffing of my briefcase carefully, and made a little sleeve on the bottom, and brought the briefcase to a shoe-repair man to have the bag sewn up properly so it would look right. I could slide the metal file in and out easily. It was a small gesture. It was much less than bringing in a gun, something that seemed far beyond my capacity and that might get Martinez caught, as well as me. It was the most efficient act of rebellion I could think of, and I brought the metal file in to Martinez on my visit in the morning.

—⊸⟨⟨⟨◯⟩⟩⟩⊶—

For two months, Martinez took that file which I had brought to him and he scraped and pulled and concentrated the edge of the metal blade against the bars of his cell. On the night of his breakout, he waited until the guards came by on their final round of the evening, before the prisoners were supposed to go to sleep, when the guards made their final roll call. The guards called out the names of each prisoner in each cell. They tapped their batons against the metal bars of each cell, echoing the names of the prisoners, and then it was lights out. A guard came and said Martinez's name, specifically. Martinez made the loudest sound he could, a squeal that was high-pitched, approximating a "yes." He knew when to say his name when he felt the vibration of the other prisoners in his cell calling out their names.

The night was unusual because it was September 15, the night everyone in the prison had just completed celebrating the independence day of the country, the equivalent of the U.S.'s July 4. On this night, all the prisoners were brought into the main courtyard at the same time to watch a concert. It was one of the few times the prisoners were brought out all together, and one of the few times they were entertained together. The daily life of the interior of the prison was run by the warden, in outward appearance. But a high-level narco, from the north of the country in Monterrey, who ran a large cartel on the outside of the prison, was the real head of the day-to-day life. He had been convicted, but his links to the outside world were still strong. He brought in information and got out his plans for his cartel, and he told the prison warden who he wanted for the Día de la Independencia music. He chose Los Tigres del Norte, a popular band that toured the country. The inmates had all hooted and hollered listening to Los Tigres. The Tigres knew better than to bring in any women with the band, or a riot might ensue. Hundreds and hundreds of tacos and cans of Coca-Cola were downed. The garbage piled up in bag after bag, loaded into extra trash cans in the corner of the central courtyard.

When the last of the guards went by, and Martinez had called out his name, and the other prisoners in his cell went to bed, he pulled at the two cuts he had filed on a single bar, pulled out the bar, and shimmied himself through.

I had discussed the breakout plan with him. Martinez had initially thought he could dress up like a member of Los Tigres and waltz out of the concert with the rest of the band in the heat of the mayhem of the prison-mate fans. He was good at acting, and a perfect mime, but the chance he could fool the other band members and the guards as they went out was far too risky, I had told him, so he had scrapped that idea. Instead we had agreed the large quantity of garbage from the get-together was the key to his escape.

From his place of freedom outside of his cell, he ran in the dark, unchecked in his small space for the first time in five years. He ran like a cat freed from his enclosure. His body moved with energy, with the training of a professional mime, keeping to the edges of the shadows and out of any few splotches of light. He ran and felt the ground, listening with his hands for the vibrations of any of the guards as they made their rounds. I knew nothing about the layout of the prison, other than what I had seen on my five previous visits, but Martinez was able to tell me where the garbage was gathered and thrown out every night from the high-walled building. He ran to the garbage containers, which were more than usual, from the party, as he had expected, lifted the lid of one of the large containers, climbed inside the gray plastic container, took one last big breath of unfetid air, smelled the residues of sauces and of soda cans, the sticky sweet residue of Coca-Cola mixing with the warm decomposing smell of corn and chilies, and he buried his whole body beneath the mess, breathing through a plastic bottle that he had cut the bottom off of.

It was similar to the trick the famous narco El Chapo Guzmán had used, making it out of prison in a laundry basket. Martinez had thought of that possibility, too, but after Guzmán had used the method, all laundry baskets were inspected entering and leaving prison. But the garbage wasn't suspected. Martinez had figured that out. It was considered too disgusting. He sat in the container for four hours, until four in the morning, when the garbage was always brought outside, each container wheeled out and left for the garbage trucks to come an hour or two later, in the early dawn.

Along the north edge of the prison, when the garbage canisters were wheeled out and left by a single man whose job it was to do so, I waited thirty-five yards across the street, in the shadows, with a motorcycle, watching with binoculars. When the last of the large plastic canisters was wheeled out, and the man whose duty it was to remove the garbage had gone, I watched intently to see if Martinez had made his break. I saw one of the lids of the canisters push up. I saw Martinez leap out. I flashed a flashlight, twice, at the man covered with garbage. We had agreed his chances would be almost zero if someone didn't come pick him up. The most dangerous moment for a prison breakout was just after the prisoner had found a way outside the prison walls. That was when they stood out, looked unusual in prison clothes, and were so dazed from the adrenaline rush of their escape that other people ran into them, saw something suspicious, and reported them. Or the prisoner went off, running cockeyed.

This was the moment when Martinez had asked me to come get him in a motorcycle. A car was too big. A car might be spotted by one of the watchtowers.

And this was the moment that I had hesitated, for a moment, in the planning. Was I really willing to risk my whole life in Mexico and to fully commit myself to this man? Yet here I was, fully committed, fully taking action for the first time in my life. I wore a black ski mask, like the crooks who had genuinely committed the crime Martinez was accused of. The mask hid the white baldness of my head. I had given Martinez the one signal with the two quick flashes, and he came to me, where the motorcycle was hidden in the long underbrush on the far side of the road. Martinez jumped on the back of the motorbike. I barely looked back at him in the rush of the moment. I focused on balancing him on the back and rushing away as quietly as I could, then racing down the big hill from the prison toward the north of the city. I felt his arms grip my waist. I smelled his body, the residue of the garbage, and the smell of his fright. There was a smell in the night unlike any I had ever smelled before, the smell of a man rushing with all of his fright and elation to freedom. We rode the back roads at first, and then hit the main *eje* boulevards that break through the city. The red lights blinked, from stop to green, and I cut north through the night like a man bringing a slave in the United States north on the Underground Railroad. And like the people who took a risk bringing those slaves north, I brought him into my home first, briefly, to wash and change his clothes, so he wouldn't stand out as he made his journey to freedom. He stuffed his clothes into the kitchen garbage container in my apartment in La Roma. He scrubbed his body in my shower. He cleansed the last of the residue of the garbage, and of the prison, off his body. He put on some clothes, which I had bought for him. It was too risky to give him my own clothes, or anything that might give me away as helping him if he were caught, and too risky to ask for any clothes from his family. His family would be kept in the dark about his escape until he was settled in a new city, months down the line.

He washed, and he ate the food I gave him, he wrote down on a piece of paper explaining exactly how the escape had gone, and accentuated the words on the paper by miming some of the scarier moments. Then he jumped on the back of the motorcycle, not waiting longer than an hour, since the prison would find out in the dawn he was gone and they might signal a search to begin. But by then, as the first light of the morning came out strong, as the chickens cockled in the morning, as they do in the streets of Mexico City even in the biggest, most densely inhabited neighborhoods, I had brought him to the bus station and placed him on a bus bound for Oaxaca. The price of his freedom would be exile from his home city, where he had grown up. It was too dangerous, even in a city of twenty million, for him to pretend to melt into the fabric of Mexico City. Someone would eventually see him. Someone would eventually recognize his face. He would have to leave the city, where he had spent almost every day of his life for thirty-three years.

Standing by the bus, after I had bought him his ticket, I gave Martinez a hug. He clasped me like a wiry feline. He rubbed the back of my bald head in appreciation, leaned back, looked into my eyes, and I could see him hold back tears. I couldn't hold back my own. I wept as he took one last look at me and then as he turned with only a small bag, with some peanuts and one extra pair of clothes I had left for him and a few hundred dollars in pesos. He would need every peso to start his new life. I had no idea, exactly, where he would go in Oaxaca. We had agreed it was best for me to know nothing about his final destination. Someday, far in the future, when he was safe, he would write to me, but we had agreed there would be no specific day when.

I felt lighter as I rode home on my motorcycle. It wasn't just the lack of an extra passenger on the back of the bike. It was the lack of the fear I realized I had always carried with me. How much does fear weigh? How much does the fear of righting the wrongs of our daily life weigh? More than I could ever have known. When I got home, I made myself a cup of coffee. I brought it out to the balcony of my small apartment. I looked at the men and women preparing for the rest of their day, sweeping up the ground, cleaning their food stalls, and carrying their heavy loads as they made their journey. I saw the hum of the city, and I felt like I was flying above it all, floating over the metropolis. I would not be able to save each prisoner, each person who had been wronged, but at least I had saved one.

# THE ESCAPE FROM MEXICO

Looking back, the summer when I was twelve—I am in my early forties now—a young, horrible man, the head of a gang, tried to kill me. The day it all began, if you can really pinpoint a single moment when an avalanche begins, was on the soccer field, or what we called in Mexico the fútbol field, behind my school. Now I am an American, an immigrant of thirty years in the U.S. with my mother, but at that time I was a relatively poor Mexican. My mother worked as an elementary school teacher. My father was more or less a good-for-nothing, even then, someone who tacked from one side to another of quick jobs he made up and small entrepreneurial projects. He believed in making the fast buck, a deal for a small plot of land or to buy a bunch of tires, from a scrap heap, and turn them around to sell to another fool who might think lead had been turned into gold.

The soccer field was so used, it was nothing more than dust. Grass was never planted on the field in any case; that was the kind of school I went to, a dusty building without grass, and as the players ran down the middle of the field, a cloud of dirt would slowly gather around the players as they duked it out and would follow the players, cycloning around them, until the curtain ebbed and flowed to and fro, moving toward me, the goalie, where a breakaway player would suddenly run out of the cloud and shoot with full force at me, a round, chubby boy, a bit taller than the others, and certainly wider, with thicker arms that might stop the ball from reaching its goal.

The other boys sometimes called me Fatty, or Gordo, though I wasn't really fat in the way of a boy who couldn't move fast, and certainly not the way Americans, who are fat now, look. You see, at that time, to be even a bit chubby meant to be fat, because there really was no extra food and because everyone had a nickname. I was Gordi the Goalkeeper. The *portero*. My hands were very wide for twelve. I lived for soccer. I stood on the line and lunged with all the energy I could muster, when they kicked the ball. I pretended to be someone much older, one of the players in Europe who played in the World Cup or in the leagues of Spain. My favorite goalie was Toni Schumacher, a monster from Germany who led the German team in 1982, leaping in the air and snatching the ball from the other players, accidentally hitting a couple of them in the head as he waded through his opponents, saving the German team, almost winning them the Cup. You could say Schumacher was rough, and some said he was an animal, but I knew he had simply done what he had to, which is the way the game of life is actually played.

The day my life began to turn, all the players had left their watches at the edge of the field, next to me, just in the back of the tattered net, with me in the center. That was what every player did, so they wouldn't scrape the faces, arms, or legs of the other players as they jumped in the air, or as they practiced their slide tackles into the other players, like sliding in to first base, trying to gain the approval and praise of all the others. So, all the watches were left by one of the goalies, and everyone trusted me, El Gordi, the most. My nemesis in this story, a thin, tall player for his age, who at fourteen was two years older than me, with a bare chest that was already as big as a sixteen-year-old's and with black hair always gelled back, neatly combed over and over, who could be pretty like a model with his body, if he hadn't been so ugly in his face and if he didn't have a tendency to sneer, was a guy named El Farito—The Lighthouse. He was called El Farito not only because he was taller than the rest but because he swiveled his head further than most could, to hit in a header goal. El Farito was also the head of a gang, whose territory included all the area that surrounded my immediate house, to the east side of the school. The west side of the school belonged to another gang.

If this sounds strange, that one side of the school could belong to one gang and the other side to another, it is really no different than many other artificial lines in the world. As I tell you this story, I am now a bass player, who regularly plays in the back section of some of the best orchestras, and the line between the first violin section and the second violin section, or between the cellos and violas, is as clear as night and day. The audience sees only "the orchestra," but the players know your whole life is different if you are one of the violinists slogging along the underlying melody in the second violins, or if you get to be the first violinist who plays the bright solo moments.

The gangs in my neighborhood fought over who controlled each inch of the immediate city. El Farito was one of the leaders of a gang called the Nacos. *Naco* is generally a pejorative term for someone who is a complete good-for-nothing, an uneducated, trashy person who has no respect for others; but they wore the badge proudly. El Farito's watch was plated with gold. He said he had bought the watch himself, and then another time he said his grandfather had given it to him, but everyone knew he had stolen it from one of the watch stands at an outdoor market that went up on Sunday mornings and down on Sunday afternoons. He walked around with that watch like he was a king. The king of Los Nacos. The rest of his outfit was completely incongruous, a sweatshirt with the skull-and-bones of his gang spray-painted by hand on the back, and some wide bell-bottom pants, even though bell-bottoms had gone out of style in the late '70s and this was 1983.

If only I had watched the watches as much as I concentrated on the soccer ball. I will never know how the watch of El Farito disappeared. The watches of all the players were left next to me, at the very back of the net. I jumped and lunged, trying to reach the crossbar and the far corners. And in one of those lunges my whole life must have changed, as someone came and stole the watch of El Farito from behind me. Some son-of-a-bitch took it, claiming it for his own, just as El Farito had claimed the watch, initially, for his own, but you can see that in the eyes of a gang leader, what he himself has done to another isn't what he sees as the same being done to himself. I imagine one of the sixth graders—or even younger, a boy I wouldn't suspect as I was playing, looking forward—sneaking his hand into the back of the net, seeing the gold plating of El Farito's watch glisten in the sun that barely peeked through the dusty clouds that day when my life changed, and I imagine him thinking the watch would bring thousands of pieces of candy if it were grabbed and sold, or maybe the child was thinking more practically of how to get more food for his grandparents and family.

However it happened, when the players all came back to get their watches at the end of the game, El Farito said, "Where the fuck is my watch, Gordi? Where did you put it? Show me your pockets." He came up to me, standing a full eight inches above me, sweating, his hair momentarily out of place until he would get his big blue plastic comb, and he put his wide hands around my chubby neck and told me that if I didn't find his watch he was going to kill me.

This wasn't a fake threat, coming from El Farito. It was well known, in those days, that to be a member of the Nacos each gang member had to beat someone up until they nearly died, and occasionally, when the battles between the rival gangs of the neighborhood got particularly bad, someone pulled out a knife and stabbed another person, or if things turned really ugly out came a gun and a couple of the opposing gang members were shot. You see, death was a very real thing in my neighborhood. Not the death of old age and natural dying, but death chosen like savage animals marking their territory, peeing on it, like dogs. The goal of all the marking wasn't just to be the bad boys who were the sexiest, but to make money, to survive, to find a millimeter of space and class and sexiness in a world that didn't give a shit about anyone in my neighborhood. We lived far away from the nice neighborhoods of Polanco and Las Lomas. We lived in Iztapalapa, on the edge of the city, where people from the wealthy neighborhoods were afraid to even say the name of my neighborhood. For the people in the rich neighborhoods, ours was forbidden territory, a place known about only in the newspapers where crime happened and the animals fought amongst themselves, and where a "civilized" person, someone much whiter than I was in skin tone, would simply never enter.

For the life of me, I could not figure out how that watch was stolen. As I played, when I wasn't looking at the dusty cloud of players as they moved down the field, I would occasionally look back to make sure everything was there. But without eyes in the back of my head, I had missed the—probably—young thief that took the watch, and El Farito didn't blame the thief, he blamed me. In the neighborhood where I lived, "don't shoot the messenger" had a literal connotation. It was assumed that if you had bad news to tell, you were the bad news, or you were hiding some kind of bad news you had caused. I was in the goal. Therefore, I was the thief. El Farito said, "I don't care how you get the watch back, but you get my grandfather's watch back by the end of the day, or I'll kill you."

And, as ridiculous as that might sound, that's how the bullying of me—the following of me by El Farito and his gang—started. Naturally, I couldn't find the watch. I looked everywhere around the goal. I lifted the net and kicked the dirt, and asked everyone else around if they had seen who'd stolen the watch, but everyone that had been watching the game looked down at their feet or said "no" in that lying way we all knew we lied to each other. You didn't snitch in my neighborhood. The only thing worse than snitching was failing to defend your mother's honor if someone said something nasty about her.


BEFORE THE LAST class of the day is done, a math class that I need to concentrate in harder or I might fail the course, I run out the back door of the classroom, looking left and right down the hallway, hoping none of the members of the gang have noticed me. Three weeks have passed since the day when the watch disappeared, three weeks during which I have begged for anyone who knows what happened to the watch to tell me, but no one tells me. I don't take the books out of my desk. It's too dangerous for me to pick up my books to study, later. I take an unexpected exit from the building, not through the front door but through the gymnasium in the basement and out through an exit where they bring in food to the gymnasium to sell us snacks. I squeeze through the crates where milk is kept for the students, and crouch behind the crates, waiting like a frog hoping not to be eaten by an eagle swooping down from the sky. And like a little mouse, I finally run from my hiding place, outside, zigging and zagging, hugging the walls of buildings and houses, not stopping in the little stores where I would normally stop to buy a bit of candy, because those days are over for good, and I feel my chest filling with air, my lungs punching in and out, trying to support my legs running, as I stop and start, springing down the back streets convinced that around the next corner I will find El Farito. Faster, faster, I think. Cut left. Stop. Look around the corner, run more. They will see me. The walls of the city are full of people who will tell them. Is that man selling tacos on the street in cahoots with them? Is he informing them? Who isn't informing them? Everyone in the neighborhood has some relationship with the two gangs. They cooperate or they are punished. The smallest punishment is spray-paint on their stores. People pay up, extortion money, or their windows are broken. Or, the bigger guys, the ones above the gangs, the real crime syndicates might come in, tipped off by the gangs. The city is a web of punishment and obeying. I am only twelve, but even at that age I already know you obey or they do with you what they want.

When I am not running, when I lie in my bed at night, trying to sleep but failing, I dream of buying a gun. A gun is what I need to make El Farito and his guys realize they shouldn't fuck with me. A gun is not easy to find, a gun is illegal, is almost impossible to purchase, especially for a boy like me who has no more than a few savings stored in a clay pig that was given to me by an uncle from Guadalajara. There are coins in there, stuffed until they have filled up the pig, and a jar, but the coins are of small denomination and there are no bills; the coins are from my parents, coins they have given to me or coins I have taken out of their bedroom at times when they are not looking.

The coins I usually use to buy some candy, but I have been saving them up for a long time to buy an instrument, an electric guitar that I have seen in a store in the center of town, far away from my neighborhood where they don't sell items of luxury like electric guitars. I listen to heavy metal music in my room when I am alone, closing the door that my parents tell me to leave open, not to hide, and I have posters on the walls of AC/DC and KISS and Judas Priest, and I play records because this is the era before CDs and we wouldn't have the money to get a CD player until much later, in any case, long after most kids have CD players, and I throw my hands around in the air, standing with my chubby body in front of the mirror of my room, imagining I am a rock star. The music pulses through me as I run—electric screeches and jams and scales—and this is the first taste I get, as I run and run and run, hoping to come closer to home, that music can be the thread that saves us, that literally comes down from the sky into the brain like a gift from God, even though I am not a believer in God, but at that time the music came in a pulse of a gift to keep my legs running to give me faith that there might be some way through the slim streets and alleyways. I stop. There in front of me is El Farito. He tells me, "Why do you bother to go running so hard? You know we can find you anytime we want. There's no escape."

"I don't have your watch," I say. "I confess I don't have it. I wish I had it. I didn't steal it. Someone else has stolen it. I told you that. It's the truth."

"But everyone knows the watch was mine. And who would dare to do something so stupid and brave and foolish, but you?"

He has called me brave. Maybe there's a chance. Maybe he wants me to join his gang. Maybe he will not try to find me in the hallways anymore.

"And brave is stupid," he says. "Do you know that? Brave is what gets a little punk beaten up."

Maybe I can reverse, run back from where I have come from, but the time it will take me to turn will give him the time to come on my heels and tackle me. So I run forward, thinking that with the music in my ears like a crescendo of harsh, scraping, rising notes I can break through him to the other side, behind him, floating in and around and above and over, back to my home, and I run as fast as I can, straight at him, straight into his stomach with my head down, like a torpedo trying to ram into a ship that I hope will disappear, a move so unexpected I hope he will let me pass through. I am only twelve and foolish and full of hopes, and he steps aside, and with my eyes closed as I run it seems he will let me go because I have not hit him yet, but then a foot comes out and he trips me and I fall flat on my face with my chubby chin hitting the ground.

El Farito towers above me and I can't see him because I am splayed forth on the ground, lying like a dead man on the pavement. "Tomorrow you will bring me all of your money. Every peso you have. You will come to me, personally, and give me the money. I'm sick of watching you run, Gordi. This time, I'm letting you lie on the street like a baby. I could run over you and stomp on you. But I prefer to watch you squirm. Bring it all, tomorrow, and don't say anything to your mother or your father about this, or I will truly kill you."

All this he says with his voice much deeper than you might expect for a guy so tall. His words come from the depths of his body like from the depths of a sewer, bubbling slowly up and out. He comes from behind me, where I lay on the pavement feeling the wet of the rain of earlier in the day mixing with the dirt of the street, and he kicks me in the groin until the sight in front of my eyes switches from the grains of sand and dirt and the black of the pavement to a momentary yellow, a flash of pain. One kick and he is gone. I hobble home, dragging my legs, bent forward, feeling the pain in my crotch. When I come into the house, my mother is there. She looks at me and her eyes well up in tears, a glossiness I hate to see, which comes only in the worst of times I have seen on the face of my mother before, and she says, "Gordi. Tell me now. Tell me, finally. You haven't said a thing for three weeks. You have barely eaten for three weeks. What is going on?"

But I won't tell her. I don't want her to worry. There is nothing she can do. There is nothing my parents can do. My father is barely present, in any case. He comes home, frequently drunk. My mother is the one who meets me at home with snacks and food made just for me. She teaches kindergarten, and she is home, early, before me. She has a plate of tortillas with cheese and green chili sauce waiting for me, and a freshly blended glass of carrot juice, but I can't begin to imagine having any of this now. I go to my room and shut the door.

My mother comes to the door and opens it, and I have already thrown myself on the bed with my face down, crying into the bed. There is no escape. None. There is no way out of this trap except to get a gun or to tell El Farito that I will join his gang. Join his gang. Get a gun. Join his gang. Get a gun. I go from one to the other, considering the only two options.

My mother peers into the doorway and she says, "Gordi. I am going to come each day to school and pick you up. I will take you home each day. What are you running from? Whatever it is, you can't run forever. Whoever it is, they'll get you, if I don't pick you up. I will come for you every day."

I don't respond. They are the sweetest words my mother could say. But nothing can save me, unless I can find a watch that has disappeared. No, I must get a gun.

WHEN I THINK of what happened to my mother, later in this story, I wonder what would have happened if I had never made the choice to look for a gun. What if I hadn't been so obsessed with the idea of finding the piece of deadly metal? What if I hadn't thought that a gun could solve all my problems? Certainly, I never would have ended up in the U.S., and certainly I would not have had to see the initial indignity my mother was brought to. But when you are twelve and a life-or-death situation seems to be knocking at your door, you knock back, seeking to protect yourself in any way you can. So I took all my money out of my piggy bank and jar, and, since that wasn't enough, I took money from a can where I knew my mother was storing up money for a rainy day, and I went to try to buy a gun.

My mother had been picking me up at school for two weeks when I went. She came like clockwork, waiting at the front door a few minutes before the final bell of the day rang. Despite the protestations of my math teacher and his stern warnings, and despite the fact I was failing his class more and more, I would leave early and hurry out to the car, where my mother would meet me where she was waiting with the motor running, and she would receive me like a mother back into the womb, protecting me as if she could be a large umbrella keeping me from the rain. I would tell her, "Mom, this cannot go on forever. You know that."

And she would say to me, "Forever is made up of individual points, one by one, and if you are good today, then things will work out in the end."

Those two weeks were, in some ways, the happiest of my life, in that I could see how much my mother truly loved me. Every child wants to believe their mother really loves them, wants to believe their mother loves them even more than their mother loves their father, that they are, deep down inside, the most important thing in the world to their mother, but few get the chance to know so clearly the complete devotion of a mother as I did in those days my mother picked me up from school.

It was like walking among a graveyard of the dead. El Farito was outside sometimes, or other members of his gang, and once they threw a rotten egg at the windshield after my mother had taken me safe into the car. Another time, one of the tires was punched flat, mysteriously, while my mother waited for me in the car. It would have been too dangerous for us to get out of the car to change the tire, so my mother drove home with only three of the wheels working, the other flapping against the ground, the tire air that was missing letting me know this couldn't continue much longer.

So I went to el Señor López's house. Señor López had been a police officer in his younger days. It might seem like surely I should have known I should try to buy a gun from someone much more nefarious, and I did know that, but I also knew I didn't really have enough money to buy a gun on the real black market. The cost of a gun was not the price itself, it was the price of the risk the seller was taking in selling a gun to someone. If someone was a professional crook, no one thought twice selling the weapon to them, because they knew that person would never lead the authorities back to them. But who wants to sell a gun to a chubby twelve-year-old who stands out like an innocent baby in a field of violence? The seller knows he will be traced to the boy who buys the gun in no time at all, when the foolish, innocent-looking child fails to use the gun properly. So when I had tried to buy a gun on the black market, at first, speaking to people on the street corners who I knew could sell me a weapon, everyone told me, "It will never happen, Gordi. You're just a kid. You're just a punk."

In my desperation, I went to el Señor López. He was eighty years old, and I told him El Farito was chasing me. The old man lived above a small bodega where they sold rice and eggs and other staples, and he had nothing to do, now that he was old, except to watch the television with the volume cranked up too loud.

"Why don't you go to the police?" he said. "They can help you."

"Excuse me, Señor López, but you know the police will not believe me if I tell them my life is in danger because someone took El Farito's watch. To them this will seem like nothing. To them, I am just a flea, a tiny story while there are big crimes going on. But for me, I know that if I don't get this gun, El Farito and his gang are going to kill me."

"How much money do you have?"

I laid out all of the money from the piggy bank, jar, and my mother's can on his grimy kitchen table. He was turning blind in his old age. He fingered the bags of coins, and then he fingered the bills I had taken from my mother. He seemed to retreat into the cloud of sound coming out of the TV, some cop show, a rerun of *Starsky & Hutch*. I thought of taking all my money back and running to find someone else. This old man was useless to me, and even as a twelve-year-old I felt he was wasting my time, but then he moved around his kitchen, feeling his way in the dim fluorescent light that harshly lit up his house. He went to his back bedroom, and I watched him crouch beneath his bed. He rummaged around, pulling out stacks of old, musty girlie magazines that he kept and must have once masturbated to, and from behind the magazines, wrapped in a piece of worn red velvet, pulled out a gun.

"This isn't a toy," he told me as he unwrapped it. He put the gun on the bed and I wanted to grab it. The gun looked like a miracle machine that would save me. "Do you know how to use this?"

"Yes, of course I do," I lied.

"Of course you don't," he said. He took out six bullets and put them into the police revolver. It had a thick, black plastic handle, with harsh texture; it felt like a handle that had been held firmly to lord it over criminals and to make sure Mr. López received his small bribes when he was a police officer, as almost all the cops took bribes to survive.

He put the bullets in the gun and spun the barrel of the revolver. He took the bullets out again. Then he had me put them in one by one. I tried to spin the revolver as he had, and the metal in the barrel seemed like lead in my hands compared to in his. The barrel barely moved.

"Don't get cocky with this gun. You're not a cowboy. Use this only in the worst cases, in the very last instance, if you have to. A gun is only as strong and smart as the person carrying it. If you try to be a show-off with this, I guarantee they will get you in two seconds flat. Hide the gun in your pant leg. And only if you absolutely need it, take it out."

He was telling me much more wisdom than I could know. The only thing I saw was what felt to me like my salvation. I held the gun, and the weight of the machine seemed to me to offer strength and power and definite protection. I would have kissed Señor López if it weren't so inappropriate. So I simply told him I would bring him more money every week for the next four weeks, as we'd agreed, since the money I had was insufficient.

THERE IS A long gash that runs down my right arm. The gash is hidden under my tuxedo when I play the bass in orchestra concerts, but the gash is always there. It is something music cannot hide. Playing music, as I hold my bow, I can only represent the scar of my body in the slow, sad sections when the plaintive sound of the bass over-whelms the audience, in those long, sighing underlying interludes which a great composer like Beethoven gives a bass player to remind the audience that sorrow is the underlying note of a life as it seeks higher ground.

Three days before I escaped from Mexico with my mother, I met El Farito and four other members of his gang out on the soccer field where the watch had first disappeared. One of the shortcuts home from school was to run out back to the soccer field and jump over a fence at the end of the field, behind the goal where I had defended my team when the watch had disappeared. Jumping down the fence, hanging in the air and then jumping down a concrete wall, saved a couple of minutes on the way hurrying home. This was the first day my mother had failed to come get me. She failed because she had to be in her school late that day to meet the parents of her students, and if she didn't stay at work she would lose her job.

So I was left to run home, on my own, that day. I brought the gun with me. I had the gun with me every day since I had bought it. The gun was heavy and must have made my pant leg look unusual to anyone who saw me, but I tried to hide it completely. I was out on the soccer field hurrying, at first, toward the back chain-link fence to climb up it, when the rush of the game of soccer that I loved, so much, overtook me. For a second, rather than hurrying on my way, I put myself in the goal to feel the thrill of the space that I wanted to defend. I put my hands in the air, pretending I was stopping balls. I felt the urge to jump from side to side, leaping toward the corners, as I had once jumped every afternoon and as I hadn't done since the day El Farito's watch had disappeared. It was impossible to jump with the weight of the gun in my pants. So I took out the gun, after looking around to see if anyone was coming, and I saw no one. I put the gun in the back of the net, where the watches had been the day they had taken the watch from El Farito. The net was still torn. It was a pitiful net, with holes as large as grapefruits, and the orange netting loose in its fibers like an old net that has been used too many years on worn-out ships at sea. But to me, in that moment, I felt like Schumacher, who had captained the German soccer team in the World Cup. I jumped high to the upper left and felt my body fall to the ground, pretending I had snatched the ball. I got up, dusted the dirt off my thighs, slapping my legs, crouching in the pose of a great fútbol player ready to block a penalty kick in the finals of the World Cup. The crowd chanted my name, "Gordi, Gordi, Gordi!" and I looked out at the wide plain of dirt and imagined the ball coming high and straight at me. And it was in that moment of pure fantasy that I lost sense of time, until in front of me, instead of my fantasy kicker, El Farito and four of his gang members were out on the field. I will never know where they came from, because it seems I should have seen them before they could get so close. By the time I saw them, they were only twenty yards away. I turned and reached for my gun. I didn't have time to think. I turned toward them and fired the gun, but I had no idea what I was doing and the bullet went nowhere near any of them. The loud clap of the gun surprised me. I shot again, and the next bullet went further into nowhere. I saw a ping of dust in the distance. The bullet must have hit the ground. The young men ran up to me. I shot again and hit the arm of one of the boys and he grabbed his arm, but he was in no mortal danger. And the next thing I knew I was on the ground and one of the boys had a machete, and they held the hand I had held the gun in, the gun now in El Farito's hand. And he said to me, "Where the fuck did you get this gun, you idiot? You don't even know how to fire this weapon. You are going to be in our gang now. But not before we teach you a lesson . . . Cut his arm," he told one of the gang members. "Let him know he will always be a fucking idiot. From now on, if you can live, you are going to do whatever I tell you. That's your payment for the watch. You are going to be one of the Nacos and you are going to tell your mother you don't belong to her anymore. You're a man now. Tell your mother you're not a baby anymore. Watching her come to pick you up in her car, it's such a pathetic sight to see." He raised his hand and held it in the air. The boy with the machete raised his blade in unison with El Farito. El Farito threw his hand down at the ground, where I was pinned by two of the boys. The one who had been shot was barely bleeding, barely grazed. And I saw the blade, as I looked up at the blue sky, which made it seem like the day was as pure as it could be, but was blue in the way of someone who feels they are going to die and be sucked up into the heavens, and out of that blue sky I will never forget seeing, as if in slow motion the black metal blade, thick and wide like a blunt club yet sharp at the edge coming down into my arm, a harsh swack, a smack and slice that caused blood to leap out of my arm, a gash halfway into my arm until it was stopped at the bone. They left me lying on the field, bleeding to death, a future Naco if I could survive, a dead man if I could not.

I still cry when I see that scar, the thick crude stitching up my arm, the long gash that never leaves me. I passed out soon after they cut me, after they looked down at me, laughing, the last image I can remember before I lost consciousness. The dust of the field floated around them, it crept into my wound as blood pulsed out onto the dirt and as I tried to close my hand, reaching for the revolver I no longer had, a phantom reaction, reaching for the weapon I had thought would protect me.

—◄◄◄( )►►►—

The door to the embassy loomed like a gaping maw before me, Marisa—Gordi is my son—in downtown Mexico City. I had traveled first by one of the small peseros, which look like small buses, and then by a real bus for two hours to get to the building along the Avenida Reforma. The gang in the neighborhood had spray-painted the car with Gordi's name and had slashed a line over his name. They had punched out all the tires. They had spray-painted the house. Gordi's body had been delivered to me by a nurse from his school, with a lone police officer. I had shouted at them that they should have brought him to a hospital first. What were they thinking? But they told me that if they had taken the time to take him to the hospital he might have died on the way, and the local hospital did not like to get involved with the gang fights. Sometimes they let patients die, intentionally, to avoid having the fighting infiltrate into the building. It was crazy having a hospital that could deny service to its own people. It was certainly illegal to do so. But who was there to check anyone was following the law? The law was what any hospital administrator decided. The choice of whether a gang member who was hurt lived or died could be made by a resident at the hospital in the middle of the night, on a whim. So the nurse had put a tourniquet on his arm and brought my Gordi to me.

The nurse was a young woman, no older than twenty-five, and she stayed in the house beside Gordi, checking his wound, putting on fresh strips of bedsheets that she wrapped around his arm, as she removed all but the tourniquet. I knew Gordi didn't believe in God—he had told me so, once, such a strange thing for a young boy to claim to know at such a young age—so I went for my own candles with the image of the Virgen de Guadalupe to burn around his bed inside the house. In the first hours he was home, he didn't know who I was. He barely could identify anyone, the nurse, or my husband.

"We can't keep him here," my husband said. "He'll die and he'll bring the gang into this house."

The nurse said, "Señor, if he goes outside now, he will definitely die. He will not be able to take being transported to a hospital. Let him rest."

"Who knows what kind of criminal activity he has become involved in?" my husband said. "He has brought near death for all of us into the house."

"Oh, shut up, José Manuel," I told him. "He's just a boy, for crying out loud. He's a boy. They have hurt my boy!" I kneeled down by the side of Gordi and stroked his head. How could they do this to my boy? My boy. My boy!

"Then act like his mother and find a way out of this trap. Do something," José Manuel said. He was nervous and said he was going to look for a gun to protect us.

"A gun?" I said. "The last thing we need is more guns. Can't you see Gordi's gun got him into this trouble to begin with?"

"I'm going to get a gun," he said, again. And he left the house with me imploring him not to do so.

The nurse told me she would look after Gordi, she would protect him, and I went upstairs and put on my best clothes and lipstick and looked for all my money, which was less than there had been in the jar where I normally kept it. I realized Gordi must have taken some of the money to buy the gun. There were no reserves to fall back on. There was nothing except my ability to persuade, I knew, and I made the lipstick shine brighter on my lips and ironed my dress before I went to catch the pesero and bus. It was 4 a.m. and we had been up all night with the nurse and in a vigil with Gordi, and José Manuel had just left. I looked into the mirror and asked God to help me and made the sign of the cross. There was only one solution I could think of—to fly away, to go to America, to get the hell out of this neighborhood, to leave El Farito and the gangs and the cancer of Iztapalapa. We should have gone before, I blamed myself. I should have known to get Gordi out of his school, before. My sweet, my love. I went into the room and ran my hand across his face, touching his round cheeks and nose and the soft skin of his forehead and felt his slow breathing in and out, so shallow, I could have no certainty he would still be alive when I came back, but the only chance he would live not only for another few hours, but for days, and weeks and months and years into the future, was to go and flee like any other refugee I had ever seen, or the women of World War II holding their arms up in the air crying over the spilled blood of their husbands, their soldiers, and knowing they had to uproot themselves from their farms and go, go, go.

So I went in the dark of the early morning, catching a pesero crammed with the people of the neighborhood, the muchachas that had to travel far across the city to get to the private homes where they worked, far away across the metropolis. They said little on the pesero in the morning, too tired to chat in the way they would chat coming home. A thin, tiny wisp of a light burned from the ceiling of the bus, the bodies crowded together, even at that early hour, and I made my way until I stood in front of the security gate of the American embassy, where the guards put me in a line, with others who waited, each like a begging ghost in the dawn as it lifted, against a snaking wall, each with hopes, until after a very long wait, it was finally 9 a.m. and the line began to move toward the large metal detector at the front, and white doors that reflected like a mirror back at all of us the hopes we felt and the barrier of the glass.

"Do you have an appointment?" the guard asked.

"No," I had to admit. I was sent to another line and to another waiting room. For four hours I sat in a room with faint blue paint on the walls and fluorescent lights, with no windows to give me any sense of the passage of time and no hope there was any way out of the room. It was a trap, a box with one way in and it felt like no way out. The numbers in red, digital, primitive shapes—yet which looked so new to me then, like another world, outside of the world of analog where I lived—changed slowly. They were a sign of hope that this country, while cold and with barriers, might be something different, completely, from the neighborhood back home where Gordi, I hoped, was healing. This was before the days of cell phones. There was no way to check up on Gordi. I waited with all the papers I could think of that I might need: his birth certificate, my birth certificate and the certificate of José Manuel, a deed to the house we owned, which was worth almost nothing, a letter which indicated I was employed as a schoolteacher. I took what I had heard from others was necessary, a list of our single bank account and whatever else I could find that might indicate some money, which would show we were wealthy enough to be trusted to go to America and to come back.

When my turn finally came, I could feel my lipstick had worn off. Why didn't I freshen it up before I was called up to the window? From the window I was directed to an office. I followed down the dull lighting of a corridor, with white linoleum tiles that shined in a way I had never seen before, so shiny and yet so cold. I knocked on the door, which was already open.

The man behind the desk did not look up at me, at first. He looked at a folder, among stacks of other manila folders on his desk.

I sat in front of the man until he finally looked up. He looked bored, and tired, and he had a pair of black horn-rimmed glasses and a blue pinpoint shirt, and he had the look of a man who had never heard of my Gordi and would never care. I placed the envelope with all my documents on his desk.

"You need to wait until I tell you you can put something on the desk," he said.

I pulled the envelope back. How could I change this man's thinking? Should I cry? Should I show him I was a mother? Should I stand as straight and still as a fragile, obedient bird? Should I go straight to the point?

I waited until he was ready. "You may now place your envelope on the table," he said. And I did.

He spoke in Spanish, but with a strange American accent that made his words twist into unrecognizable forms. I knew very little English, only a few words from when I had studied, years before, to be a teacher. But I thought it would impress him if I could speak some of his language, so I said, "Mr. . . . Mr., I have come here today because I have a son."

"You should speak in Spanish," he told me.

I switched to Spanish, as he commanded. Long ago, I had learned you do whatever a bureaucrat wants, or nothing happens. It was the first rule to facing a bureaucrat in Mexico. And giving him a bribe.

"Señor," I said. "I am requesting a visa for tourism for me and my husband and my precious son, Gordi. He has always wanted to go to Disneyland. He wants to go to Disneyland, and my husband and I, we want to give him an opportunity to see the beautiful place of your country."

"And the reason for why you don't have an appointment?" He opened the envelope I had placed on the table and looked at the papers, as I replied. He scowled at the papers. I could see he was not going to buy my story about Disneyland.

"You know," he said, "it is a punishable offense to lie about why you want to go to the United States. I see people like you coming in here, every day, saying they want to go see the Empire State Building or the Statue of Liberty. The whole family just wants to up and go for a few days to see the Statue of Liberty. And, strangely enough, they come with papers trying to show me how much money they have, when they clearly have very little. You, ma'am, have a house in Iztapalapa. Does that sound like a place where many people, suddenly, have the money to go for tourism to Disneyland?"

"Please. I beg you," I said. "I am begging you. My son Gordi has been attacked by a gang. He is lying at home bleeding now, and I must be a bad mother to have left him, and the only reason I have done so is because I believe in your government. I believe that your government stands for the land of the free, as it says in your national anthem. I believe that you will give a chance to me and my husband and Gordi, and so I am requesting a tourist visa for us to go to Disneyland and to Miami."

"I would be fired, in a moment, if I gave you the kind of visa you are asking for because your son is trying to get out of his neighborhood," the man said. "But I will tell you what. If you will agree to meet me for a drink, then we can resolve this matter, and you and your husband and your son can go to Disneyland. A drink. One time, and at this place." He wrote an address on a piece of paper and gave it to me. "Will you do that?" He paused. He looked at me with the officiousness of a man who had no scruples. Yet what did I think? Why did I expect him to be different from any other animal? Why did I really think that just because the floors shined more brightly that this bureaucratic dog from the United States would be any different from the Mexican bureaucratic dogs who reached out for money every time we needed something—a permit to buy our house, a permit to register the car.

I knew he meant more than a drink. I knew the words, *a drink,* were a euphemism for sex. I knew he simply wanted to make me bend to his will to see if he could. I knew he was a pig of a man, who could ask to take advantage of a mother, dressed in her finest, obviously just trying to find a way to save her son and her husband and to get out of a hellhole of a circumstance. I felt like spitting in his face, but, as any mother would, I told him I would be there. I told him I would have the drink with him. I went to the address he gave me later that evening, staying in town until he was done with his day of work. I called Gordi a couple of times to see how he was doing, and the nurse said he was recovering, but nothing was certain. I thought of the gangs, like a cancer coming closer and closer around the house, circling like wolves. I thought of my husband doing who-knows-what to get another gun. And I slept with that officer in Polanco, in the hotel at the address he gave me. His breath tasted like cheap spearmint gum as he kissed me, later. His fingers moved like cold keys of a typewriter across my nipples and my chest. I had never done anything so abhorrent as to let a stranger touch my body, but I did it to get the tourist visas, to be able to take Gordi to a new land.

—«««()»»»—

My father refused to come with us when my mother came home with the news of the tourist visas. He reacted like a caged cat, pacing through the house, faced with what my mother had done. I was only, finally, coming out of the immediate shock of the blow El Farito had given me. I had missed my mother's gift, her gift of her body to another man, which she had never wanted anyone to find out, but which I found out years later, when my father wrote to me in the United States saying he had reason to believe my mother had done such a "horrible thing," as he put it. It was his reason, his excuse, for not making the trip with us. I heard him from my bed yelling at my mother, "You smell of another man's cologne." I had no idea what he was referring to, as I lay in bed, but his letter years later let me know what he was stating. How he had guessed what had happened to my mother, I will never fully know. He used this as the main pretext for not coming with us. At the time, when my mother had given me more than any son could ever hope or expect from his mother, her own sense of self-dignity, he turned on her and accused her of being unfaithful. For that I can never forgive him, but I know that what he was also afraid of was leaving the home of his birth, the country which, for better and worse, had raised him. There is a smell to the country that one comes from that is either necessary, a smell that cannot be left because it gives you your whole identity, the culture which cradles you and gives you your sense of purpose and norm and a sense of daily routine; or a smell which, for me, after El Farito struck me, would always be the smell of blood and fear.

My mother snatched me out of that fatherland, like the stork which had originally given me life and which now wanted to ensure my continued survival. With no more than a small suitcase, because my mother insisted we look like tourists and not immigrants to a new land, she made the further difficult choice of not only leaving her home country but also of leaving my father, whom she had been married to, at that time, for twenty years. She had met my father at a wedding party of a cousin, with soft mariachi music accompanying them on their first dance, but she gave up even her husband—who certainly had many faults, but for all of his faults had still been her love, once—so that she could bring me to safety.

We landed in the middle of the night, at the darkest hour just before the dawn in Miami, me with a teddy bear and my small suitcase, and my mother with an old, beat-up red nylon suitcase that was so old the back zipper was coming undone and the red had turned to a bruised reddish-black. And with no more than that in our hands we arrived in America, two tourists supposedly going to Disneyland, two members of a family now broken, my arm wrapped in gauze which my mother kept as fresh and as clean as possible.

"What's wrong with him?" the guard at the border said in the airport in Miami, pointing to my arm, looking at our passports, yet barely showing any real interest in us. Others were waiting. We had the proper visas. My mother merely said, "His name is Gordi. He is twelve years old, and he has always wanted to come play in this country."

That was enough to have the gentleman stamp our passports and, though he was clearly unconvinced, he was on to the next persons to stamp their passports.

Soon after we arrived in Miami, my mother enrolled herself in night classes so she could say she was a student, worthy of a student visa. She enrolled me in school for the fall, so I could get a student visa as well. Our long climb with the immigration service of the government began, and we stayed in the United States, and I grew up in the country, first as a rebellious kid who, once my arm healed, began to play American football, and then, oddly, I received a minor football scholarship to Southern Methodist University, but the year I arrived at the university their football program was shut down and all of their money was put, temporarily, for a few years, into promoting music instead. In high school, because I had wanted to play the bass guitar in a band, I had started taking stand-up bass lessons in the public school orchestra. I was late to begin the instrument, but the bass is not like the violin, which you have to begin as a child to play well. I played the anchoring notes, and traveled with the orchestra, and became interested in the deep, underlying sounds that seemed to resonate with some inner pain I had kept from my days in Mexico, even though I had grown into a boy who talked a lot and who joked a lot with others in the hallways of my American school.

**TODAY, THIRTY YEARS** have passed since my mother took me, bravely, to the United States. Thirty years to the day, and the United States is finally giving my mother her U.S. citizenship. Had we come completely illegally, we might have been able to become U.S. citizens much earlier, but ironically, by coming with official visas, by working through the legal system as you are supposed to, my mother had signed papers with fine print that said when we came as tourists we never intended to stay as immigrants. It has taken this long to work her through the legal system.

I live most of the time in New York, where I eventually attended Julliard for a master's degree, but I have bought a house with my wife down in Florida. She is a composer, and she finds the escape from New York a source of calming, a place where it is easier for her to compose. I follow my wife, who is far more famous than me, around the world. She is the star. I am her supporter, her biggest fan, just as my mother was once my biggest fan, saving me. I pull my wife's suitcases through the airports. I check her in to hotels, as she is brought to compose music for some of the biggest orchestras and quartets in the world. I am a nobody, but I know my wife loves that I am so supportive of her. I live for my wife, as my mother has lived her life for me.

To celebrate my mother's thirtieth year in the United States, and the envelope that came in the mail this morning, announcing that she is now, formally, a citizen of this country, I take her to the mineral springs that I love so much, near our house just outside the

town of Englewood, Florida. The place has the feeling of a spa. When
you walk in the door there are lawn chairs spread out on the wide-
open, manicured grass. Palm trees sway in the air.

As is my habit when I am down in Florida with my wife who
is composing, she works in the house, locked away from me in her
room, while I go to the mineral springs. I like to wear a thick, white,
plush bathrobe, which I stole from a hotel in Germany when we
were on tour for one of her musical compositions. I have a second,
equally plush robe that I give to my mother. We have lunch first,
and I order plate after plate of sandwiches, fresh orange juice, beer,
borscht soup, since the local Russians like to come to this artesian
spring, and then I order a plate of caviar and black bread, which is the
most expensive item on the menu. I like to celebrate everything in
life. I like to take in every opportunity to have fun, to taste, to play
music with friends, to feel just how good life can be.

My mother, looking at all of the food I have ordered for us, as we
sit under a large sun umbrella at the café of the mineral springs, says,
"You eat like you are always running away from something, Gordi.
You eat too much."

She is right, of course, in some ways. But I tell her, "It is not running away. It is taking in everything, sucking the marrow of the
bone." I feel my scar under the plush cotton cloth of my robe and
pull the sleeve of the arm up, involuntarily, until I can see the scar.
My eyes get watery looking at the scar, the deep gash where El Farito
almost killed me. I think of my father, who only came once to the
United States to see me, six years ago, when I was married to my
wife. It is the only time he has ever come to see me. He came on the
day of the wedding, though he hid from standing in most of the pictures because he was uncomfortable that my wife is Jewish. There is
odd, lingering anti-Semitism there, another story for another time.

Me, I have never been back to Mexico. I can never return. I have
no desire to go back to the place where I was almost killed, and to
those times of running away from the gangs of Iztapalapa. I order

another orange juice and down it in three gulps. My belly is round, but it is a happy belly, not a slothful belly. I take in life. I play in the back of the orchestra, letting my arm sway widely to and fro. "You look wonderful today, Mamá," I tell her. And she does look happy. "I can never thank you enough."

She smiles at me, gets up from the table for a second, leaning forward with her relatively small body next to me, her little bear cub, who is now not so little, with some gray around my temples, and gives me a kiss around the back of my ear. When we are done, and she is sitting in the chair with her eyes closed, leaning back, looking calm, I leave her and I walk out into the deep pond of the mineral spring. I walk into the water that others might think is full of muck, burbling up from the origins of a swamp, which is so deep the bottom cannot be seen. It is said the hole of the mineral spring goes down hundreds of feet to another place, to other origins, to a place so deep the bones of dinosaurs can be found there. The explorer Ponce de León passed near the place in 1513 when he came looking for seven fountains of youth and gold, which he never found, but which I lay floating in comfortably in the deepest part of the water, looking up at the sky as it breezes by. Floating in this water is my favorite activity when I am down in Florida. I like it even more than floating in the ocean. I feel the power of the healing minerals as they swish and move around my body, into my ears and over my scar, and the waters soften the scar, as time does—I should never have bought the gun, my mom and I will always be refugees, I think—and I feel my mother nearby, right next to me even though she is fifty yards away, the calm of another beautiful day in Florida, the calm of a mother's love for her child.

## ACKNOWLEDGMENTS

**THANKS TO** Tessa Hadley, Jaime Manrique, Edie Meidav, Susan Burmeister-Brown, Linda Swanson-Davies, Albert Goldbarth, Tom Perrotta, Nathan Roberson, Philip Spitzer, Lukas Ortiz, Christopher Merrill, Jennifer Clement, David Lida, Peter Nazareth, Chris Walsh, Mary Sullivan Walsh, John Matthias, the National Endowment for the Arts, the Hermitage Artist Retreat, Patricia Caswell, Martin J. Sherwin, Marc Nieson, Sherrie Flick, Peter Trachtenberg, James Alan McPherson, Frank Conroy, David Hamilton, Steve Almond, Thorpe Moeckel, Margaret Dawe, Levente Sulyok, Bradley Narduzzi, Roberto Espinosa, Jessica Poore, Rafael Moreno Arnáiz, Dušan Sekulović, Dena Wetzel, Maria Elena Barron, Sandy and Bronwyn Barkan. In memory of my father, Joel Barkan.

## ABOUT THE AUTHOR

JOSH BARKAN has won the Lightship International Short Story Prize and has been a finalist for the Grace Paley Prize for Short Fiction, the Paterson Fiction Prize, and the Juniper Prize for Fiction. He is the recipient of a fellowship from the National Endowment for the Arts, and his writing has appeared in *Esquire*. He earned his MFA from the Iowa Writers' Workshop and has taught writing at Harvard, Boston University, and New York University. With his wife, a painter from Mexico, he divides his time between Mexico City and Roanoke, Virginia.